★

Jacob's Baptism

★

A novel of the War Between the States

Mark Randolph Watters

Jacob's Baptism

King's Way Press
3721 New Macland Rd.
Suite 200-141
Powder Springs, GA 30157
www.kwp-books.com

ISBN-13: 978-0-9988367-4-4

Cover artwork "Battle of Spotsylvania" circa 1887 by Thure de Thulstrup

*F*or my parents, hurdlers of hard times and lovers of life. Thank you for your sacrifices.

Jacob's Baptism

★

Jacob's Baptism

★

A novel of the War Between the States

Mark Randolph Watters

Mark Randolph Watters

On September 4, 1862, General Robert E. Lee's Army of Northern Virginia, awash in the glory of their sweeping victory over General John Pope's Army of Virginia at Second Manassas (or Second Battle of Bull Run), began its crossing of the Potomac River at White's Ford. Confederate spirits were at their apex. Northern morale, on the other hand, could be summed up with this, from a Union soldier: **"The whole army is disgusted . . . you need not be surprised if success falls to the rebels with astonishing rapidity."**

Though the Confederates were ill-fed and physically depleted, Lee believed the immediate post-Manassas weeks were vital to luring Lincoln's beaten army from Washington, away from its supply lines, and onto ground of Lee's choosing. Plus, Lee needed to draw the war away from Virginia and onto northern soil, to take advantage of a war-weary north's call for peace, and to attract foreign recognition.

In preparation for this, Lee issued **Special Order 191**, detailing the deployment of three columns of the Army of Northern Virginia for the purposes of capturing Union garrisons at Martinsburg and Harpers Ferry. Lee believed he could accomplish this risky movement in light of Lincoln's decision to return command of all Union forces to General George McClellan. Lee was keenly aware of McClellan's sense of caution and love of self.

As the fates of war dictated, however, a copy of Lee's Special Order 191, intended for Major General Daniel Hill, was lost. Found in an abandoned Confederate campsite near Frederick, Maryland by members of the 27th Indiana, the lost orders were wrapped around three cigars in an envelope. These orders gave McClellan unprecedented access to Confederate high command and thus the key to destroying Lee's fragmented army piecemeal.

True to character, McClellan delayed his reaction to this gift of military intelligence, allowing Lee time to consolidate his forces on the ridges near the town of Sharpsburg, Maryland. The Battle of Antietam (or Battle of Sharpsburg), fought on September 17, 1862 from dawn to sundown, resulted in the greatest number of single-day casualties in American history. Twelve hours of combat. **A baptism in blood,** its magnitude seen never before or since. 3,654 killed outright. 17,292 wounded, many of whom would die in the weeks to come. 1,771 missing. More than 29 men hit every minute. One man hit every two seconds. This rate of human destruction included several lulls in the fighting, between phases, after the opposing forces had exhausted themselves.

Arguably the most important battle of the entire war, Antietam, though a military draw, gave Lincoln a tactical victory and a point of launch for his Emancipation Proclamation, giving the war a completely different complexion, a completely higher reason for blood and sacrifice.

★

Jacob's Baptism

Lee's Lost Order
Special Order 191

Jacob's Baptism

**Dead Confederates in Hog Trough Road (Bloody Lane),
September 19, 1862 (two days after the Battle of Antietam).
Piper's trampled cornfield in background.**

Photo by Alexander Gardner

Jacob's Baptism

"Deep, unspeakable suffering may well be called a baptism, a regeneration, the initiation into a new state."

-- Ira Gershwin

"In our youths our hearts were touched with fire."

-- Oliver Wendell Holmes

"Now the wind is still;
In a moment it will be raging.
Now my soul is young;
In a moment it will be aging."

-- Dan Fogelberg

Jacob's Baptism

Antietam Battlefield, Sharpsburg, Maryland. Modern-day view of Hog Trough Road (Bloody Lane), southeastward leg. Point of view is at intersection of Roulette's Lane and Bloody Lane, looking down the Confederate line of battle. Confederates faced left, rifles rested on stacked fence rails, awaiting the advance of William French's and Israel Richardson's Divisions.

Photograph by Mark Randolph Watters

★

Jacob's Baptism

★

Prologue

The ninety-day rebellion turned

seventeen months in September, 1862, the same month Jacob
turned seventeen years, without fanfare and with scant
observance. The war plodded along like wheels through spring
mud. Lincoln urged men to enlist their patriotic duty, to rise to
their manly call and tend to the national emergency. Jacob
plowed through his duties, his day-to-day routine, without fail,
one eye affixed to the frenzy of wartime activity surrounding
him. Laughter, shouting, exhortations to hop aboard the glory
train rang as clear through the valley as the peals of a church bell.
Friends succumbed to the call, filled with glee, taking leave of
family and boyhood innocence to join local militia units, their
bright uniforms and brighter rifles worn as proud symbols of a
cause most could not articulate, except through emotions
generated.

And the casualty lists. Filled with names of real people with
real lives, people with whom he was well acquainted, men
hobbled with sickness, shot, missing, wounded, killed. Jacob
wondered about the laughter, the exhortations, now that war was
real.

Jacob's Baptism

Each morning across the valley of the Antietam—alas, the whole of Maryland—folks awakened from their lofts of dreams and descended promptly into the abyss of reality. Loved ones of soldiers afield charged over farm lanes and through meadows, beelines made to community nerve-centers and courthouse steps. Here, tacked to posts and walls, or handed to reaching fingers like bread to the starving, casualty lists scribed with the names of thousands met with eyes of frantic families searching madly, hoping for no news. For no news, indeed, was good news, good news suggesting their citizen soldiers had survived another bloodletting.

Maybe.

Blood gushed like the floodwaters of spring and had reddened the watered eyes of families from Maine to Texas. Places meant for the nooks of obscurity instead flourished in infamy.

Manassas.

Shiloh.

Gaines Mill.

Savage Station.

Malvern Hill.

Manassas, again.

Cedar Mountain.

Harpers Ferry almost weekly.

The war of the rebellion, an uprising once believed in need only of a tamping, like restless children in a church pew, thrashed now with the fury of Ares. And now, just a few miles away, the growl of thunder riding waves of summer heat and acoustic shadows, its angry staccato occasionally spilling into local ears, came the fighting on South Mountain, the prelude to an elephant of mammoth proportions.. The clutch of war closed in on the serenity of Sharpsburg and the valley of Antietam Creek like the inexorable crush of claustrophobia, and nothing anyone said, nothing anyone did, could prevent its advance.

Rolling waves of emerald and gold gave form to the September breeze pushing the fields' fertile foliage, corn and wheat swishing the sweet air. The Antietam valley was an idyll, a panoramic tease of divine brushstrokes set against the ominous backdrop of a nation at war with itself, gray clouds stalking a blue sky. The waning summer coursed through the trees, over pastures and fields rich with crops, through towns and homesteads, giving the reassurance of strength to weary residents and retreat to hints of Confederate dominance. Such reassurance was short-lived.

Whispers of change, of Lee's advance northward, indeed his army's splashing across the Potomac River into the border state of Maryland, spoke instead of the coming rage, of the nagging sense of waning well-being.

It was a citizenry squeezed between the throat-held grip of devils and gods. The quiet roads of Sharpsburg and the meandering Antietam crossed dead center within the crosshairs of a struggle destined to redefine the savagery of warfare, with an outcome far from certain, of a burden borne by a generation born to settle with blood the issues of slavery and the futures of two nations.

These were the days of contrast, at one turn as predictable as the seasons and at another as fickle as the weather. These were the days of tranquility and explosion, as interchangeable as milking buckets. The valley of the Antietam offered a haven of plenty for hungry, march-weary soldiers and hence a fine spot for the business of war. On that point, in this September of whispers, Lee, McClellan, and the thousands of men in their commands, agreed.

The valley of the Antietam drifted through its moments of routine turbulence, like a butterfly caught up in a March gust. Mid-September thunder marched across the lightening-lighted horizon, creating a troubling crescendo of alternating piano and forte. Indeed, a storm lurked like none other. Such loyalties as boasted behind shields of untouchable homeland hearths gradually transformed over the months into whispers of war.

Total war.

Chapter 1

Devil's darning needles, clinging

one atop the other in nature's dance of domination and submission, zipped around Jacob and Rachael.

"Watch out, Rachael!" Jacob yelled, teasing. "They'll latch on to your ears, suck your brains out!"

"That's just plain silly!" Rachael squealed, dodging the unpredictable maneuvers of the six-legged projectiles. "Where'd you hear such a thing as that, anyway? Dragonflies ... AAHH! ... are as gentle as butterflies, just not so ... pretty!"

Jacob laughed. "Some of 'em are, I reckon ... like the ones on your back. Its wings are as blue as the midday sky."

"Get it off!" Rachael screamed, taking awkward swats at her back.

"Keep on talkin, Denia! Else them things might just knit your lips together!" Jacob insisted.

Hand over her mouth, just in case, Rachael desperately evaded the swerving paths of the insects, ducking her head, veering her hips left to right, and grabbing hold of Jacob's arms, swinging him side to side as her shield.

"That one there's a *Yankee!*" she said through her fingers. "He's chasin that Reb fly like a wild mare; gonna take *him* prisoner and suck *his* brains out!"

"What are you *talkin* about?" Jacob asked.

"As if you didn't know, Jacob Hoffman. You're the one that started all this darning-needle silliness and talk of brain-suckin an' such."

"Rachael, you're waltzin around here like a spooked chicken. Never knowed you to show fear of no dragonfly. Just what are you up to, anyhow?"

"Oh … a little of *this*, a little of *that*," she sang, "a little of why-don't-you-come-over-here."

"What kind of talk is *that* on a Monday afternoon, anyhow?"

Rachael bent and picked a dandelion, resigned that Jacob again had failed to receive her subtle hint. She blew the feathery seeds and watched as they caught a gust and scattered across the meadow.

"Just talk." Rachael sighed. "What you got against Monday? It ain't like you're about to be baptized or nothin. Speakin of which, what happened with *that* anyhow? I thought yesterday was the big day for you."

"I … I overslept. Daddy didn't wake me, an' I overslept."

"Overslept? Ain't you got a couple dozen roosters, each of 'em wakers of the dead? I reckon they overslept, too?"

"Three roosters, an' I reckon they did."

"Jacob, when are you goin to be baptized?"

"I *am*. It's just that—"

"It's just that you're *embarrassed* to, bein dunked in the creek three times, like rinsin some dirty shirt. You should've done this when you was nine or ten, before you knew what embarrassment was all about. It's ain't nothin but gettin wet, is all. You do that everyday, just workin in them fields."

"I think the Brethren would have put it off anyway," Jacob said. "All they do these days is meet at the church an' talk about the war, about how close the fightin's comin to Sharpsburg. Reckon they ain't got the time for one trine immersion."

"Could it be your fear of water, Jacob Hoffman? After all, it ain't been that many years since you *fell* off the Rohrbach Bridge, smack into the middle of the Antietam, kickin an' screamin like some three-year-old. If *that* wasn't your trine immersion, I don't know what was!"

"Hush up, Rachael. I didn't *fall* off; I was *pushed*, by Roswell. Water's ten or twelve feet there, an' I had on some heavy clothes, an' a fishin pole to boot. I *ain't* afraid of no water, an' I ain't *embarrassed* to get wet. It's just that … well—"

"I know, I know. You overslept. Maybe next Sunday?"

"Maybe," Jacob answered, tossing pebbles toward a stand of sycamores. "What's it to you?"

"Anyway, I hear tell Roswell's joinin up with Lee's Virginians," she said, head tilted one way and eyes the other, eyebrows arched. A bouquet of blue phlox and black-eyed susans drooped in her hand.

"*Roswell?* Ain't no such a thing!" Jacob said, yanking up a handful of clover and picking through the bunch for four-leafers. "Ros ain't no more'n sixteen, and besides, his Daddy would hunt him down like Saturday's rabbit, skin him six ways from Sunday."

"Not what *I* hear," Rachael said, hands on hips. "Boys a lot younger'n sixteen are runnin off everyday to join the trail to glory. I hear tell of drummer boys no older than twelve, eleven even. What you got to say to that? Ain't all I know, neither."

Jacob stared at Rachael, the first girl for whom he ever felt more than a passing attraction, a girl he affectionately called Denia, after the sweet scent of gardenia, he'd say to her delight, but more likely because her spunk reminded Jacob of his deceased mother, whose given name was Denia. Rachael, too, possessed uncanny knowledge about the goings-on of this war, about the conduct of Lee's Army of Northern Virginia and McClellan's Army of the Potomac, before newspapers reported such things, things Jacob believed only insiders or spies could know. Maybe it was her precocious attention to political ramblings and the porch talk of old men. Maybe it was nothing more than her luck of the Irish.

"Trail to *glory?* For *who?* Politicians and musket-makers, maybe. How do you know about eleven-year-old drummer boys? What parents would allow—"

"I have my sources, Mr. Jacob Hoffman," Rachael boasted, "and don't you wish you may have them, too?"

"Did Ros *tell* you *hisself* he was joinin?"

"Didn't have to," Rachael answered, sniffing the phlox. "I could see it in his eyes, and those eyes said he's doin it, maybe today."

Jacob studied Rachael's changing expressions, like watching the rise and descent of afternoon thunder clouds. "When did you get close enough to Ros to hear what his *eyes* was sayin'?"

Rachael gave a quick smirk but avoided that question. "I hear he's been spendin time over at Packhorse Ford, just sittin and watchin the river like it was whisperin his name."

"The river's *whisperin?*"

"Maybe so. You jealous?"

"Of hearin voices from a *river?* I don't think so."

"It might do *you* good to be so sensitive, Jacob Hoffman."

Jacob scoffed at the notion. "Anyway, it's all because you *dared* him, Rachael, just like you done me. Ros has always liked you, an' well … he'll do just about *anything* to impress a pretty girl."

Rachael curled a slight smile of acknowledgement, and, handing Jacob her bouquet, flicked her hair and turned her back to him.

"What else you know of?"

"I like a man in uniform," she confessed. "You'd be right cute yourself—without the flowers, of course."

Jacob blushed, almost tossing the flowers to the ground, but he stopped short. "The only *uniform* I ever seen on a reb was a suit of patchwork *rags.* Have you *seen* these rebs? Shoeless skeletons, most of 'em. Look, Rachael, just because the rebs licked Pope at Manassas—"

"Again!"

"—don't mean the war's over. Fact is, it's just *beginnin,* but I don't reckon it'll be lastin much longer, what with McClellan in charge again. Them rebs're out-*gunned*. Most of the ones I've seen ain't totin no more'n squirrel guns, flintlocks even. Some ain't got nothin' at all, 'cept a Bowie, maybe a pike. I hardly ever see one with a Springfield, and I *won't* 'less they pick 'em up off dead Yankees."

"Or capture them at Harpers Ferry."

Jacob sighed, silently conceding that if anyone were outgunned, it was he. "Well … what *artillery* they have ain't nothing more'n a few smoothbores, everyone of 'em out-ranged by our rifled guns."

"*Our* rifled guns?" Rachael noted. "Takin sides, are you?"

"You know what I mean, Rachael. Maybe I *am* takin sides. Not only that, they're out-*manned*, they're out-*supplied,* they're—"

"But they ain't out-*spirited*," she countered.

"Out-spirited?

"That's what I said."

"What else you know, aside from uniforms and whisperin rivers?" Jacob repeated. "It'll take a passel more'n—"

Ka-CHAM!

Chapter 2

Jacob's bouquet burst into a powder of yellow and blue as he jerked back his hand in reaction to the explosion.

"What the—"

"*Roswell!*" shouted Rachael, eyes beaming.

"Damn, Ros, you tryin to *kill* me?"

"If I was *tryin* to kill you, you'd be dead now," Roswell answered, walking toward the pair, smoke rising from his musket, tilted barrel groundward, a rebel flag draped over his shoulders. "You put it out there, Jacob, an' well … I couldn't resist such a *yellow* target."

Rachael giggled. "How'd you sneak up on us like that?"

"He's half *injun*, Denia," Jacob said.

Roswell smiled. "Got me some Shawnee blood in these veins," he explained proudly, chin up, rubbing his musket-kicked shoulder. "My mama was half Shawnee. Heck, weren't nothin to it, really. Y'all goin on like school children made it pretty easy. If I'd been a rattler …"

"An' why are you haulin that ol' reb flag around with you like some child's blanket?" Jacob asked. "Might as well hang a target on your back. Some folks in the valley're liable to string you up for *less*."

Roswell ignored the question. "Well?" he baited.

"Well *what?*" Jacob replied, flicking pieces of black-eyed Susans from his shirt and face.

"You ain't heard?

"Heard *what?*"

"I'm *leavin*."

"Leavin?" Jacob asked, pretending this was the first he had heard. "Where to? When?"

"This evenin, after supper, I spect."

"To join Lee?" Jacob glanced toward Rachael.

"Right. To join Lee. So you *did* hear." Roswell lifted his gleaming Springfield. "Got my rifle cleaned an' ready. Works right good, wouldn't you agree? How 'bout you, Jacob? You ought to come along with me. Can't you just smell it?"

"Smell it? Smell what?"

"Fightin, Jacob! They's more yanks and rebs around here'n ears of corn! I don't think them boys're here to shake hands."

Rachael beamed.

"I aim to be a *part* of it," Roswell finished. "You comin?"

Jacob fidgeted, tending to missed flower debris. "I don't reckon my daddy ... I spect I ought *not*, what with the corn needin harvestin an' such."

"Harvestin! You ain't got *that* much corn *to* harvest, Jacob. Ain't Bigun an' his family takin care of such as that?"

"Well, yeah, they're helpin, as usual, but there's the wagon business an' all, and, well—"

"He ain't goin, Roswell," teased Rachael. "Isaac won't *let* 'im."

"My daddy ain't got *nothin* to do with this!" Jacob insisted. "This is *my* decision. There's the corn, and deliverin wagons to the Furnace ... an' who *knows* what else. More goin on around here than just some war."

"War's the *only* thing goin on around *everywhere*, Jacob. When you goin to understand that?"

"I got things that need tendin to first, Ros. Anyway, the time just ain't right. Maybe in '63. Next summer, maybe."

"By then it'll all be *over*," Roswell observed, rubbing with a corner of his flag fingerprints smeared on the barrel of his musket, "and you'll have missed it. I never understood your old man, Jacob. Never understood you neither."

Jacob stepped up to within a couple of inches of Roswell's face and placed his palm on Roswell's chest. "Me an' my daddy ain't on this earth for you to understand, Ros."

"What I mean is," Roswell said, clearing his throat, knowing that an unloaded Springfield was little defense against Jacob's superior ire, "here he is a *slave-owner*, yet he waves Ol' Glory around like a trophy. He shows *Union* and practices *Confederate*. Just seems he's a might confused. Like you, maybe?"

"Watch yourself, Ros. An' keep my daddy out of this, or you might just find that musket of yours bent 'cross your skull."

"No need gettin all riled, Jacob. I meant no disrespect. Here," Roswell said, extending his rifle-held hand, "how 'bout you take a shot? I'll load it for you."

Roswell took a cartridge from his pocket and with his teeth ripped open the top of the paper wrapper. Black grains of gunpowder painted his lips. Quickly, he poured the powder into the muzzle, followed by a drop of the conical bullet. Jacob watched the practiced precision of the process, marveling at Roswell's speed. Roswell seated the barrel's deadly contents with several swift plunges of the ramrod.

"The only thing I'm confused about is your eagerness to go an' get yourself killed, an' for *what?*"

"Eagerness? I ain't eager at *all* for that, Jacob."

"Then for what? You *did* hear what happened at Shiloh, didn't you? Yankees whipped 'em good. And at some place called Malvern Hill, too. Case you ain't heard, Ros, this here's a *real* war. Men dyin all over the place. How come? To keep their slaves? To take their slaves? To hold together this here Union? Reasons seem as slippery as Hog Trough Road in a spring rain, is what *I* think."

"I reckon you heard about what happened at Manassas? Lee's got himself a *real* army now. Dyin's for boys who ain't learned to shoot straight, Jacob. Or duck. I reckon I can do both. Here you go." Roswell handed Jacob the rifle. "You seen what I done to your … flowers," Roswell said, muting his chuckle. Rachael smiled. "Me an' Sally ain't *about* to let some Yank up and kill me."

"Sally?"

"My Springfield." Roswell patted the rifle's lock plate.

"You named your rifle … *Sally?*"

"She's my girl. To have an' to hold—"

"—'til death do you part," Jacob finished.

"We'll see about that," Roswell said, pulling the hammer to half-cock and pointing to the nipple. "Only thing left to do is to snap on this percussion cap. Right here." He smiled.

"I *know* what to do, Roswell," Jacob replied with irritation, feeling Roswell's one-upmanship played out in front of Rachael.

"Boys, boys!" feigned Rachael, her desire for a tussle rising. "Let's be … civil."

"Civil, my corn-fed *butt!*" Jacob mumbled.

"Jacob, you've always *wanted* a new rifle," Roswell said. "Just as *I* have. An' now I *got* me one."

"Where'd you get this, anyhow?" Jacob asked, sighting the rifle at a sycamore branch some fifty yards away.

"Around," Roswell answered, implying nefarious means. "Come on with me to the river and I bet them rebs'll even let *you* have one, straight from Harpers Ferry."

"Harpers Ferry's in reb hands again?"

"Well … not at the moment. But it will be soon, right where it belongs. You gonna shoot that gun or what?"

"Give me time. So, you're joinin up with Lee, are you? At the river?"

"Army of Northern Virginia, they call it now."

"Why the *river*? Rebs're all over the place, *here*. Bound to be a regiment in Sharpsburg that'll take you in."

"I'm aimin to meet Marse Robert hisself. I hear his headquarters is back toward Packhorse Ford. I gonna present him this flag," Roswell announced with peacock pride.

Jacob stilled his aim, taking sight of a hornet's nest wedged atop the sycamore's branches. He pulled the hammer to full-cock.

"I don't spect Lee has the time or the patience to tend to some fool kid's dreams of glory. This war'd be over in a month if the Yanks had *Lee* instead of McClellan. You believe slavery's right, Ros?"

"Slavery? Ain't give it much thought, I reckon. My daddy don't own none. Wouldn't want to *be* one, I know *that* much. Whatchu aimin at anyhow?"

"The rifle? Oh, I don't know. That sycamore maybe. I don't see the sense of fightin, Ros, especially dyin," Jacob said, "for the sake of a country that keeps human beings in bondage." Again, he steadied his aim.

"Me neither, Jacob. But, it ain't *just* about bondage," argued Roswell. "It's more about *states* decidin their own way, without the national government buttin in. Wait a minute. You ain't aimin to hit that hornet's nest, are you?"

"Afraid of a few hornets, Ros? Think of 'em as them bullets you figure on duckin from."

"It don't matter. You ain't *that* good a shot!"

"I thought all men were created equal," Jacob replied, parroting something he had heard from the mouths of cracker-barrel pundits. "Seems to me the South don't want the black man free. *Ever.* So, what'll you give me if I *do* hit that nest?"

"I agree with you, Jacob, but the *states* should have the right to decide that for *themselves*, not some faraway Federal government. I'll give you ... um ... I'll give you this here *flag*. But that won't happen 'cause you couldn't hit a sunnin pig if you was standin in slop *next* to one."

"What if," Jacob argued hypothetically, "Alabama sees fit to remain a Confederate state but, for economic reasons—say, sellin cotton to England, hell, to New Yorkers even—also sees it fit to abolish slavery? And what if Georgia don't go along with that?

Before long, Georgia slaves will hear about the *free* state of Alabama and will skedaddle there like miners for gold."

"Centralized government can't always be about what each *state* wants, is what he means, Ros," chimed Rachael.

Jacob and Roswell turned toward Rachael. "He *knows* what I mean, Rachael. Go pick some flowers."

"Says you, Jacob Hoffman." Rachael took a few paces away from the boys but kept a sharp ear turned.

"One state's *right* is another state's *problem*. What are there, thirty-three, thirty-four states? Can't have each one goin its separate way, Ros, like it was some whole other country. They'd be bumpin into each other left an' right." Jacob licked his thumb and swabbed the sight. "An' speakin of bumpin, Ros, you just watch *this*."

"I guess that's why they're fightin this war," Roswell said, his voice fading to a whisper as he looked across the breeze-swept field, catching for the first time a mental glimpse of the war's drivers. "Sure as the sun sets, they're bumpin into each other right now. It's a mess."

Ka-CHAM!

Rachael jumped. The oval nest exploded into a cloud of gray powder, sending angry hornets in all directions seeking their tormentor.

"An' I just can't sit this thing out," Roswell whispered unheard.

"You were sayin something about a *sunnin pig*, Ros?"

"What? Oh ... I spect you'll be wantin this flag."

"Keep it, Ros. It's a powder keg, with a lit fuse."

"Anyway, since when did you give a wit about bondage?" Roswell countered. "Bondage is what keeps your Daddy's wagon business a goin concern, food on your table. Besides, bondage is all them people know. Give 'em a little freedom and see how far they get. They *need* the Confederacy."

"*Need* the Confederacy? I think you been dippin in the cider again, Ros."

"The Union would just let 'em go wanderin around like sick puppies, beggars and thieves, to die on city streets and country lanes.

"Your Daddy's just foolin himself, wavin them stars and stripes while flauntin his slaves. South wins, they'll take away Bigun, ship him down to the Mississippi delta or the South Carolina low country to pick cotton. North wins, Bigun goes free. Mess, all right."

"Ros," Jacob asked, "if you had a wolf by the snout, would you keep holdin it or would you let it go?"

Roswell sidestepped the trap. "I wouldn't be a-holdin that wolf in the first place, but some believe they ought to have that right. When Lee whips the Yankees—and he *will*—he'll take Bigun down to the plantations of Mississippi, maybe even Charleston," Roswell said, as if he'd drafted the South's post-war intentions for border states, "and scatter Bigun's family to God-knows-where, leavin your daddy with *nothin*. Maryland's a border state *now*, but you wait an' see. She'll come around soon enough, I reckon. I give 'er a month or two. You, *too*, I spect."

"Aw, Ros, you're just flappin your jaws," Jacob replied, handing Roswell his rifle, "like always. Nice gun, by the way. Sho' 'nough do want *me* one."

"Then *come on!* Call it flappin all you want, Jacob. But, mark my words. You'll see. Come on with me, while you got the chance."

"He's got the chance *now*, Ros," Rachael chimed again. "Had it since *July*. You are aware that Lincoln has issued a call to arms for another three hundred thousand men."

"I'd heard such," Roswell replied. "You gonna be one of them Yankee boys, Jacob?"

"Slavery's plain wrong, and you *know* it. Even *Rachael* knows it, an' she ain't but fifteen! If I *was* gonna fight, it wouldn't be with Lee's army. I can't fight alongside soldiers that *support* holdin an sellin other humans. It ought to be the *people*, *each person*, decidin their own course, blacks included, not the wealthy politicians and plantation owners on our behalf. Besides,

Ros, you ain't gonna go join no rebel army no how. Come on, Rachael. Gettin late."

Rachael sauntered, hands clasped behind her back, feigning disinterest. "What'd you say, Jacob?"

Jacob grabbed Rachael's hand, whisking her in the direction of Jacob's home. "I said come *on!*" he whispered loudly. "You done talked too much as it is."

"Go on an' pick your wildflowers, Jacob," Roswell shouted. "We'll see who comes out smellin like a rose!"

"I'd rather *pick* flowers than *push* 'em outa the ground, Ros. You still comin to supper tonight?"

Rachael turned toward Roswell and with a tilted head gave him a coy wave and a wink. She wanted nothing more than to see Roswell tangle with Isaac Hoffman at his own supper table. No better fun, she figured, than to watch Roswell's sapphire almond eyes penetrate the ire of Jacob's daddy.

"I'll be there. Seven o'clock?"

"Seven prompt. You know how Jesse gets when folks ain't around to eat her cookin. She's whippin up some potpie."

"Chicken?"

"Ain't *no* other kind worth eatin! Jesse's the best chicken potpie-maker in the whole valley. If we could just get Lee an' McClellan to sit down an' enjoy some Jesse-made chicken potpie, the war'd be over before sundown."

"You're right about that!" Roswell shouted as he rammed home another round.

"Ros, you best watch where you're shootin that rifle!"

"Don't aim to shoot it, Jacob. Just keepin it ready, is all."

"And fold up that flag! Somebody's liable to mistake you for the enemy, for somebody who ain't holdin no *flowers!*"

"Shaw!" Roswell said, dismissing the possibility. "See you at seven."

"Make it six-thirty. Got some cats' eyes if you wanna go a round or two before supper. Hey, I hear you been talkin to rivers!"

Roswell stopped. "Talkin to … *what?*"

"To *rivers!* You an' the Potomac good buddies?"

"Might do you some good to give that river a listen, Jacob. Good place to reflect. Says more'n you might want to hear, though."

"Yeah, like *'Here comes the big bad Lee,'* whispers the river." Jacob tossed a stone and laughed.

"He's done crossed it, Jacob. Spect we'll find out soon enough what he's up to!"

"What he's up to is *plunder*, takin anything to feed his men!"

Roswell gave a sweeping wave of his arm and draped the banner around his shoulders, covering his back, and with a song of Dixie from his lips, he set off for Packhorse Ford.

"Somebody's goin to up an' *shoot* that damn fool!" Jacob said. "*Look* at 'im. He looks like some farmer's *barn door* walkin across that field. Billy Yank's *granny* could hit that."

"I think he's right *cute*, Jacob Hoffman," Rachael said, admiring Roswell's gait. "You'd be, too, with a flag wrapped across *your* backside. Even holdin a bouquet of flowers."

Jacob pulled the remnant of wildflowers he had stuffed in his pocket just before shooting Roswell's rifle. He looked at the shattered remains and threw them to the ground. Rachael giggled.

"Yeah, well, you think a slop hog's cute. Come on. I got to get on home."

Rachael snatched up a sunflower and slapped Jacob's back.

"Ow! Careful, Denia! That ain't no *flower* you're slingin. That's a dang *dinner plate!*"

Both laughed as they flung flowers and pebbles and stumbled through the fields toward Landing Road and Jacob's home.

Meanwhile, Roswell topped a bluff overlooking Packhorse Ford. The mighty Potomac River bent through the panorama like a sunning snake.

Ten days earlier, Roswell had watched another Roswell, Confederate General Roswell Ripley lead his four brigades in a spirited splash across the Potomac at the Point of Rocks. Men in gray and butternut sang "Maryland, My Maryland" as they negotiated the shallow, swirling waters. Shouts and laughter, a proud and arrogant sound, filled the air with confidence, as if these men knew something the rest of the country did not.

Roswell again witnessed the gathering gray bands in Frederick three days later while on a day trip with his daddy. He had a notion to join the Rebel army then and there, and would have, had his daddy not seen him cavorting with rebel soldiers near Rosenstock's Dry Goods and Clothing and yanked him away to lunch.

Groups of loitering rebels laughed upon seeing Roswell tugged by the collar. As his daddy pulled him into a restaurant, one rebel hollered, "Come take up a rifle when you can shave!" Those words rang in Roswell's ears like the percussions of a smoothbore.

Roswell knew Confederates patrolled the west bank of the Potomac, near Shepherdstown. He was anxious to prove his mettle in the eyes of the army he wished to join and thus began his wade across the river to return the Rebel battle flag he and Jacob had found a week earlier on the Harpers Ferry Road near the Antietam Iron Furnace. He sat on the Potomac's east bank, the barrel of the Springfield propped against his forehead, and stared at the water's swirls, just as he'd done day after day, contemplating the feat.

I'll show them rebs I'm as good as they are! He thought. *I'll bring 'em this flag, holdin my rifle high, an' I'll do it in front of Yankee eyes. Hell, they might even make me a Captain.*

He issued a sigh and rose from his perch. Securing the flag under one arm and the rifle in hand, he descended the hillside toward the slapping waters.

Halfway across the shin-deep shallows, Roswell heard the echo of a shout garbled by distance and space. He stopped and turned, seeing three figures atop the bluff, each holding a rifle. One waved his arm, motioning for Roswell to return to land. Not understanding why, Roswell shrugged and continued across. Again the shout came. Again he ignored it.

Shloop! Shlurp!

Roswell heard the sound, like stones splashing water. Echoed reports of rifle fire followed. Roswell turned.

"Yankees!" Roswell shouted between cupped hands, his rifle tucked in an armpit. "Go ahead and shoot, boys!" he shouted. "Y'all lucky to hit this *water!*"

As the soldiers reloaded, they again yelled something distorted by the ripple of water over rocks. The soldiers leveled their rifles. Roswell saw three puffs of dusty white smoke.

Shlurp! Shlurp! Shloop!

Three more shots sliced through the water, this time much closer, close enough to sprinkle his face. Roswell still believed the distance too far and his movement too swift to pose any real danger of being hit.

He raised high with one brazened hand a corner of the flag, enough to reveal its blue Southern Cross and white stars. He flaunted his rifle in the other hand, daring the soldiers, as if to imply he possessed immortality or a daunting superiority of firepower. He shouted a few obscenities, and his momentary stillness was all the soldiers needed.

Jacob and Rachael arrived home, arm in arm, to the smell of chicken potpie, potato soup and cornbread, specialties of Jesse's.

"Git on in here, Missuh Jacob, Miss Rachael! Wash on up and find yo' places," Jesse instructed, a scold in her tone for her suspicion of their childish indiscretions.

Jacob stopped and cupped an ear. "Did you hear that?"

"Of course I *heard* her. She's standin right there. Scruffy as ever, she is, but she's a sweetheart," answered Rachael.

"No, Rachael, not *Jesse*. Listen." A minute passed. "*That.* That, right there. Hear it?"

"Sounded like artillery, toward the mountain."

"Closer'n that. It's been buildin', Rachael. Somethin's about to blow. I can feel it."

Rachael looked at Jacob, his eyes toward the ridges east of the creek, excited words spilling from his lips. She turned her attention toward the river beyond the western horizon. Like the last wisps of evening light, Jacob's voice faded from Rachael's

Jacob's Baptism

world. A breeze passed through her hair, tossing the strands about and shuffling the leaves beyond. Her soul perked, her brows arched, as if she had heard the whisper of another's name.

Chapter 3

Evening orange passed into twilight gray. Jacob struck a match and lit the hanging lanterns. He looked down the wagon path and issued a long sigh as he resumed his seat at the shucking table. A steady breeze helped evaporate the sweat of his shirt, giving him an unexpected chill. Corn silks clung to his lap and lay scattered about the planks surrounding him. Thunder rolled from the distant north and west, clashing on occasion with the scattered rumblings of artillery from the east, reminding Jacob of something Rachael had said earlier in the meadow.

"Denia, you mentioned something back there about knowin *more*. Just what more *do* you know?" Jacob asked. "An' whycome you know so much about this war anyhow?"

Rachael grinned as she stroked with her brush tip freshly applied colors.

"More?" she asked, feigning forgetfulness. "Oh, that. Well, it's simple, really. I just … *fiddle!* Can't get this sunset to set right." Rachael took a step back, assessing the progress of her painting. "Too orange, more'n it need be. Reckon more purple'd do, pink maybe? Tell me what you think, Jacob."

Jacob craned his neck. "Red."

"Red? Are you sure?" Rachael turned her head sideways, imagining more red. "Maybe a touch, right about here. But ain't it still the prettiest sunset you ever did see, Jacob Hoffman?"

"Needs more'n a *touch* of red," Jacob replied, yanking away another husk. "Slop some red on it. Draws attention."

Rachael sighed. "What's that you're unravelin?"

"This paper?"

"What's in it?"

"This."

"Jacob Hoffman! When did you take up cigars?"

"Right about now, I reckon." Jacob scratched a match across the porch planks, its flame brightening the gray. "Ros gave me this one last Friday."

"Ros? What's your daddy gonna say?"

"Nothin. He ain't gonna know."

"You don't think he'll smell it?"

Jacob pondered that thought a moment. He gave the flame a puff, extinguishing it. "Reckon I'll smoke it later."

"Anyway, that cigar put me to mind of an answer to your question."

"What question?"

"The one about me *knowin* more, that's what question!"

"So tell me."

"Well, Lincoln's call for more men, for one thing. Askin for three hundred thousand more. For another, Daddy and me went over to Frederick last Thursday, to see my Aunt Vera. She's showing her age an' needs some help now and then. Comin home, we stopped to take a look at McClellan's grand Army of the Potomac. What a sight *that* was! As if the sky had swapped places with the ground! Looked like Lincoln had found every last one of his three hundred thousand, then some." Rachael paused, her eyes dancing at her memory of the occasion, as if careful to omit certain details destined ever to remain locked inside her vault of secrets.

"No sooner had we spread us a blanket in the meadow grass of somebody's farm, to take us some lunch, some soldiers millin about did the same thing, takin their rest, that is. About that time, somethin white caught my eye over by a fence rail. I went to over to see. Turned out to be a piece of paper folded around some cigars ... three, I think ... or was it four?"

Jacob ripped the stem off another ear and sighed, impatient.

"About that time, a corporal from the 27th Indiana walked up to me and introduced himself. Barton was his name."

"Barton? A *corporal?* The 27th Indiana? Pretty sure of your details, aren't you? Count the freckles on his cheeks, did you?"

"That's how he *introduced* himself, Jacob Hoffman. Barton was his name," Rachael noted, masking a slight smile.

"You *said* that. The *point,* Rachael!"

"I'm gettin to it. Hold your horses. Before he came over to me, I had the chance to take a peek at the papers wrapped around the cigars, four papers, actually. *Three* cigars. Jacob, I know this sounds crazy, but I think I found me some reb orders!"

Jacob stopped shucking. "What? You think you found ... *what?*"

"Reb orders, written by Lee hisself, orders directin his army's commanders, the movements of his whole army! And it appears that Lee's army, just a few days ago, was scattered over the countryside like leaves in a windstorm."

"No, you didn't!" Jacob shouted, annoyed by Rachael's grandiose claims, this one stretching skin-thin the notion of truth.

"I *read* them, Jacob, what I *could,* anyway, before Bar ... the *corporal* came along. Jacob, Confederates were all around us, *everywhere,* not just in Sharpsburg. Harpers Ferry, Hagerstown, Boonsboro ... South Mountain. The orders directed the movements of his entire army!"

"How do you know they were *Lee's* orders?"

"Said so on the papers. Special Order somethin. Well, sort of. The papers were copies of Lee's orders, copied by General Jackson. I reckon it was Jackson's handwritin. Had his signature right on it."

"Stonewall," Jacob muttered. *"Copies?* More'n *one* copy? What'd you do with them papers?"

"Gave them and the cigars to Bar ... the corporal. He seemed more impressed with the cigars than the papers, lightin up one an' takin big draws, shovin the other two in his pocket, before he even took a glance to them papers."

"Just *gave* 'em to him? Rachael, do you realize what you've done?"

Rachael looked at Jacob, the answer not apparent.

"That's why McClellan's camped across the creek, as we *speak!* Thanks to those lost orders, the Yankees were *bound* to have learned exactly what Lee was up to, where they was going, which is *here*."

"Just by what's written on this scribbly piece of paper?" Rachael asked, pulling the script from the bosom of her dress.

Jacob stared in disbelief. "That's ... that's the *orders?* I thought you gave it to ... to the corporal!"

"I *did*. But, like I said, there wasn't just the *one* copy. Figured I'd keep one of them copies for myself, to show you and Roswell, since y'all never believe a word I say. Here. Maybe you'll believe me now. Tell me what *you* think the scrawl says, Jacob Hoffman. Pretend to be McClellan."

"Yeah, right," Jacob replied, secretly relishing the notion of viewing the war through the eyes of the commanding General of all Union forces, feeling for the moment as if fate had handed him the course of victory for the nation, as if Lee's fate, the Confederacy's fate, rested in his palm and required only his words to invoke the actions necessary to surprise, overwhelm, and destroy the mighty Robert E. Lee. He snatched the folded papers from Rachael's hand.

The feeling fleeted like a wisp of smoke. Jacob knew the copy Rachael had given to the corporal had, no doubt, already found deliverance up the chain of McClellan's command. The armies, after all, were all but face to face, on the cusp of battle, the intelligence value of the lost orders now moot. His thoughts shifted to feelings of shame such as one might experience upon prying without permission into another's diary and consuming

revelations not meant for his eyes. Pulling on the papers'
corners, he hesitated.

"Go on, Jacob. *Open* it!"

"I *am!* Give me a minute."

With all deliberation, Jacob squinted and pulled back the tidy
square folds of the stiff parchment, indeed, the folds of his
curiosity. The words struck Jacob like ethereal bits.

'Confidential'

'Special Orders 191'

'Sept 9, 1862'

'Sharpsburg'

'Harpers Ferry'

'Copy by Genl Jackson'

'By command of Genl R E Lee'

"Dang if it *ain't*," he gushed in whispered excitement.
"Some fool rebel's gonna hang by the neck for losin *this!*"

"So, what's that paper sayin? What they gonna do, them
rebs?"

"Hush up! Give me a minute!"

Jacob read in places, paused in others, taking deep breaths,
discerning the confusing bits of military jargon into a sensible
whole.

"Daddy'll want to see this. Maybe *this'll* convince him."

"Your daddy's pretty set in his ways, Jacob. It'll take
more'n *that* to change his mind."

"Maybe not, Denia. He ain't never seen the war from *this*
point of view. Best he sees this now than wait until it explodes in
his own front parlor."

"Wait, Jacob."

"What *now?*"

"You *can't* show that to your daddy."

"An' just why not?"

"Don't you *see?* Word ever got to the rebs that a *yankee* girl
in Sharpsburg was in possession of *Confederate* orders, why
they'd hang *me* as a spy, quicker'n April lightnin!"

"A *yankee* girl?"

"You *know* what I mean, Jacob Hoffman! Soldiers comin and goin all over this part of the country, reb and yank. Gonna be quite a tussle, an' *soon!* Wouldn't want any of 'em thinkin *I* helped bring about this ruckus." Rachael was nothing if not self-important. "You ain't goin to tell him, are you?"

Jacob stared at Rachael, her jade-green eyes brimming with the sparkle of youthful persuasion. "I reckon not. But I'll be keepin these orders for now." Jacob jerked his arm away as Rachael tried to snatch the papers from his hand. Just then, the canter of hooves announced Isaac's return. Jacob shoved the wad of papers into his pocket.

"I got some news, Jacob. *Bad* news," Isaac said, dismounting his horse, his voice competing with the squeaks twisting from a homemade porch rocker.

"*Bad* news?" Jacob asked through a hollow grin. "Worse news than a cold supper an' us hungry, waitin' on you?"

"So have Jesse warm it up," Isaac said, as he looped the reins around a porch rail, giving Rachael a fleeting glance suggesting *she* should have kept supper warmed. "Hear me out, son. I'm late for a reason."

"It's okay, Daddy. Ros is late, too; expected him two hours ago. Probably shootin off his rifle, like he does his mouth."

"Son, I've been talking to the Chief Burgess. 'Fraid this concerns you, too."

Chapter 4

Jacob looked out across the dusk-draped fields as he whipped husks and silk off cobs, tossing the corn into one basket and husks into another. Rachael flicked the paint-wet brush across the canvas of her half-finished horizon, waiting to see what might emerge.

"Concerns *me?* What news, other than cold suppers, could possibly concern me on a day like this?" Jacob pulled the collar of his shirt to his forehead and soaked up the rising sweat. He sighed.

"Couldn't Jesse keep supper on a low fire, 'til I got here?"

"Reckon she could've—heck, *I* could've. She's got Bigun and her kids to feed, an' I got more corn to shuck than Lee's got soldiers. I don't mean to sound complainin about you bein late, Daddy. Just didn't think we ought to start without you, is all." Jacob lifted his eyes toward the western horizon and rubbed a bead of sweat dangling off his brow. "It's more this September air. Hotter'n the iron furnace, an' I still got me about fifteen bushels of corn yet."

"You got the cool of the evenin, son, and Bigun to help you in the mornin, after he rims those wagon wheels. 'Nother pair of hands would be nice," Isaac said, again his gaze turned to Rachael, "and I'll lend you that hand right after supper."

"I 'preciate it," Jacob acknowledged. "We saw Ros earlier this evenin, totin a sparklin new Springfield an' that old reb flag we found. Shoot, except for Ros showin off his rifle and spoutin off about joinin the rebs, today's been—"

Jacob stopped. He noticed the unflinching glare in his daddy's eyes and the tight pressing of his lips.

"Concerns me, you say?"

"It does, son."

"It's Roswell, ain't it?"

"Yes, son, it's Roswell. He's been shot."

Jacob paused as still as a cornered squirrel, absorbing the punch of his daddy's words. Then, as if nothing had been said, Jacob rubbed corn silk off his hands and reached for another ear of corn, avoiding an eye-to-eye acknowledgement with Isaac, his singular link to truth and the reality at hand. In a moment of sudden acceptance, his fidgety fingers stilled. Filled with growing frustration with this emerging truth, he lay to rest the silk-draped ear onto his lap. *"Damn,"* he whispered.

"Roswell's ... he's *dead?"* Rachael uttered inaudibly, tears welling against the rims of her disbelieving eyes.

She stirred her paints faster, straining as always to appear indifferent to the conversations between Isaac and Jacob. Not that she didn't care. This was Roswell, after all, whom she admired almost as much as she did Jacob. Roswell played as Rachael's marionette, her toy for use in manipulating Jacob to her liking. She loved Jacob and made no secret of her desire to have him as her husband. Someday. Perhaps after the dust of war had settled, after the Bartons of the army had slipped her grasp. Caught now in the crosshairs of Isaac's revelation, her attention piqued, though she dared not let it be known. Facing her canvas and clearing her throat, she dipped her brush into the red oil on her palette and pushed strands of hair behind her ear.

Isaac considered Rachael and her scheming ways an odious distraction to his son's sense of proper direction, as obvious to Isaac as the blue of a cloudless sky, despite his son's blind attraction to her. He believed Jacob's feelings toward Rachael little more than boyish lust, and he thought it only a matter of time before Jacob saw beyond the fog of her physical beauty. Rachael, Isaac believed, knew well her ways of playing with the minds of watchful males, sashaying her pubescent body around like the Sirens of Jason, casting her silken strands of hair to the wind like the nets of fishermen. Sharpsburg's adolescent males flocked to such like ants to sugar, and Rachael seemed quick to oblige.

Rachael spent much of her spare time goading Jacob and Roswell to pick a cause, as long as that cause involved the dash and glory of the Rebellion, marching with the invincible legions of Lee's Army of Northern Virginia. She did thus with the full knowledge of Isaac's staunch objections to the endorsement of either cause, north or south. She did not oppose Isaac, per se; just the futility of his anti-war tirades in the midst of the tide of a war irreversible. Seemed fitting to Rachael that a man who owned slaves ought to be investing in the defense of the practice, else denounce the hypocrisy of it and dispose of his slaves. She stared at her easel and pretended to apply a curl of red to her evening sky.

"When? Where did it— Is he ...?" Jacob asked, stumbling over each question.

"Yes," replied Isaac, answering Jacob's unfinished question. "This afternoon, on the river, down near Packhorse Ford. Way I heard it, Union soldiers, scouts I reckon, saw him wadin across the river and thought he was secesh. They called for him to surrender, even gave a few warning shots. He ignored 'em; they shot 'im."

"*Secesh?* Why, Ros weren't no more a Rebel than a chicken is a fox. He mentioned a curiosity about *both* sides, claimin the glory of war was temptin. *Me, too!* Who amongst us bucks ain't done *that* a time or two! Both of us wondered what it'd be like marchin and fightin an' kissin girls an' such. But *joinin* up? Not *Ros.*"

Rachael raised her eyebrows and resisted the urge to fling a loaded paintbrush at Jacob. She had not figured *'kissin girls an' such'* into her goading.

"There's more, son."

Jacob closed his mouth. He struggled to hold back the angry tears in his reddened eyes. He knew the rest of the story.

Why'd Ros go pretending to be a soldier and get hisself shot! He flaunts that rifle like a sack of gold! I told him so. Fun and games is one thing, but this? The jackass! Jacob's postmortem admonitions drowned away his daddy's voice, until he heard mention of the flag.

"He was wavin that fool Johnny battle flag y'all found near the iron furnace last week, waivin it plain as a full moon, just *darin* 'em. That's the same as fightin words, and he ought to have *known* better. Yankee soldiers all *over* the place around here. Confederate, too. A battle bigger'n Jericho's about to explode. I can feel it, what with all the soldierin goin on. I told you so." Isaac took a breath.

"Daddy, Ros told me today that he was fixin to join Lee's army. Made up his mind. I spect he was secesh after all, always talkin about states' rights an' such."

"Roswell was a fine boy, Jacob, but he let his ideology get the best of him. I reckon he got what was bound to be comin to 'im." Isaac paused and considered the boys' closeness. "What if *you'd* been *with* him! They'd a-shot you, too. Yankee soldiers don't take kindly to flag-totin boys, and they ain't going to stop and ask no questions. *Damn* fool kid! This is what war *does* to folks, Jacob, and when you're fightin your own people … well, it takes on a whole other level of hatred. Strange truth, I know, but hate's never meaner than when it's thrust upon the ones we love most. I told you it'd come to this."

Anger welled up inside Jacob. Roswell was dead, his best friend in all this world, aside from Rachael, and he had his doubts about her. He paced over to Rachael and stared at her sunset painting of Hog Trough Road and Ole Whooey's tree, images of innocence and once upon a time, of ideals now beyond his grasp.

She peered at him, not wanting to know his thoughts but knowing them nonetheless. She managed a smile, looking for a measure of reassurance in return. He glared at her, brows furrowed like fence rails, a scathing bolt of contempt she knew was payback for her relentless urging of Jacob and Roswell to join the army and fight like men, men in uniform.

Jacob knew his daddy was right, but adolescent pride shouted for a lashing out. He checked his rage and turned. His lips tightened like a dam at the push of floodwaters.

Nothing irritated Jacob more than his father's smug pacifism. Isaac Hoffman loathed the war, all war, as was expected of any faithful Dunker Baptist. Worse, Roswell's killing seemed Isaac's vindication, ammunition for his war against war.

This war was different, Jacob believed, the kind of war so different that it demanded not only a stand on ideology, but an active exercise of principles, even at the sacrifice of life. As far as Jacob could see, Isaac had only hollow principles, the sort of principles one flaunted unchallenged for selfish purposes at meetings of the Brethren and among like-minded pacifists. The purity of Isaac's principles—"Union first", freedom, peaceful reconciliation—blurred when confronted by the sanctity of his prosperity.

Jacob knew little about this war between the states, politically and militarily. He had heard the same rumors and glory-filled bravado and speeches meant to move men to action. He'd read newspaper accounts of battles and had glimpsed at casualty lists. But the drivers of this dissolution of the Union, the machinations that so split the nation like a stick of pinewood, seemed as esoteric and filled with the unanswerable as trine immersions and the Will of God.

Units of Union blue, like waves of an ocean's tide, washed toward the eastside bluffs and hills of Antietam Creek. Southern troops, their loins girded, poured into the western side of the valley of the Antietam, into Sharpsburg itself, like migrants, homeless and hungry. The village and its adjacent ridges and fields were awash in butternut and gray and brown, human form given to soil that seemed to rise from the ground.

Jacob's Baptism

Despite the near constant presence, since the war's outset, of some elements of the opposing armies, war and its vagaries held a fascination for Jacob, like the smoky imagery of campfire lore. He hadn't considered with any serious effort the stench of powder, of blood, of death, the waste of lives and futures, the reality of bodies turned inside out. Lincoln vowed to preserve the Union, with force if need be; the South vowed to create its own nation. And so it was.

Union; a house divided; force; secesh; slavery; rebellion; high-browed browbeating; young men fighting politicians' wars. All this hoopla seemed to Jacob no more than a husband whipping his wife into submission just to prevent her divorcing him. Divorce was inevitable.

Just let the South go, thought Jacob. *Give 'em their slaves and let 'em go!*

The issue of slavery, when given its proper consideration, stirred Jacob's soul like nothing else. The institution divided Maryland as it had divided a nation. Isaac, a Union loyalist and Lincoln supporter, owned four, and thus embodied a microcosm of the wedge of division. Jacob's attempts to justify state-sponsored servitude only made his long Hog Trough Road walks longer, spinning his tired mind for answers.

Rachael was right, Jacob knew, in her tirades against the institution of human bondage, part of why Isaac despised her so. If the Union had any reason to take up arms against its Southern neighbors, perhaps no nobler a cause than forcing an end to the ownership of human chattel provided reason enough. Maybe ideology and its dutiful exercise—a stand—was as simple as that.

Maybe Rachael was right, too, about joining. The Sharpsburg Rifles needed men. Maryland needed protection, though from whom, Jacob was unsure. He was sure slavery needed ending.

On the other hand, Roswell was dead, Jacob learned, shot by a soldier from the army of a nation bent on injecting its will, not only upon the policies of states but upon individuals as well. The ideological question, its fog having lifted just minutes before, now seemed again irrevocably thick.

The issue of slavery demanded resolution, Jacob concluded, if the Union were to survive, but he struggled with accepting one tyranny as the replacement of another. Better, he thought, to allow the South to deal with its ugliness alone.

Too late.

Maybe John Brown was right, Jacob thought. *Maybe the crimes of this guilty land will not be purged away but with blood.*

"Come on, Rachael, let's go for a walk," Jacob said, taking her hand.

"What about your supper, son?"

"Reckon it can wait a bit longer. We'll be back directly," Jacob replied. "Go ahead an' take yours."

Rachael stood, her hip knocking the paintbrush to the porch, its red goo splattering the planks. Isaac sighed.

Jacob and Rachael reached Hog Trough Road, a stretch of farm lane connecting the Hagerstown Pike to the Boonsboro Pike. The lane's high embankments afforded the pair a sense of privacy, their favorite place in the valley. Hand in hand, they walked its length, maintaining their silence, alone in their thoughts as they kicked loose stones.

"Remember when you'd come down here and paint, Denia?" Jacob asked. "All day, you'd do that, an' I'd sit and wait, chewin on grass and flingin rocks at Ole Whooey." Jacob spit out a laugh. "Never could hit that ol' bird. He'd sit on a branch, still as a statue, wide-eyed, *darin* me to hit 'im, like he knew I never would. Let's go see what Ole Whooey's up to."

"Makin ready for his hunt, I spect, night fallin like it is." Rachael sighed as the last glitter of sunlight vanished, puffs of clouds an amber orange. "Some of my best work was done here. Remember the time Ole Whooey swooped down and picked one of my brushes, plucked it right out of my hand, like it was some field mouse? He circled his tree a time or two and dropped that brush when he realized he couldn't eat it." Rachael chuckled.

Jacob issued a brief smile in response.

"Why'd he do it, Rachael?"

"Because he *had* to."

"Because you made him *think* he had to."

"Jacob, I did not *make* him. Ros had a mind of his own. He was just a bit too eager to act on his thoughts."

"Some of his thoughts grew from seeds," Jacob suggested. "Reckon who *planted* them seeds."

Rachael stared at the ground.

"John Jacob?" Rachael cooed after a few minutes of silent walk.

"Yes, Rachael Erin."

"Ever notice how cherry blossoms blow to the ground, while still white as snow?"

"Yes. Most trees' blossoms do."

"Not like the cherry tree's."

"What's your point?" Jacob asked, aware that the only relevant point was Rachael's poetic ramblings, her way of dealing with the discomfort of adversity.

"Don't know, I guess. All I know is that folks don't want blossoms to brown on the branch," she said, looking at a cherry tree bordering the road. "I reckon trees don't want that, either. Folks don't want them to fall white, leavin the tree and clutterin the ground."

"What are you gettin at, Denia?"

"Don't want 'em to fall at all, I reckon. Just stay on the tree, white, forever. I guess folks have to decide whether *they're* going to brown on the tree … or brown on the ground. Either way, seems the brown's always coming. Ros didn't want to brown either way, did he?"

Jacob knew Rachael had slipped into her Miss Emily persona. Such was Rachael's only way of making sense of a senseless world. Better to nod his head, he thought, to feign understanding, than to scrunch his eyebrows and beg explanation.

Jacob touched her chin with a finger and gently lifted it. He brushed away tears dribbling down her cheeks.

"It's okay, Rachael. I like to think Ros would have joined up anyway, without anybody's encouragement. I think that's just what he was doin."

Rachael nodded acknowledgement. Jacob kissed her forehead and took her hand into his. They made their way past

Roulette's farm lane intersecting Hog Trough Road near the point
of its southeastward bend. Piper's corn pleaded picking and
Jacob joked that he reckoned Ole Whooey might just get the job
done, swooping as he was for field mice.

Jacob's Baptism

Chapter 5

Pinkney slumped in his chair, shadows
serving as a shroud, the front rim of his slouch hat tilted
downward, fingers interlocked around his empty whiskey glass.

"Else *give* me that bottle, or *pour* me another," he demanded
of his partner, Simon. "You're smotherin it like it was your
woman! And keep your blame voice down."

Avoiding the slightest swivel of his head, he surveyed a
congregation of Union loyalists sharing a sudsy toast in a
Sharpsburg saloon.

Pinkney bent forward and lifted the whiskey glass to his lips.
"Talkin about snarin darkies is one thing," he said behind the veil
of the glass, "like braggin about some twelve-point rack you ain't
so much as *seen*, much less *killed*. But goin out an' *doin* it—
catchin a runaway—well, that's *tenfold* harder. Like deer, they
smell you comin."

He turned up the glass and swallowed fast his jigger of
whiskey, squinted, and exhaled as if he were expelling fire from
his lungs. As the crowd roared at somebody's joke, Pinkney

slammed the glass onto the table and shook his head like a dog in the rain, the slouch hat falling to the floor.

"Old Monongahela! Whoo-ee! Dadblame volcano in a bottle!" Pinkney slapped each cheek and replaced his hat. "Like I said, a black man, especially them runaways, is like a fox downwind; he can *smell* you comin, put a knife twixt your ribs, before *you* know up from down," Pinkney explained, fingering the glass of its clinging drops sliding slowly down its side. "Can't explain it. They hear you. They read your mind. So, you got to outsmart 'em, throw 'em off their guard. That's where the experienced hand of ol' Pinkney comes in.

"These belong to Isaac Hoffman. Staunch supporter of Lincoln, so he claims, and a man who prefers Maryland stay Union but *keep* her slaves, or at least *he* keep *his*. Wants it both ways, he does. Wants the protected right to own slaves, but he just as soon *not fight* for that right. He ain't much on the South and secesh, considers 'em as common vagabonds, but he sure as hell loves their ways of doin' business. I'm going to show him another way of doin' business, *my* way of business."

"How you reckon to do that, Pinkney?" Simon asked, Old Monongahela splashing into his glass.

"Simple as rain. I'm gonna take his slaves from him, same as he took 'em from me. They're runaways, sure as water's wet. I spect some plantation boss is busy as we speak, tryin to explain how them slaves come up missin." Pinkney chuckled and pressed his forefinger against his left nostril and snorted, sending a gooey wad to the floor.

"Runaways? How you know that, Pinkney?"

"Got their owner's brand on their forearms, and it ain't Hoffman's, that's how I know."

"How'd he take 'em from *you*, Pinkney?"

"*Outbid* me! Had 'em bought, I did. Claggett did too, I reckon, but then that ol' borderman Hoffman doubled the bid at the fall of the gavel. I wasn't prepared to top a bid such as that. Thought Claggett would've, but he just walked away.

"Least I could've *dealed* with Claggett, but Hoffman … money ain't no object to Hoffman. Took the whole family, an' as he drove off in his fancy wagon, like he was King of Somalia, told me I wasn't breakin up *this* nigger family."

"So how *do* we get hold of 'em?" Simon asked.

An arrow of late morning sun spread its inexorable shaft across the table. Pinkney tilted his slouch hat forward to shadow a scar that traversed the arc of his left cheekbone from his ear, under the eye, up to the bridge of his nose, like a path of jagged, pink corduroy. Conspicuous scars across one's face spoke of unsavory encounters, perhaps 'Wanted' bills, and Pinkney found no value in drawing attention to that voice.

The saloon chatter huffed and barked like the bellows of the Antietam Iron Furnace. Despite the cacophony of wartime banter, folks had a way of recognizing above the din any talk of slaves and slavery, like discerning a tornado from a dust devil.

His wary eyes upon a group of farmers at the end of the cherrywood bar, Pinkney said to Simon, "You know of the underground railroad?"

Simon leaned closer and stared blankly into Pinkney's eyes. "Can't say that I do, Pinkney." Taking the whiskey glass to his lips, rivulets dribbling down his chin and to the table, Simon gulped, exhaled and wiped his mouth with a single broad swoop of his forearm. "Ain't never heard of no train takin underground tracks."

"An' I don't spect you'd give a newspaper a decent read if someone was to *pay* you," Pinkney observed, shaking his head. "Allow me once again to teach you a thing or two. This kind of railroad is a network of abolitionists stretching from Florida up across the Mason-Dixon all the way to Canada. They provide sanctuary for darkies runnin from their masters north to freedom. A railroad's what they call it, but it ain't no ribbon of steel.

"This railroad's somebody's cellar, somebody's attic, somebody's closet. This railroad's like the North Star, a guidelight and passage through the dark of night; it's symbols painted on tree trunks; it's lanterns hangin on hitchin posts. It's treachery and deceit. It's escape from bondage. It's a taste of hope for those not meant to know its flavor. It's downright *treasonous* to our beloved Southern way of life is what it *is!*

Jacob's Baptism

"Which is why *we*, acting as the instruments God that Jeff Davis intended …" Pinkney declared, almost standing, his blood up, "… well, we have got to *sweep* these darkies back south, to their rightful place." He clenched his fist around his glass, and poured another shot. "That, and there's a heap of money to be made from the effort. A man's property is a man's *property*, even if that property is a man. We are merely providin a service to a market in distress. What's worse, my friend, is that Lincoln has spoke of creatin *Negro regiments* from runaways. Armed slaves fightin their betters. The very thought … We got put a *stop* to it."

The revelry in the saloon continued unabated. Excitement filled the smoky stench. Men and boys pushed through the swinging doors like couriers, delivering the latest rumors and gossip.

Townsfolk shared eye-witness accounts of the two great armies camped within a shell's lob—fighting distance—of the town. Lee had brought his men over by way of Boonsboro from the rumble at South Mountain and had scattered his men along the ridges bordering the east side of town, the Potomac River to his back and within a spit's distance of Antietam Creek in his front. Longstreet's men were seen streaming toward the northern end of the valley, down from Hagerstown. General McClellan was on Lee's heels, just east of Antietam Creek, endless waves of blue splashing up clouds of beige stretching from Smoketown to Boonsboro.

Confident his legions could destroy McClellan anytime, anywhere, Sharpsburg was Lee's chosen ground for such work. So confident was Lee, he opted not to construct earthworks or other manmade means of defense, relying instead on the land's natural fortifications, its rock outcroppings, its patches of woods, its sunken lanes.

Exhausted gray soldiers, many shoeless and all hungry, poured throughout the day through village and valley, their numbers growing into a formidable line three miles in length along Sharpsburg Ridge. Pendleton's batteries held the high ground on the northern end of Lee's line, at Nicademus Hill.

A panting lad burst through the saloon's doors. Eyes and ears turned as the boy delivered word that Stonewall Jackson's men had captured the twelve-thousand-man Union garrison at Harpers Ferry, a half-day's march south, along with an equal number of small arms, dozens of field guns, wagons of provisions, and crates of ammunition. The rear of Lee's army now secure, despite its back to the Potomac, imminent battle had come calling on Sharpsburg's fields and parlors.

Families streamed in response out of Sharpsburg northward toward Hagerstown and southward along the Harpers Ferry Road. Talk of a great battle simmered to boiling on street corners and front porches, like summer stew. Pinkney and Simon cooked stew of their own.

"Hoffman gives his slaves, especially the big one—hell, they even *call* 'im Bigun—a day of freedom every week. Lets 'em go wherever they please, long as they're back before suppertime."

"Sounds like Hoffman's slaves ain't exactly ... *slaves*," Simon observed.

"Not by Southern standards, they ain't. Like I said, Hoffman wants it both ways. He likes the convenience of their labor, but he don't want 'em runnin off to Philadelphia or Boston or Canada. So he lets 'em run loose down here for one day a week. Lets 'em taste freedom tethered near the comforts and safety of three squares an' a roof. That way, he figures, they won't risk uncertainty in a North growin angrier each day with Southern victories."

Pinkney paused and snickered.

"Know what else? I hear tell he's lettin the big man *buy* his own freedom. Buyin his freedom will do that black man about as much good as a bible at a lynchin. It'll take him 'til the moon turns green to earn that freedom, an' then he ain't *free*, nowheres near. Yessiree, he's better off right where he is. Yankee mamas are losin their sons fightin to free these slaves."

"Fightin' to *free slaves?*" Simon asked. "I thought this war was about preservin the union."

"Was at first, but it's gettin bigger'n that, so I'm told."

"Such as?"

"Such as England ain't gettin so much Southern cotton no more. Such as they're givin thought to givin aid to the Confederacy, military aid to break up the Union blockade so the cotton can get through. Such as some up north are of a mind to just let the South have their slaves and their country, especially after Pope's disaster at Manassas last month. Northern folk ain't takin' kindly to the idea of restorin the Union as it was, not at the cost of all the blood and battles lost.

"Anyway, if Hoffman's any kind of a businessman, he's threatened to sell his slaves to parties South if they *do* try to run away. Plenty of soul-drivers around these parts to run 'em down if they do run. Ain't nothin like the specter of a Southern plantation to unfrizz a darkie's hair."

Both men laughed, an outburst overwhelmed by the ruckus of the latest news concerning the surrender of Harpers Ferry. Pinkney downed his fourth shot of whiskey and poured a fifth. Simon drained what little remained straight from the bottle.

"Barkeep!" shouted Pinkney, between coughs. "Another bottle of this firewater!" His demand went unheard and unheeded.

"How big ... how big is this Bigun?" Simon asked, rolling shreds of tobacco into a cigarette.

"Big enough to break *you* over his knee. Claggett's the only man I ever knowed that might bring Bigun down. *Might*, I tell you. We got to get to Bigun before Claggett does. I hear Claggett's comin to collect on a certain debt. Might be here already."

"So, where you reckon Hoffman's niggers're off to today?" Simon asked. Smoke oozed from his nose and mouth, framing his face as he spoke.

"I seen 'em in Sharpsburg this mornin, Bigun and Hoffman's boy, poles on their shoulders. Bigun's family was taggin behind. Fishin in the Antietam, I spect, over at Rohrbach's Bridge. I reckon we'll head that way first."

"*Rohrbach's?*" asked an unnerved Simon, reaching to take another swallow from the empty bottle. "What about all the soldierin goin on over yonder, goin on *everywhere?* Fightin's liable to break out any minute.

"I spect Bigun and the Hoffman boy don't care nothin about that, else they'd be skedaddlin, too! I figure they'll mosey on down to the creek like it's a Sunday afternoon. Anyhow, all this battle talk's just that—*talk!* Ain't gonna be no *battle*, not like folks are sayin. They'll fire a shot or two and stare at each other, is all."

"But the place is *swarmin* with soldiers," Simon observed. Lee's placed some of his guns up yonder at Nicodemus's. Some say McClellan's got his Grand Army of the Potomac's just across the creek. Smellin like a battle to me, a big'n at that."

"They've been soldierin around here, more or less, for goin on two years now," Pinkney said dismissively. "Ain't nothin come of it yet, 'cept that little spat at the mountain yesterday. They're just a couple of big ol' barn roosters showin their spurs is all."

"How we gonna catch 'em?"

"We're going to walk right up to 'em, ask 'em how's their luck," Pinkney replied with a broad smile of cratered, yellow teeth, "an' take 'em."

"Just like that?"

"Just like that."

"I thought you said snarin a slave's as hard as takin down a deer; they smell you comin," Simon said, confused by Pinkney's confidence.

"It is," confirmed Pinkney, "but once you got 'em down the sight of a barrel, game's over. Of course, I'd rather not do it that way. Makes 'em all persnickety an' mad. We got to make 'em *think* we're deer, that we're their friends, *blend in*. They won't see the trap 'til it's sprung."

"I'm listenin," Simon said, wanting details. "But don't seem to me they're gonna see *any* white folk as friends."

"We're going to wear the masks of the very people they *have* come to trust, the *abolitionists*," Pinkney said as he scratched a match across the table and set it under the tip of his cigar. "Convince 'em we're tracks on the railroad, lanterns on the posts.

Tell 'em we know this fine upstandin family up Boston-way
lookin to take on some house servants, pay 'em *wages*. No more
sweat of the field, we'll tell 'em. No more threats of bein sent to
the cotton states. Cool Boston summers and a chance for some
real education. Bein house niggers sure beats the snot out of
dawn-to-dusk field-farmin, blacksmithin, and barn-cleanin, even
when you do get one day a week free."

Simon pondered Pinkney's words.

"So … what say we go bag us a twelve-pointer!" Pinkney
drew heavy on his cigar, blowing the cloud of smoke toward the
ceiling.

Simon smiled. He pulled his Remington from its holster and
clicked through the cylinder, affirming its fullness.

"Let's move." Pinkney slid back his chair and slapped
Simon on his back. He flipped a silver dollar onto the table as
they rose. The coin struck the tabletop, spinning on the wood
tabletop as they departed. Heads down, the two men slithered
unnoticed past the chattering groups. The dollar kept spinning,
dizzily spinning, slowing to a wobbly cadence, tails up.

A man standing a few paces back in a darkened corner of the
saloon nursed his glass of beer. Finishing, he wiped droplets
from his chin and sauntered up to the silver-dollared table. He
lowered his thick palm onto the coin, picked it up, and placed it
inside his shirt pocket as he watched the pair exit the ever-
swinging doors.

Antietam Creek carved a gentle, winding trough through
rock-strewn foothills just east of Sharpsburg and in the shadows
of South Mountain. Its shallow waters, swift in spots, serene in
others, its purpose certain and lean, flowed in peaceful constancy,
a contrast to the might and bluster of the armies simmering near
her banks.

Jacob accompanied his daddy's slaves to the creek this
Tuesday, as was his practice on their 'free' days, after completing

his share of chores, not to watch for their possible flight, but because they shared mutual enjoyment of each other's company.

Isaac Hoffman owned six slaves, two of which had died of malaria two summers prior. Bigun's family of four, including a wife and twin girls, remained. Isaac believed 'slave' too oppressive a term, meant for those beaten into submission and otherwise deprived of social and familial rights, and he resented the relentless description.

An unwavering Unionist by his own reckoning, Isaac purchased his slaves from bounty hunters in 1853 at auction in Hagerstown. He paid $4,500 for the lot of four, all captured runaways, doubling the bid of Claggett Parker's at the gavel's fall.

Isaac justified the purchase as an act of rescue, preventing the inevitable and irrevocable scattering of the Negro family. His action purchased also the undying devotion of the slaves, each preferring bondage, even death, to separation. Isaac further justified the legality of human holdings in his divided border state as measures of charity, acts of benevolence, as humane as taking in stray dogs. An impoverished people, possessors of no rights under the law, if released to the jaws of freedom, he reasoned, stood no chance amid an increasingly angry and war-weary populace.

Keeping slaves—'help', his preferred term—from the sticky hands of slave-hungry Southern coastal plantation lords was nothing less than an act of common morality and noble sacrifice, Isaac believed. That he derived financial benefit from their services, he also believed, was at worst, coincidental, and at best, a fair return. Isaac would, on rare occasions, wield the threat of the slave family's division and delivery to points south should any of them "cross the line", a term intended vague in what might constitute such a crossing, but certain in the effects of its message.

These human cattle, and one seventeen-year-old son, Jacob, allowed Isaac, in addition to his farming activities, the financial benefit of maintaining a lucrative wagon-making operation. Isaac carried on the family business of manufacturing farm wagons and wheels, a family tradition begun 1795 with the manufacture of Conestoga wagons.

Bigun, nicknamed such by Jacob upon seeing the man lift the rear-wheel end of a loaded Conestoga, worked as Isaac's blacksmith. He possessed the enviable skill, among others, of wrapping red-hot rims of iron around wooden wheels and hammering them into place.

As for the Confederacy, Isaac considered it and its armies little more than bawdy bands of outlaws. Beyond treason, Isaac believed, their sole purpose was the pillaging and plundering of not only his crops, cattle, and furnishings but of his help as well. He gave his help three meals a day and a roof over their heads, more surely than they could get south of the Mason-Dixon and probably better than fending for themselves in the free North. Isaac trusted that Lincoln would not strip the border states, Union states, of the right. Isaac Hoffman considered himself a sort of savior, righteous in his brand of morality without the recklessness of John Brown.

Jacob, meanwhile, had yet to cast commitment regarding his desired course for the war, though his curiosities of war bubbled up in his mind with increasing frequency, taking over his unspoken thoughts, pushing him closer to a decision. He was a boy on the edge of manhood, a lad caught between the pull of innocence and the push of responsibility. Experience had taught him to think, and thus he was not without his opinions, though pliable as taffy.

He viewed the Confederacy through clouded lens. States should have the right, he believed, to declare independence from the Union. The ownership of men by other men, he also believed, was the work of the devil and a lesion upon all of humanity. If the South insisted on keeping her slaves, let the South keep also her country. Let the practice and the nation sink alike under the weight of injustice. Let the lesion be severed.

The stretching shadows of war spread a pall of gloom over Maryland, over Sharpsburg, and over the valleys of the Antietam, the Potomac, and the Shenandoah, despite the successes of Lee and Jackson, perhaps because of them. Virginia played stage center in the war for Southern independence, and her resources strained to keep up. Battles at Manassas, the Peninsular, and the Seven Days had dispelled the notion of a quick war.

Christmas was a short three months away. Soldiers wondered unavoidably if the Christmas of '61 had been their last. The boredom of encampment, interrupted by brief, ferocious spurts of battle, had hardened hearts into believing the only hope for escape from the ordeal was, indeed, an enemy bullet.

Southern high command, flush with summer victories at Manassas and the Seven Days, believed the time had come to push the issue northward. Late summer brought harvest time and renewed hope that Southern troops had only to replenish their bellies, haversacks, and cartridge boxes for the final push to Washington and the winning of their country. And the keeping of their slaves. They held fast and proud to their growing sense of invincibility. Second Manassas provided all he evidence needed. Such an attitude had carried inferior armies to heights of superiority. The Army of Northern Virginia, gathering and camping on the high ground east of Sharpsburg, was such an army.

The man holding Pinkney's silver dollar was such a man. He turned the coin between his fingers as he watched Pinkney and Simon mount their horses and ride eastward on the Boonsboro Pike.

"Mister?" said the barkeeper, tapping the man on the shoulder, "I reckon that dollar belongs to the house."

The man wheeled around and, taking hold of the barkeeper's chin and jaw, touched the tip of his Bowie knife against the barkeeper's throat. The wide-eyed barkeeper lifted his hands to shoulder height. The man said nothing as he dropped the coin to the floor and returned the knife to his belt.

"Claggett," whispered a patron.

"Claggett? Claggett *who?*" asked another.

"You don't know?" the patron asked, surprised anyone living didn't know. "Parker. Claggett Parker. But the first name's all you need to know. Used to work over at the Antietam Iron Furnace. These days, buys an' sells slaves up in Hagerstown.

Did, anyway, 'fore they run him off. Been gone half a year, what I hear, delivering a load to a Savannah plantation. Mean nail-eater, I hear. Folks say he'd kill his mama if she come between him an' a slave deal. Wonder what he wants in Sharpsburg?"

Claggett reached into his pocket and pulled out a five-cent coin to pay for his beer. "Much obliged," he said, the words rumbling from his tongue like distant thunder. He placed the coin on the bar.

The crowd disbursed piecemeal from their tables and conversations, like intermittent gusts of autumn breeze through piles of leaves. Claggett walked away, not once turning his head to see who might be staring at him. Two Remingtons, like soldiers awaiting orders, kept the belted Bowie company on his hips. The man mounted his horse and yanked its head eastward, toward the creek, and spurred it to a gallop.

Chapter 6

Jacob and Bigun sat atop one of the stone walls along the span of Rohrbach's Bridge. Their pole lines bobbed in mid-creek, more in response to the occasional nudge of a ripple of water than to nibbles of fish. Squads of Confederates marched past, establishing positions on the bluffs and high ground overlooking the southeastern banks of Antietam Creek. They dug their rifle pits and constructed breastworks amid spits of laughter and jabs of profanity and occasional queries of "Havin any luck?", as if begging to borrow such luck.

Other soldiers, skirmishers, ventured out into the fields on the opposite bank, probing for enemy positions. Jacob gazed at the surreal sight, the kill-me-if-you-can exposure of men offering up their lives in return for knowledge that might help the army, aid the coming fight, and he thought of Roswell.

Sprinkles of rain, just enough to offer a taste of relief, fell from sun-silvered clouds. Jacob heard the hollow roll of distant thunder and surveyed the sky. The smell of imminent rain, an odor like wet cotton, filled the air.

"You know de Robert E. Lee?" Bigun asked. "Talk to 'im, I mean?"

Jacob's Baptism

"I know *of* him," Jacob said, "but I ain't *never* talked to him." Jacob's eyes widened at the utter improbability of such. "I don't think General Lee come all this way to Maryland to strike any conversation with me. Best you get a wiggler back on your hook an' give it a bath, maybe slap a wet *cloth* 'cross your head."

"Yassuh," Bigun said, a smile of tease across his lips. He baited the hook and slung his line back into the stream.

"But, Lee, ain't he gawn need a place to hide when dese Yankees whup 'im? I figured he might come a-knockin' on *yo'* do'e," Bigun said, after which a laugh burst from his white-toothed smile.

"You're a funny one, you are," Jacob said, smiling, pulling up his line in response to a tug. He sighed. "Ain't bitin', Bigun. What say we go on down to Snavely's."

"Spect they ain't bitin there none, neither, Missuh Jacob."

Jacob heard the rumble of hooves and caught a glimpse of several horse-drawn cannon atop the bluff. "I'm sure you're right." Jacob patted his belly. "Gettin' hungry. Let's get on home an' eat."

"Sound *real* good to me, suh. Lemme gathuh up my folk."

Jacob smiled. "Will you stop it with the 'Mister Jacob' and 'sir' stuff! I'm your *friend*, not your better." Jacob extended his hand to Bigun's shoulder. "Fact is, I know of *no one* better'n you, Bigun, white or black."

"Thank you, s—"

The pair pulled in their poles and packed their bait. A few civilians walked the hills overlooking the creek, leaning from time to time to whisper thoughts in companions' ears, their curiosity with the gray soldiers directing their steps. The soldiers ignored these lookers except to warn them away.

Pinkney and Simon huddled amid the bramble at the base of a sycamore on the bank of the Antietam near the bridge. Pinkney slid his Colt from its hold and checked each chamber of the cylinder.

"Let's catch us some slaves," Pinkney whispered, and he kissed the barrel.

"What about them rebs up yonder, an' the civilians?" asked Simon.

"Ain't gonna be no shootin. Besides, we're too far away for our words to be heard, an' them rebs don't give a hoot's hooey about us no how."

A blue heron flapped awkwardly into the air, hinting of the men's presence, splattering creek water like a summer rain shower. Pinkney tapped Simon on the arm and nodded. Both men arose, as if appearing from thin air, and stepped around the scrub. They walked up the creek bank, slapping dust from their pants, startling Jacob and Bigun.

"Gentlemen!" said Pinkney, smiling, waving, his eyes following the pair's movements. "How's your luck this fine mornin?"

Bigun sensed immediately their mischief, noticing the long Colts strapped to their hips. He eyes shifted from the sidearms to Pinkney's scar. The smell of whiskey filled Bigun's nostrils. He took a periphery view of Jacob, who had no consideration for the trouble brewing.

"Been here most of the mornin, sir," replied Jacob. "But the fish ain't bitin, barely nibblin. Must be all the commotion goin on 'round us."

"Reckon so, young man," Pinkney said, lifting his hat and scratching the back of his head. "Certainly is a lot of … a lot of commotion, all right. What … whatchu baitin with?"

"Grubs, bark, stems, stuff like that. Whatever'll fool them suckers," Jacob said with a laugh.

"Nothin shiny?"

"Not really. Don't spect it's the bait, though. More likely them rebs kickin up the water, fillin their canteens. Lot of that goin on, soldiers back an' forth to the water. Y'all think we in for a battle?"

"Could be, son," Pinkney said, adjusting the brim of his hat, "but I wouldn't go worryin much about that if I was you. Unless you're thinkin about *joinin* 'em, seein what they're *up* to."

Jacob returned a short chuckle, his thoughts turning to Roswell.

"Thought we'd head over to Snavely's Ford, try our luck there, but we done heard a louder call for lunch."

Pinkney smiled. "What's your name, boy?"

"Jacob Hoffman, sir."

"Hoffman ... Hoffman. You wouldn't, perchance, be Isaac's boy."

"Yes, sir, I am. He's my daddy," answered Jacob. "Makes wagons over in Sharpsburg. You know him?"

"Indeed. And a fine craftsman he is. Say, your ... your black friend there ... he wouldn't by chance be a ... be a slave, now, would he?"

Jacob's smile lowered slightly. He turned to Bigun.

"This man's my daddy's helper. He's a blacksmith in the wagon shop. Name's Jim, an'—"

"You can call me Bigun, suh," he interrupted, the tone rolling from his lips like a snorting bull.

"My, my, indeed you are a ... big-un, aintchu?" noted Pinkney scanning Bigun's frame with a buyer's eye. "Well, Jim ... pardon my manners ... Bigun ... if you *happened to be* a man of bondage, despite Jacob's description to the contrary, then what would you say to a ride on the train to freedom?"

"Train to freedom, suh?"

"Well, not exactly a *train*, but damn close. And freedom, certainly. Allow me to explain—"

"Come on, Missuh Jacob," Bigun said, grabbing Jacob's arm and turning away.

"Wait, Bigun. Please. Go with us, sir, and we'll deliver you to Boston, Massachusetts, to a man of considerable wealth— exporter by trade—who will promptly put you in the employ of one Samuel Vanlandingham, a prominent Boston physician in the immediate need of a *paid* house servant. That's right ... *paid*.

"I am prepared to compensate your master—if a slave you be—quite handsomely and deliver you myself to Mr. Vanlandingham," Pinkney continued, glancing over at Jacob. "Shall we begin our journey, *your* journey, to freedom?"

Bigun stared. "I'm a blacksmith, suh. A wagon-maker. I ain't *nobody's* house nigguh."

Pinkney cleared his throat and smiled. "I'm sure that …
what I mean is, Mr. Vanlandingham can *accommodate* your skills
to their most advantageous use, inside his house or outside. The
important thing is that you will have your freedom. Freedom to
move about as you wish. *Paid* freedom.

"Of course, there are some *risks*," Pinkney continued.
"What would life be, after all, without *some* risk, right? Slave
catchers slink over this countryside like wildcats, and, well, much
of your journey must be spent in inconspicuous cover, out of
necessity, you understand.

"I presume you, Jacob, will deliver my compensation to Mr.
Hoffman?" Pinkney asked, reaching into his pocket as if to
retrieve his wallet.

Simon placed his thumb on the hammer of his revolver,
neither man intent on paying a penny for Bigun.

Aware of the mischief at hand, Bigun turned to Jacob and
gave him the slightest shake of his head. His honed distrust for
white men, armed white men in particular, heightened Bigun's
sensitivity to proposals from strangers such as these. Jacob's
eyes returned acknowledgement.

"Bigun ain't for sale," Jacob said. "An' he ain't interested
in your … that train you spoke of."

Pinkney's prop of a smile fell and his eyes squinted at
Jacob's resistance. He glanced in the direction of the Rebel line.

"Well, son, we're not *buyin* him. We're merely
appropriating reasonable consideration for your daddy's property.
It's a personal financial sacrifice from Harriet Tubman herself. I
assure you the amount will be sufficient to replace Jim twofold,
maybe even get your daddy three breeders. We ain't lookin for
no trouble. All we want is to provide this … this gentleman a
way to freedom, freedom due him from this great land. Why
don't you let Jim speak for himself? What say *you*, Jim?"

"Name's Bigun, suh, and what Jacob says here be the gospel
truth. I's bought a slave all right, my family an' me, but Missuh
Hoffman don't treat me like one, not like they's treated down
south. An' I ain't no fool. No, suh, Missuh Hoffman's a
hon'rable man. He own me, true as rain, but he treat me wit'

respect an' trust. An' he lettin me buy my freedom, my family's freedom, work off what he gone an' paid for us."

"Fool, sir? Why, of *course* you're no fool. Wouldn't dream of *thinkin* such. A man of your obvious intelligence and skills livin among those who profess to be your betters can be *no* fool, I assure you. No, sir, you are no fool, just as you say, but you *are* a slave, still the property of another man. Why do you think two mighty armies are gatherin right here in your backyard? So they can break bread together? They're fightin for *you*, boy," Pinkney said with a jab of his finger, belying the trust he had hoped to instill. "Jacob, you look like a man of reason. Here now. Take this draft for $2,000, Federal. Give it to Isaac." He turned his gaze toward Bigun and whispered, "This is *one* nigger our boys ain't dyin for."

"Like I told you, sir, he ain't for sale," Jacob repeated. "I don't believe slavery to be right myself, but—"

"That why you're on *this* side of the creek, away from them rebs? Spect one of 'em might just have you in his rifle sight, hankerin to put a bullet in your head, take your slaves for nothin, boy."

Jacob watched the Confederate activity across the creek. "Them I trust. You I don't," Jacob answered. "Why ain't you goin directly to my daddy, make *him* your offer face to face? Seems to me maybe you got dubious intentions. Bigun here, he ain't for sale—for no amount of reasonable consideration—to nobody."

Pinkney smiled and wiped his mouth. He turned to Simon. "I reckon we'll have to substitute more persuasive means, Mr. McMillan."

"I reckon," replied Simon, his hand gripping the Colt handle.

Bigun squeezed the shaft of his cane fishing pole and waved off his approaching family.

"Boy," Pinkney said, watching the approach of Jesse and the girls, "we're takin this slave, all of 'em, whether you agree to our terms or not. It's in your best interests to accept this draft and kindly step aside."

"Slave drivers, that's who y'all are," Jacob said. "You ain't aimin to set nobody free, in Boston, in Canada, nowhere."

A pair of eyes watched the drama from the perch of a bay horse standing aside trees on a ridge two hundred yards from the bridge, opposite the Confederate line of battle. The rider twirled a silver dollar between his fingers and waited.

Bigun turned to his anxious family. "Go home!" he shouted.

"Bigun, we's—"

"Jesse, git on *home*, I tol' you! *Now!*"

"Wait a minute, here, Jim," said Pinkney, "your family's goin with us, with *you*. The boy's wrong. We got freedom for *all* of you."

"You is a *liar*, suh! Go *home*, woman!"

Bigun's family stepped backwards a few paces, Jesse's hands pressed against her children's chests, then turned and broke into a full uphill run. Simon started after them.

"Never mind, Simon!" Pinkney shouted, "Let 'em go. We'll catch up to 'em."

Simon and Pinkney pulled their Colts, the click of the hammers echoing over the bottomland. Sprinkles of rain patted the rims of their hats.

"Step aside, boy. Your nigger's comin with us. He's all we care about anyhow."

Jacob took an instinctive step forward, to protect Bigun. Simon thrust his revolver straight against Jacob's forehead.

"Don't even think about it, boy," Pinkney said. "Simon here ain't killed a man since … I don't know … First Manassas, I think, and, well, I spect he's gettin this *hankerin*, if you know what I mean."

Jacob stared into Simon's eyes. The cold end of his revolver's barrel pressed against Jacob's skull.

"Well, then, Bigun," Pinkney said, sensing submission. He reached inside the saddlebag draped over his shoulder. "I'll just slap on these wrist irons, and we'll be on our way. On the ground, boy, your belly."

Jacob knelt, lying on his stomach as instructed. Granted this flash of distraction, and with the swiftness of a rattlesnake, Bigun swung his cane pole, smashing Simon's wrist. The revolver flipped to the ground, inches in front of Jacob, the impact discharging the weapon. Confederates digging rifle pits and penning letters home stirred to arms.

"Hold your fire, boys!" shouted a Colonel on the ridge. "This ain't about us."

The ball grazed Jacob's shoulder, tearing away a swatch of his shirt and searing a burning path along his skin. He cringed with pain but managed to place his body over the weapon, out of Pinkney's sight. Bigun sent Simon sprawling unconscious with an uppercut that caught him squarely under his chin, shattering his teeth and breaking his jaw. Surprised with Bigun's display of quickness and strength, Pinkney pointed his cocked pistol straight into Bigun's chest, finger pressing the trigger.

"That'll do, boy!" Pinkney shouted to Bigun. "I don't want to kill you, but don't for a minute think I won't. Get up, Simon!"

Explosions rocked the air. Jacob flinched, thinking first the shot came from the buildup of men and guns along the creek. Pinkney lurched backwards, his revolver's discharge echoing into the air. He thumped to the ground, dead as a bale of hay thrown from a barn loft. Blood streamed from two holes, one in the middle of his chest and the other between his eyes. Bigun looked at Jacob, eyes as big as full moons, smoke swirling from the barrel of Simon's revolver.

"How'd you get off *two* shots, Jacob?" asked Bigun.

"I *didn't*. I—I don't *know*, I just fired the one. One of them rebs up yonder?

Both scanned the undulation of the fields and hills surrounding the creek, looking for the source of the second shot. Confederates moved about in response to shouted orders, ignoring the killing, ignoring anything beyond their preparations. Simon stirred, shaking his head and clutching his bloodied chin as he twisted his frame to a semiconscious crouch on his knees. He pulled himself to his feet.

Bigun stooped and grabbed the revolver from Pinkney's clenched fingers. Another shot cracked from the tree line opposite the Rebel side of the creek. Bigun and Jacob looked, a swirl of smoke riding the breeze. Jacob turned to see Simon on his back, a hole through the middle of his chest. A silhouetted figure on a horse, a white-flagged staff in one hand, emerged from the tree line atop the ridge and approached the pair. Jacob smiled, glad for the intervention but unsure he and Bigun weren't intended targets as well.

As the horse cantered nearer, Jacob shouted in the surprise of recognition. "Claggett!"

Jacob's Baptism

Chapter 7

"Gentlemen," the horseman said with a nonchalant drone and a slight nudge of his hat, pulling his reigns. "Reckon I was in the right place at the right time."

Like you was followin us, thought Bigun.

"I knew you was a good shot, Claggett, but, *hell*, that was two hundred paces if it was a *foot!*" observed Jacob, slipping Simon's Colt into his pocket.

"I'm obliged to ya, suh," Bigun said softly, nudging with his boot Simon's limp body.

"I know of these two, both of 'em bounty hunters," the horseman said, rolling Pinkney over with a shove of his boot. "We'll be buryin 'em here, next to the creek, where the ground's soft."

"You saved our lives, Claggett, but …"

"But what, boy?"

"Well, sir, how you gonna explain killin 'em?" Jacob asked. "What I mean is … well, what harm did they do *you?*"

The horseman tilted his hat upward. "You rather I not come along when I did, boy?"

"No sir; that's not what I meant to—"

"Might be nobody'll miss 'em. Then again, the way I figure it," the horseman answered, staring at the Confederate line, "these boys're no more'n casualties of war. They'll mix in right good by the mornin. Reckon, now, y'all owe me a favor. A ... big'n," he said, staring at Bigun.

Jacob and Bigun shifted uncomfortably. The message was unmistakable, like stepping from a rabbit trap into a stew pot. Jacob cleared his throat.

"Got somethin for us to dig with, Claggett?" Jacob asked. "To bury 'em?"

"You won't be needin this," the horseman said, taking Pinkney's Colt from Bigun. "Use these." He pulled a tin pan tied to his saddle and the Bowie knife from his belt.

"Ain't much for diggin graves with, suh," Bigun noted, taking the items.

"They'll do," he answered, "but don't go gettin ideas about the blade."

"Reckon the creek bank *will* make a good spot," Jacob said, clearing his throat and kicking the soil. "Ain't as dry as the ground in this field."

"You don't remember me, do you, Bigun?" the horseman asked as Bigun plunged the Bowie into the soil, loosening stones and sod.

"Remember you from what, suh?"

"The auction. Up in Hagerstown. Almost had you."

Bigun remembered but said nothing. The pace of his work hastened as he channeled his energy into digging, his thoughts into burying the Bowie deep within the horseman's chest.

A man of six feet-five inches, Bigun's shirtless, sweat-drenched torso glistened like waxed leather, blood-filled veins pulsating inside his treetrunk-sized arms. The horseman could not help noticing the brand on Bigun's forearm, the English-styled 𝕯.

"That ... uh ... that *brand* you got there, boy, on your arm."

"Yassuh?" Bigun's digging stopped as he glared at the horseman, daring him to take the matter further.

"I knew a man in South Carolina with the exact same brand, a Mr. Gustav Devereaux. You ... uh ... you heard of 'im?"

Bigun gave no reply.

"I'm pretty sure you have, boy. Don't much matter, anyhow," he said, shoving the Colt under his belt. He released a loud belch and lit a cigar.

"Reckon we ought to finish up, Bigun" Jacob interjected, feeling the sting of sweat in his shoulder wound. "Need to get on home. Daddy's gonna be worried, what with all the soldierin."

"All the soldierin," the horseman repeated as he sat against the stump of a hickory tree and watched, hat tilted forward.

Jacob scraped away the dirt and rocks freed by Bigun's Bowie twists, the depressions deepening and lengthening little by little. Their eyes alternated, from the sweat-dampened muck to the horseman's shifting repose. Clouds thickened and offered some relief from the press of the September sun.

Finished, they dragged the blood-washed bodies and rolled them into the depressions, faces up. Bigun pushed dirt over their bodies, leaving their open, blank eyes staring skyward, uncovered. Jacob scattered leaves over the dirt. Confederates shouted unintelligible barbs at Jacob and Bigun, teasing them.

"Done," Jacob declared, wiping his forehead and tamping the graves with his foot. He squeezed the fingers of his blistered hands and handed the horseman the pan.

"Nice work, boys," the horseman said as he rinsed his pan in the creek water. "Now, Jacob, let me have that Colt you got."

Jacob looked at Bigun.

"Gimme the Colt, boy!" the man shouted. "I know you have it. Slowly now, handle first."

Jacob handed the man the gun. As he did, Bigun tucked the Bowie inside his pants, above his buttocks. Bigun stood, arms by his sides and waited, giving no indication he still possessed the knife.

"Now, I'm takin Bigun with me. First time it dawns on me you or your daddy are comin after him—after me—Bigun an' his family die." The horseman tied Bigun's hands together and the rope's opposite end to the horse's saddle. "Now, then, Jacob, I reckon you ought to be skedaddlin on home, what with all this soldierin. It's gonna get hot here real quick."

"You can't just up an' *take* 'im!" Jacob shouted. "He don't *belong* to you. At least those two were gonna *pay* me."

The horseman laughed. "You really *believe* that, don't you. An' he don't belong to your daddy, neither."

"My daddy *bought* 'im'," Jacob shouted.

"He *does* belong to Mr. Devereaux, who paid for 'im first. You see, boy, Bigun here's a runaway. I'm returnin him to his rightful owner. Besides, Bigun's got a little matter of John Brown to think about. Ain't that so, Bigun?"

Jacob looked at Bigun. "What's he talkin about?"

"I ain't goin witchu, suh," Bigun declared, his feet firmly planted.

The horseman laughed and spat. "You ain't got no choice in the matter, boy, unless you want to be *dragged*. Now, move!"

Bigun stood defiant, chin up.

"Nigger, I'll shoot you where you stand. What'll your family do then, with you stone dead?"

"Spect if I go witchu, suh, I won't be havin no family no mo' anyway," Bigun replied calmly. "I reckon I'll be stayin here."

The horseman, hewn of thick bone and heavy muscle, equal to Bigun's physique, felt a rush of temptation to strip Bigun of his binds and engage him with fists. He thought better of it. The distraction of a physical confrontation with the younger and quicker Bigun might not return the desired result. He opted instead for a solution less consuming of energy and more to the point. Lifting his long-barreled Remington .44-calibre revolver from his holster, he thumbed its hammer, pointing it at Bigun's head.

"Move!" the horseman shouted.

"No, suh!" Bigun confirmed.

The horseman stepped back at double arms-length and pulled the hammer, which clicked like the popping of knuckles.

"Last chance, nigger," the man grumbled.

"Claggett!" shouted Jacob.

"Shut up, boy!" the horseman said.

Bigun stared at the revolver, its cylinder filled. He tilted downward and spat.

"Bettuh dead now than go witchu."

The man fingered the trigger. Bigun stared at the man.

"Go on!" Bigun demanded, closing his eyes. "White man kill the unarmed slave. Won't be the first time, and I spect it won't be the last."

Bigun flinched as a shot shattered the tense air. The horseman re-holstered his weapon, smoke oozing from its barrel. He spurred his horse to a trot, Bigun in tow, struggling to keep pace at the end of the taut rope.

"Keep up, boy," the horseman shouted, "lest you be dragged."

Weaponless, Jacob watched as the horseman and Bigun entered the thicket of trees. When Jacob no longer could see them, he followed.

Chapter 8

Jacob pushed his way through the grass, hardwoods, and intermittent tangle of brush, following as best he could the trail left by the horseman and Bigun. He recalled the employ of Claggett Parker at the Antietam Iron Furnace a few years prior, as well as Claggett's strained relationship with Isaac.

Had something to do with a question of the price for an order of wagons, of Claggett's disagreement with the specifications of the wheels. Turns out, Bigun rimmed the wheels according to revisions made to specifications provided by Claggett, who had advanced to a position within the Furnace's management hierarchy to authorize such revisions.

When challenged by Furnace ownership to explain the altered wheel specifications, who at first withheld payment to Isaac for the finished wagons, Isaac produced his copy of the original order from Furnace officials, as well as the change order. Original wheel specs had been altered by Claggett, whose signature approval appeared on the change order. The Antietam Iron Furnace, recalled Jacob, honored the changes and paid Isaac in full for the order, after which they dismissed Claggett, withholding his pay.

Jacob stopped. He cupped his ear. He heard through the foliage a muffled whinny.

No too far ahead, he thought, stooping low to prevent the Parker's notice of Jacob's red shirt.

"Why we stoppin?" Bigun asked.

"A man's gotta piss. I reckon so do you," Parker answered as he dismounted. "I'll let you have first honors. Means I'm gonna have to untie you."

"Obliged," Bigun replied, his thoughts swirling with opportunity.

Parker reached for his Bowie, feeling its absence from its usual spot. "What'd I do with that damn thing?" he muttered. Then, he remembered. "What'd *you* do with my knife, boy?"

"Lef' it on the ground, back at the creek, suh."

"Is that so." Seeing no evidence to the contrary, Parker reached inside his saddlebag and retrieved a smaller knife.

"Prob'ly got too dull to cut rope wit' anyhow, suh, what wit' all dat diggin."

"Best knife there is, the Bowie. Durable, strong, *never* dulls. Could dig a *trench* with one and still split hairs. Won that knife is fist fight, back in Lawrence, Kansas. Now we got to go back an' get it." Parker's voice rose with his frustration. "Stick out your hands! I'm gonna cut the rope with this." Parker removed one opportunity, his Remingtons, from Bigun's reach. "Don't try nothin, boy, or this knife's liable to slip."

Bigun complied. Parker cut the knot and stepped back, re-holstering one Remington and training the other on Bigun, who nursed wrists rubbed raw of skin.

Jacob inched closer, his view of the two men unobstructed.

"Go on, now," Parker said, "make your water!"

"Yassuh," Bigun answered, pretending to adjust his pants in preparation, looking for any hint of opportunity.

SNAP!

Parker lifted his eyes and turned. "That *you*, boy?" Parker shouted in reference to Jacob.

Jacob pressed his back to the cover of an ancient oak, eyes closed, breath held, and praying his presence remained undetected.

Parker took a few steps toward the sound. He pulled the Remington's hammer. "Sit down, Bigun," he instructed, not turning his view from the woods in front. "I reckon we got us a visitor."

Parker stopped, motionless, listening.

"If you try to follow me, I *will* see you," Parker announced, his words echoing, "an' when I do, you can be sure the big man here dies. Then, it'll be *your* turn, boy. *Don't* try me."

Parker listened for any reaction to his threat. Hearing none, he turned his attention to his captive.

"You finished makin'—"

"You lookin' fo' *dis*, suh?" Bigun asked, thrusting, twisting the Bowie deep into Parker's chest, pulling Parker closer, saliva spraying Parker's face, the men's eyes nearly touching.

Parker's eyes bulged round, filled with shock of the sudden drainage of life, of precious blood wetting his torso, of pain rifling through his body, of the spurts of realization that this slight distraction had cost him his life. Grabbing Bigun's shoulders, mouth wide and wordless, gasping for air his lungs could not breathe, Parker slid to his knees, his brain desperate to salvage consciousness, helpless to reverse the irreversible.

Bigun stepped back. The man crumpled lifeless to the forest floor, his weight pushing the blade through his body, out the middle of his back.

"Get up here, Missuh Jacob!" Bigun shouted, his voice echoing through the forest's depths.

"Bigun, you okay?" Jacob said, running, panting.

"I is now, Missuh Jacob."

Jacob stared at Parker's powerless, blood-soaked body. "*Jesus*, Bigun. You had the Bowie the whole time?"

"It do look that way, suh. Hid it in my pants, after at the buryin."

"He would have shot you dead if he'd found that knife on you. But ... *how?*"

"We stopped to make water, an' then he heard you comin up. Took his eyes off me, an', well … there he be." Bigun smiled.

"There he be, all right," Jacob echoed. "Now what're *we* gonna do? We come to fish and end up with three *dead* men."

"Fish may not've been bitin, Missuh Jacob, but dem sharks sho' nuf was."

Despite the echoes of military preparedness stretching across the shadowed valley, the area surrounding the Rohrbach Bridge retained an eerie, purple silence, like a child holding its breath before the tantrum. Bigun suggested the man's body, in the days to follow, would find the companionship of worms and anonymity among military casualties.

"I hope you're right, Bigun," Jacob said. "Ain't *no* tellin' what kind of trouble we might be in."

"You mean what kind of trouble *I* might be in," Bigun argued. "Dis right here would be self-defense, fo' de *white* man; it just plain ol' *murder* fo' dis nigguh."

"What are you *talkin* about, Bigun? We're both up to our necks in this."

Bigun sighed and sat on a pine stump. "Spect now's as good a time as any to tell you."

"Tell me what?"

"Dat Claggett got sump'n on me, suh. Spect he done tol' de world who he was goin aftuh," Bigun said, his voice fading to a mumble. "Ain't no tellin who knows about it by now."

"About *what?*" Jacob asked again. "If you mean the auction in Hagerstown all them years ago, well, stuff like that happens all the time. If Claggett had wanted you, he'd have *paid* for you. Besides, Claggett can't hold *that* against you."

Bigun scanned the area, his instincts as the hunted reinvigorated. Then Bigun's face stiffened.

"Casualties of war, Bigun," Jacob said, observing the extent of Parker's wound. "Maybe Claggett was right about that. Maybe these fields and woods'll be covered with 'em come tomorrow evenin. Won't nobody know the difference."

"Ever'body knows Claggett ain't fightin this war. He just makin money from it, is all. An' ever'body know by now he was aftuh me." Bigun paused.

"Why was he after you? I told you the Hagerstown auc—"

"This ain't about the auction, Missuh Jacob, not directly."

"Just Jacob, Bigun. Misters and sirs are for old men. Ain't got time to worry none about this now, anyway. Let's get on home, away from this place," Jacob said, scanning the trees for movement. "You can tell me then."

As the two left Parker's bent body in the dark of the trees, they stopped, hearing the sharp ***satch, satch, satch*** of feet trampling through leaves just ahead, the sound diminishing with distance.

Jacob's Baptism

Chapter 9

Bigun stared into the woods, studying the movement's sound, trying to discern its source, its direction.

"You reckon …?" Bigun said.

"Hooves, Bigun. It was a deer."

"Sounded mo'e like *two* feet, not fo'."

Jacob listened, the sound softening. *Satch, satch, satch.*

"Just a deer. *Had* to be. Who'd be out here now, what with all the soldierin and such?"

Bigun looked at Jacob.

"Oh," Jacob said. "I guess … I guess *we'd* be out here now."

Tha's right, an' so might somebody else. I tell you, Missuh Jacob, we done been *seen*, a black man killin a white man."

"Now calm yourself, Bigun. Ain't necessarily so. We don't know it wasn't a deer or some stray, an' … an' if it *was* a person, it likely was one of them rebs lookin for food. Lord knows by lookin at 'em, they ain't had a decent meal since they left home."

"I don't know, Missuh Jacob."

"Probably wasn't nothin more'n an ol' hare. Heck, if I was an ol' hare, I'd be runnin, too!" Jacob smiled. "You done *good* back there, Bigun. You done what you *had* to do. As much as I

hate to say it, you were stolen … property … defendin yourself,"
Jacob said, head bowed, catching himself upon the realization
that indeed Bigun was a slave, owned as a man owns a wagon.
"You got me as a witness, should any of this ever come to light,
which it *won't*."

"I hope you right, suh."

"Come on."

"Wait!" Bigun said.

Frustrated, Jacob started to ask why another delay, but just as
quickly realized the reason for Bigun's concern.

"Oh, yeah," Jacob said. "We better take care of that."

"Yassuh, we bettuh."

Jacob returned to Parker's body. He looked, finally spotting
the white cloth Parker had used as a cease-fire flag back at the
creek. Ripping it from its staff, Jacob handed it to Bigun, who
spat repeatedly onto the cloth to dampen it before noticing
Parker's canteen hanging from the saddle horn. Grabbing it,
Bigun spilled water onto the cloth and wiped hard the coagulation
of blood covering his shirtless chest.

"Reckon we ought to do sump'n with his ho'se?" Bigun
asked, still wiping.

"Can't bring it with us," Jacob said, rubbing his chin,
"though it *would* make a fine work animal."

"Don't even *think* it, Missuh Jacob. They hang us for ho'se
thievin."

"Tie it to this branch," Jacob replied, wrapping the reigns
around a low oak limb. "Someone'll come along soon, in a day
or two, an' let him loose."

The two tramped back to Rohrbach's Bridge, toward
Sharpsburg.

"*Snake fangs!*" Jacob said in a flash of recall.

"What *is* it?" Bigun asked.

"I remember Daddy sayin he was to meet with Claggett this
very *evenin*, and here you done gone and *killed* the son of a
biscuit!" Jacob chuckled as he realized the bit of irony nestled
within this turn of events.

Bigun paused and pondered. Then he smiled, saying, "I reckon he'll be late."

"Claggett an' my daddy weren't exactly drinkin buddies, if you know what I mean, not after the Hagerstown auction. A lot of folks know how I feel about that man, too. Somebody's *bound* to make the connection, if someone finds his body before tomorrow. I wonder what they were meetin for?"

"What if yo' *daddy* gets the blame for dis?"

"You think Claggett was goin to let you live, your *family* live? He'd a-killed you out of *spite,* chalked it up as a cost of doin business, before he returned you to that Devereaux fellow. You *had* to kill 'im, Bigun."

Bigun wiped harder at the hardened, stubborn crusts of blood. "I know, but, like I said, what if yo' *daddy* gets the blame for dis, folks knowin the relationship an' all?"

"Wonder why?" Jacob asked, ignoring Bigun's concern.

"Wonder why *what?*"

"Wonder why Daddy is goin to meet—*was* goin to meet— with Claggett this evening?"

"Reckon Missuh Isaac 'bout to sell me? Maybe that be de reason Claggett decided to just *take* me."

"Naw!" Jacob replied. "I spect Isaac's in the market to *find* you some *help* in the wagon shop. Orders for wagons, wheels, and parts're bound to pick up, now that the war is pickin up. Much as he despises Claggett Parker, it's *still* about business."

Jacob stiffened in thoughtful silence, his mind jabbed by the awareness of Bigun's question. *What if Daddy does get the blame? Could be any one of us gets the blame,* Jacob thought. A pall of reality overtook him. Beads of sweat prickled his forehead. Three men dead. Three. One by his hand, one by Bigun's. A swirl of violence, like battle, and the two had emerged with no more than a slight bullet graze to Jacob's shoulder and a pair of rope-rawed wrists. These were not mischievous episodes of eggs tossed through Reverend Abram's window or the pelting of Widow Marly's cat with slingshot stones. Murder or self-defense, in Jacob's mind the distinction draped insignificant, the consequences swelling like a snakebite.

"We got to get *out* of here until this blows over," Jacob blurted, his tone reversed from mere minutes ago. "We got to get *you and Jesse* out from here!"

"Whatchu sayin, Missuh Jacob? Up an' leave Missuh Isaac's wagon bidness?"

"What if there *was* a witness, Bigun? Maybe what we heard *wasn't* a deer. Maybe we ought to lay low a few days, until the fightin's over."

"Wha's yo' daddy gawn do when Claggett don't show?" Bigun asked.

"Nothin, I reckon. What *can* he do?"

"He can find another *buyer* is what," Bigun asserted.

"Calm yourself, Bigun. Daddy ain't about to sell you to *nobody*. You're his *hardest* worker, the *finest* blacksmith in the valley, the best friend a body could have. You're the reason his wagon business is doin so dadgum good. No sir, Isaac ain't *about* to sell you," Jacob said, thinking of the running heard back in the woods. He paused. "But, truth is, you *are* a black man. An' as much as it pains me to say, a slave. We've got to *change* that part, an' now's the time.

"I hear tell folks're scatterin over creation, for the Furnace, up to Hagerstown, over to Boonsboro, even to Killing's Cave until this battle's over. That's where you and Jesse go, to the cave. Then, *you* can decide where you go after that. Ain't *nobody* payin attention to a wanderin black family, not in these parts, not *now*. Make for Philadelphia, Boston. This battle, here in Sharpsburg, is an open door for you, Bigun."

"Nobody but the soul drivers," Bigun replied.

"You got a good eye for the drivers, Bigun," Jacob said, "an' when they cross your path you'll know what to do."

"You talkin 'bout *freedom!* Fo' *me?* What I gawn do wit' freedom, Missuh Jacob? I done *kilt* somebody. Could be *lots* of folks payin attention," Bigun noted, "but dey only needs be one."

"Stop makin so much sense! Let's get on home and get started," Jacob replied.

"About the bidness, Missuh Jacob."

"What about it?"

"Missuh Isaac done lost some orduhs lately," Bigun revealed. "They's another wagon-maker up near Boonsboro. Makes mo'e wagons an' fo' less money, too. Missuh Isaac's bidness ain't doin as good as you say. I spect he's lookin to cut his losses. Tha's why he meetin wit' Claggett, I spect."

Jacob looked at Bigun. "Lost some orders? He never said any … *never mind* that. Let's stop at Renner's. Reckon what five dollars gold'll buy us?"

Jacob's Baptism

Chapter 10

"You *brung* the *coin?*" Bigun asked.
"My, my, Missuh Jacob, if you ain't in trouble fo' killin one of
dem men—an' bein wit' me—you *sho'* nuf in trouble fo' takin
dat coin. It's yo' gold all right, but it might as well be gold off
God's own teeth! Missuh Isaac'll skin you alive if he ever gets
wind. That gold coin's as sacred as that time piece give you by
yo' gran'pap."

"I ain't got the coin *with* me, but that's … wait a minute. Of
course! The time piece. It's got more gold in it than—"

"Now, hold on, Missuh Jacob. Dat onion an' dat coin was
give to you fo' yo' future, not to squander on some rifle."

"An' *supplies*, Bigun. Look, we're face to face with our
future. We're gonna *need* some things. Time to put that watch to
good use, coin too, if need be. Anyhow, I got credit at Renner's.
Come on."

Jacob and Bigun, their eyes watchful for clues anyone knew
of their earlier encounter at the bridge, arrived in Sharpsburg.
They walked streets crowded on occasion with the shuffle of
soldiers, the gallop of horses, the pull of artillery, and the banter
of battle. Townsfolk laden with all they could carry trekked the

opposite direction. Slapping their pants free of dust, they stepped inside Renner's General Mercantile.

"Jacob, Bigun! Come in! Been to the *bridge*, I hear," Renner said. Jacob's brow lifted upon learning such indeed *was* common knowledge. Perhaps Renner was not saying all he knew. "Actually, this day's like any other Tuesday, am I right? Y'all fishin, that is." Renner sighed, gazing out the door. "Confederates all *over* the place, north of town, south of town, *everywhere*. Word is, the Yankees are just across the creek. Reckon you two got an eyeful of it all. I suppose you'll be leaving town, like all the rest."

"Y-yes sir, Mr. Renner," Jacob answered, his glance ricocheting from shelves to tables. "Been to the bridge, fishin."

"Catch anything?"

Jacob did not answer.

"I said, catch anything," Renner repeated.

"Sir?" Jacob asked, distracted by thoughts of dead men, supplies, and leaving home. "Uh … no, sir. Weren't bitin, I reckon."

"Too bad. Well, let me know if I can help you fellows, but you might want to hurry it up."

"Thank ya, Missuh Rennuh. We much obliged," Bigun said.

"More'n welcome, Bigun."

"We'll need blankets," Jacob whispered.

"Whatchu talkin 'bout! It's *summuhtime!"*

"Shhhh! I *know*, but it might rain, and there ain't no way to know where we'll spend our next few nights. We need supplies, blankets and … bedrolls … lamp oil … some coffee, flour, beans … maybe some …"

"*Wet* blankets'll give us our death of cold," Bigun said.

"So, we'll make us a shelter, maybe go to Killing's Cave," Jacob replied.

"You runnin away fo' *good*? Whatchu gettin all dis stuff fo' anyhow?" Bigun asked. "An' what's Miss Rachael gawn say when you don't come back?"

"Bigun, you're goin with me. Now's as good a time as any, *better* than any probably, to get you off to freedom, maybe even to the Yankee army. Maybe *both* of us to the Yankee army," Jacob said, thinking of Rachael.

"*You*, in Missuh Lincoln's army?"

"Why *not?* I been givin the matter a lot of thought lately. Ever thought about wearin a blue suit and killin Rebs?"

"But I thought you was mad at the Yankees for killin Roswell."

"I was. Still am. But, that wasn't *entirely* the Yankees' fault. Seems Ros sorta asked for it, like Daddy said. Way I see it, the bigger sin is slavery. For me, this war's got to be about *more'n* a quest for glory. Heck, we ain't got to go to *them*. They've practically come to *us*, right across the creek! Besides, we're pretty much in a pile of dung taller'n Piper's barn. Might need us some redemption. You *with* me or not?"

"Witchu, I reckon. Yankee army, huh? Reckon dey let *me* wear de blue suit?"

"I hear tell there's a push for Negro regiments. Three squares a day. Thirteen dollars a month. An' a sparklin new Springfield. Now, help me with this stuff," Jacob said, carrying the load to Renner for tallying.

"Well, well, Jacob Hoffman," Renner observed as Jacob and Bigun plopped the goods on the counter, "if I didn't know better, I'd think you and Bigun were *running away* from home. Ha, ha. But then, ain't *everybody!* I reckon you're just getting ready to sit out the battle, right? Me, I'm going to be closing up in just a bit. Already boarding the windows. See?" Renner noted, pointing to a clumsy array of planks covering his north and east windows, as if such might block out the destruction of battle.

"Rebels been trouncing through here all morning," Renner said, "most of 'em respectful enough and willing to pay, when they're able, but there ain't much I can do with a fistful of Confederate scrip or a mouthful of promises. Even so, I ain't about to go and tell them boys 'no', if you know what I mean. Why, some of them Rebs look like they just crawled out of a grave, eyes sunken and dark. Smell to high heaven; got whiskers of grizzlies and eyes of snakes. Most are as scraggly and lean as packs of wolves, just as ready to pounce, and breath like skunks.

Of course I didn't *tell* 'em so, you understand, but they ought to know McClellan's boys are going to give them such a *whipping*. Why, I heard that—"

"Mr. Renner … sir," Jacob interrupted, "we—we really need to get goin. How much do I owe you?"

Renner gave Jacob a courteous smile and a sigh of subtle frustration at having been cut off in mid-sentence.

"Of course. Well, now, let's see. You're not going to give me any of that Rebel paper, are you," Renner asked with a wink.

"I got money," Jacob boasted. "Gold. It's back home, but I can run get it, pay you this evenin."

"Well, then. Good. Let me just add up …" Renner mumbled, scribbling the prices of Jacob's items on a piece of scrap paper. "Okay, got it. I reckon an even ten dollars ought to cover it."

"Ten … *ten* dollars? Let's go, Bigun."

"But wait. *Jacob!* What about all this stuff? Could be I added wrong. Wait!" Renner pleaded. "Probably closer to eight dollars; I'm not all that good with numbers. Let me just—"

Jacob and Bigun left Renner's doors swinging and started up Main Street, passing knots of Confederate soldiers, all of whom looked and sounded just as Renner had described them. Jacob overheard some of the buzz from the soldiers, spry of step, their words ringing with the confidence of a hard-earned reputation, belying the expected effects of their squalid appearance.

Couriers raced up and down Main Street delivering messages to waiting commanders, reigns snapping side to side in mad, dust-clouded dashes. Fleeing residents hunkered to the sides of the street to escape the brief bursts.

Jacob stared at the assortment of long rifles resting atop shoulders. Smoothbore muskets; shotguns; flintlocks, even a smattering of polished Springfields confiscated from U.S. arsenals, most likely Harpers Ferry, and from fields of the unfortunate.

Men hung thick blanket rolls across their bodies, rugs brought from home or scavenged from battlefields along the way. Jacob imagined how uncomfortable, how hot these bulky articles must be and wondered if perhaps the soldiers believed them useful as shields, their thickness the distance between the here-and-now and the hereafter. He did not ask.

Boys younger by years than Jacob carried red-bordered drums on their backs, their forage caps tilted at swashbuckling angles, sights awkward amid the flopping of tin cups, canteens, haversacks, and other accoutrements. Others held aloft red, blue-crossed battle flags, their bullet-holed fabrics flapping in the breeze, many announcing the victories of previous fights. These men and boys laughed at shared jokes and chatted more like kids on the heels of some great frolic, far from the demands and discipline—the ordinariness—of home.

The dull butternut and gray of the men contrasted sharply with the brilliant red of those flags. Some men walked with soles of feet thickened by endless marching, soles of shoes thinned by the very same. Their skin had weathered, as resilient as saddle leather. Others wore shoes burdened with holes, held together with knots of rags. Feet walked blistered and bruised, cut and scabbed, numbed to their injuries by repetition and the passage of time.

Men stopped to take their rest. They sat on porches or propped against posts and pillars, some taking gulps of water, other with pipes clenched in their pensive, smoke-puffing mouths, muffled words spoken as if they were scouting the area for home sites after the war. Moments of rest offered illusions of relief, of peace, to weary bodies, as well as chances to clean rifles and pen letters and to accept bits of food handed them.

Offbeat, contorted strains of "Dixie" and "Maryland, My Maryland" rippled through the village air. Some residents unfurled the stars and stripes in a show of utter contempt for the trespassing Southerners. Others hurled insults, verbal projectiles, at the soldiers, who demonstrated remarkable willingness to absorb the blows. These men maintained the focus of a veteran army, wanting only to conserve energy and avoid needless confrontation in the face of grim work coming.

Men drained their canteens into parched throats and onto reddened skin before refilling. Soldier issued few complaints, despite numerous personal discomforts. Each seemed as certain of tomorrow's outcome, a Confederate victory, as they were of the sunrise.

The sunrise. *For how many would it be their last?* thought Jacob as he watched.

Jacob and Bigun reached the outskirts of Sharpsburg and the Landing Road. A half hour later, they were home.

"Gettin on, Bigun," Jacob said, observing the angle of the sun. "Now listen. Tell Jesse and the young-uns that you'll be back for 'em. Assure them, one way or another, you'll come get 'em. They can stay in the cellar 'til this passes. If the Rebs take this fight tomorrow, they might just take any Negroes they find, too, so Jesse's got to stay out of sight. Prepare 'em, Bigun. I'll help you *make sure* your family gets to freedom."

"What Missuh Isaac gawn think? He gawn send us to Charleston?"

Jacob pondered the question. "How's he gonna send you to Charleston if you ain't here? No, I don't think he'll—what I mean is, I think deep down, Daddy understands. If Daddy's losin business, like you say, he ain't gonna need you anyhow. What corn we had the rebs done took. Ain't no chores me an' Rachael can't take care of, that is if she can put that paint brush down long enough. Lord knows Daddy's got his money's worth out of you. How much you owe 'im 'til you've bought your freedom?"

Bigun chuckled. "*Too* much. I reckon maybe another fo' or five years."

"So you'll pay him later," Jacob said, dismissing the matter's importance. "Won't be the first time he's extended credit. My guess is he'll forgive the debt. Seems *darn ludicrous* makin you buy your freedom anyway, after all you've done for 'im.

"Now, the minute you see the lamplight go out in my room tonight, head for the back of the barn. I'll meet you there soon after. Right now, I'm gonna go find me a rifle to buy. I figure a reb'll sell me one for gold. We're gonna *need* one."

"Rebs needs rifles, too," Bigun observed. "Ain't none of dem gawn *sell* you one, not on the eve of a *fight*."

"We'll see about that. Just may be that one or two rebs're lookin to stay *out* of that fight, take leave of this battle with some gold in his pocket. Just might be the lure I need. Call it fishin with a different sort of bait."

"Whatchu aimin to do wit' a rifle anyhow, Missuh Jacob? You got your shotgun, your revolver."

"No more questions, Bigun. Think about your freedom, your *family's* freedom."

Bigun fought off his skepticism but concluded that another opportunity this promising might never again see daylight. He turned for the barn, and some chores, to pass the time.

"Go on, now, Bigun. Here comes Rachael. She's been hankerin for me to shoot this here scattergun," Jacob said, lifting the shotgun propped on a porch post. "Who knows *why*. Funny thing about her. She loves to paint, pick flowers, and spit out poems nobody but her understands." Jacob looked to the porch planks and laughed. "I pretend to understand, but dang if I do. One minute, she's all mushy about love and Miss Emily, an' I just want to hug her 'til she can't breath. But then she can be the *tomboyest* thing I ever seen when her blood's up."

"I be lookin fo' de lamplight." Bigun started to walk away, then stopped and laughed, thinking of Rachael. "Don't *you* be goin an' gettin *yo'* blood up."

Jacob nodded. He thought of rifles and dead men and witnesses. He hurried inside to retrieve the coin and watch. He would have to find supplies in the house and from the barn.

Chapter 11

Jacob pulled away the downy quilt. His
head whipped back in reflex. The musty odor of age mingled
with lamplight-washed strands of broken spider webs, swirling
and floating about his face like apparitions. He raked his
fingertips across the carved letters of DENIA, inscribed atop the
pocked white pine, each letter polished smooth with years of
touch. He raised the lid, the two hinges emitting a slight squeak.
Shadow and light splattered the contents, heirlooms existing in
Jacob's memory of voices from his early years, heirlooms he had
never before seen, heirlooms Isaac forbade Jacob to touch until
he reached manhood. Jacob figured manhood had reached him.

He peeled layers of hand linens and quilted rectangles of
place settings, each stitched with an embellished **H**, each piece a
reverent wedge of family history preserved for Jacob's posterity.
Jacob lifted the mahogany trinket box and placed it on his
unmade bed.

Slight variations of color along the edges marked evidence of
the careful handling of the handcrafted box. The sides were
covered with carvings of arrowheads, deer, gardenias, and
personified exaggerations of the sun.

A magnificent horned owl relief adorned the lid of the trinket box, below which were cut the words "Ole Whooey – King of the Valley of the Antietam, 1778."

"Ole Whooey," Jacob whispered. *"Still* King."

Jacob stared at the carving. Inside the box rolled a few cats' eyes; an antler-handle knife; owl feathers; a pocket Colt; an assortment of dried marsh marigolds and the crumble of gardenia pedals. Beneath this miscellany rested the square folds of two beige silk handkerchiefs.

Jacob lifted the silk cloths to his palm and caressed each, as would a new mother a baby in her arms. He pulled back the corners of the first, revealing the blue embroidered letters, **JJH**, inside of which rested an 1838 five-dollar Half Eagle gold coin. The coin was without blemish, pure and unused, the gleam of its essence a stark contrast to the dreariness of the morning.

Only five years old at the time, Jacob did not remember the coin itself but did recall Grandpa Hoffman's advice on the eve of his death in the winter of 1850. He told Jacob to "buy an adventure". Isaac insisted his son save the gold for use in the event of "unforeseen calamities." As far as Jacob was concerned, "unforeseen calamities" thrived just outside his door.

Jacob saw the coin as not only the fulfillment of his desires but as giving honor to his Grandpa's dying words. Giving rationale, if not purpose, to the coin, he raised it from its hold. Isaac did not have to know, not yet anyway. He pondered his dilemma as he turned the coin between his fingers and stared at its perfection. *Daddy never checks this box*, thought Jacob.

"John Jacob Hoffman!" shouted Rachael from the front porch.

"Comin!" Jacob replied, on the cusp of a decision.

He shoved the handkerchief, wadded around the coin, into his shirt pocket. The other handkerchief looked heavier, bulkier. He lifted the object, round like the coin, but thicker.

"This must be the onion." Jacob chuckled softly at the term Bigun used to describe the pocketwatch carried by Grandpa during the Revolution. "Does have a distinct smell about it," Jacob said sniffing the handkerchief.

"You comin out here or not!"

"I *said* I was comin, didn't I!" Jacob yelled as he pocketed the handkerchief-wrapped watch and scampered down the stairs and out the door.

Rachael held Jacob's Remington revolver loosely in her left hand, shaking it like a scornful finger. Jacob stopped dead in his tracks.

"You gonna shoot this scattergun like you promised me?" Rachael whined, one hand on her waist and the other bent with the weight of the pistol. She tilted her head.

"Where'd you get that gun!" Jacob asked, remembering he had left it on the porch steps after last night's cleaning. "Put that thing *down*!"

"Worried I might pull the trigger, are you?" she said, toying with Jacob. "Relax. Look," she said, pointing to the steps.

Jacob saw the pistol's percussion caps lined along a step, like little children waiting their turn.

"Learned something new about you today," Jacob blurted, shaking his head, not sure whether to feel arousal or worry.

"What's that, Jacob Hoffman?"

"Either you know a thing or two about guns, or you don't know nothin at all, *that's* what!"

"Anything else?"

"You're full of surprises!"

"Just you wait an' see, Jacob Hoffman. You gonna shoot the shotgun?"

"You're an impatient thing," Jacob answered, lifting the double-barreled weapon from its lean against a post.

"Just you shoot it, or you … or you won't get a nibble of sugar from *me*, now or at the Hog Trough," Rachael warned.

Jacob ignored her threat and rammed buck and ball down both barrels. He glanced at Rachael. He knew full well how to steal a kiss whenever the urge struck him, with or without Rachael's permission. He took careless aim at a chopping stump twenty paces forward and pulled the first trigger. Rachael's clover-green eyes winced and her shoulders buckled with the explosion.

The shot obliterated an ear of corn wedged vertically in the stump, spitting kernels of corn and splinters of wood and scattering the afternoon lounge of nearby crows. Echoes of the blast rippled through the air, rupturing its serenity. Rachael laughed and clutched Jacob's arm.

"Satisfied?" asked Jacob, lowering the gun to waist level.

The smell of spent black powder crept up Rachael's nostrils. She closed her eyes and sniffed. "Mmmm," she cooed, as if tickled by an aphrodisiac.

"Do it again!" she demanded with delight. "The *other* trigger! *Pull* it!"

Jacob stared at the gun and then at Rachael.

"I reckon not," he said after a moment's ponder. With a sigh, he leaned the smoking gun against a porch post and scanned the eastward stretch of Landing Road. He was keenly aware of the agitation his refusal of compliance caused Rachael.

"Why, John Jacob Hoffman, I do believe you are *irritated* by my request!"

"Not irritated, Rachael," he retorted, "just manipulated."

Rachael smiled. "Then kiss me," she insisted, giggling, as she thrust forward her face, lips puckered and eyes closed, manipulation at the ready.

"In the broad light of day?" Jacob teased as he turned toward an overflowing bushel basket of corn on the steps. "I got me some shucking to do, Rachael; then I got to go to Renner's for some supplies. That is, if he ain't locked his doors yet. From the looks and sounds, things are goin downhill fast. Best you go on home."

"Renner's? I thought you an' me were takin a picnic basket to the Hog Trough, maybe pick some blackberries, like you promised. You ain't goin to no *Renner's*, you little *liar!* He's done boarded his windows, like *that's* gonna stop them thievin Rebels. You're on your way to Belinda Springs to lay down money on the cockfighting!" Rachael tugged the waistline of her calico dress.

Jacob wanted more than anything to kiss Rachael. Fact of the matter, Jacob longed to whisk Rachael to the barn, out of the prying sights of family, slaves, and drifters, and show her all the nuances of the kiss, as if he knew.

"I'm *goin* to Renner's," Jacob insisted, touching his shirt pocket. "Wanna come?" he asked, knowing she would not.

"Downhill, you say?"

"Can't you see it? Yanks an' Rebs all over the place, like skeeters. You *know* what I'm talkin about."

"I seen a *mess* of blue coats over by the creek yesterday mornin," Rachael revealed, caressing the shotgun's barrel.

"Was *Barton* among them?"

"You're so *cute* when you're jealous, Jacob Hoffman. At the bridge between Newcomer's an' Boonsboro. More soldiers than the sky has stars. Then, on my way over here, I walked right through another passel on the Pike, between Miller's an' the church, only these was butternuts, Rebels. Grimy lookin predators, grinnin *ear to ear* at me, like they ain't seen a lady their whole lives."

Still ain't, thought Jacob, a mischievous sliver of a smile on his lips.

"The ones that weren't droolin like hound dogs, bless their souls, were relaxin on the grass. Not showin a care among 'em, some scratchin out letters to homefolk; some leanin on their rifles soakin up the air; some readin a bible; some playin cards or sittin by their campfires cookin up some God-awful smellin stuff. Down the road a piece, another crop of 'em looked up an' noticed me. Clusters of men, some with actual *teeth*, spittin out hollers an' whistles. Some of 'em *were* right cute, Jacob Hoffman, in spite of themselves, yelpin like field hands at a Sunday meetin." Rachael twirled her hair and smirked.

"Rachael!" Jacob chided. "What do you know about *field hands* and Sunday meetins, for Christ's sake!"

"Well, I got them *smiles,* I did! An' the things they shouted at me, why, I *never* … What's it to you anyhow? A Sunday meetin might do *you* some good, Jacob Hoffman. Anyway, that's when I shouted some Miss Emily back at 'em," Rachael said, a confident lilt of oneupsmanship in her voice. "I looked 'em straight in their sunburned eyes, I did, and I started recitin:

'Then look out for the little brook in March;

Where the rivers overflow;

And the snows come hurrying from the hills;

And the bridges often go;

And later, in August it may be;

When the meadows parching lie;

Beware lest this little brook of life;

Some burning noon go dry.'

"That shut them scoundrels up, at least that bunch of 'em. Must've got 'em thinkin," she said with one eye closed. "They looked at each other and took to the ground, the whole lot of 'em, like they'd been shot down by a Yankee volley." Rachael sighed and gazed upon the sky. "Nobody turns a phrase like Miss Emily, don't you think? They looked at me like I was crazy or somethin, wantin more, I think, a lot like *you* do. I just laughed an' ambled on my sweet way.

"I saw a line of cannons, too, over yonder in Mumma's field across the Pike from the church."

"Cannons?" muttered Jacob, suddenly alert.

"Four, I think, pointed north toward Smoketown Road. Maybe six. A couple of 'em was still limbered, but horses an' men were runnin all over the place."

If Miss Emily's phrase-turning had not shut off the urge to kiss Rachael, talk of cannons and Rebels camped as close as the Dunker Church surely had. Shucking corn would have to wait, too.

"I gotta go. You comin with me or not?"

"Not, I reckon," answered Rachael after a moment's consideration.

"Suit yourself," Jacob acknowledged, getting exactly the outcome he had hoped for. He began a brisk walk down the Landing Road. "Tell my Daddy where I've gone an' that I'll be home directly. Bigun'll be goin with me."

"What makes you think I'll see your daddy?" Rachael shouted. "Your Daddy *despises* me, Jacob. You think I'm gonna stay here waitin for *him?*

Jacob kept walking. "He don't *despise* you. Can't stand the *sight* of you, maybe, is all."

"Hey, Belinda Springs ain't *that* way, Jacob!" Rachael shouted as Jacob scampered down the drizzle-dampened road. "John Jacob Hoffman, them Rebs *ain't* gonna sell you no rifle, and you *ain't* about to impress 'em by takin along a *slave!*" Jacob scampered on. "You an' your Daddy ought to be *ashamed* ownin slaves anyhow! What I *ought* to do, what I *will* do, is to tell your daddy you got the *coin*, that's what I *ought* to do! *Renner's?* Why, you might as *well* go on to Belinda's cockfights and throw away your money while you can! *That's* what I'll tell your Daddy, that you're about to *gamble* away that five dollar gold piece your grandpa gave you, the watch, too, then gamble off *Bigun* when you lose 'em both!"

Jacob stopped.

"You may be seventeen, but Isaac'll give you a twelve-year-old's skinnin," Rachael shouted through cupped hands.

Jacob sighed and lowered his head, again manipulated.

"I'll get the basket," he droned, kicking a rock.

Rachael smiled. She had a way of getting her way with Jacob. Phrase-turning.

Chapter 12

Jacob and Rachael walked the straight-
line path through farmer Reel's property, which bordered
Landing Road on the west and the Hagerstown Pike at its
intersection with Hog Trough Road on the east. Jacob held the
basket filled with picnic fare. A blanket curved with asymmetry
around his shoulders. He stroked Rachael's hand, thinking about
how best to reveal to her the morning's events, how her
perception of him might change were she to learn he had been
involved in the deaths of three men. He loved Rachael despite
her manipulative ways, perhaps because of them. He wanted to
tell her so, but on his terms, not hers.

In a cove of willows, a pebble's toss from the creek, Rachael
pulled the blanket from Jacob's shoulders and spread it over
Mumma's soft Virginia rye, spots of the morning dew clinging
still to its blades. Item by item, with the deliberation of a poem,
she emptied the basket, arraying its contents in neat rows, like a
stanza, its meter audible only to her. She smiled.

"When we gonna get married?" Rachael asked with a
bluntness that stilled Jacob's heart.

"Married?" Jacob asked with an excitement he had hoped
not to reveal. "What makes you think we're gonna get *married?*"

"John Jacob, there you go again!" Rachael mumbled
between chews on a piece of blueberry bread. "I know it; you
know it; the whole *county* knows it. What was that you
whispered in my ear at the huskin bee? 'Rachael Erin
Farnsworth, I love you more than I can say, and I want you to
have my children,'" she mocked, voice rising and falling, head
swaying. "Of course, I'm hopin for a more *fittin* proposal—can't
go havin your *children* without you properly askin—but I reckon
you know my answer."

Jacob blushed. Rachael's affinity for dramatic effect made
him feel naked, exposed. Marrying Rachael appealed more to his
lustful side, a means to an end, his need to burst out of the
awkwardness of adolescence, but at seventeen, his mind of minds
knew the venture was a fool's game. The awkwardness of
silence prevailed for the remainder of the picnic, interrupted once
by one of Jacob's toad-like belches.

Bread and preserves eaten, Jacob gulped his water and
strolled over to the creek bank. He flung a few pebbles into the
satiny swirl of water gurgling over stones, tickling the wings of
dragonflies. Rachael wiped the utensils and plates and folded the
blanket.

"I know what's on *your* mind, John Jacob," Rachael sang.

"You *do?*" Jacob replied as he skipped a pebble across the
creek. "Three … four … five … *six!* Beat *that*, Denia!"

"Don't you think for a minute I *couldn't*, John Jacob."
Rachael sauntered over to Jacob and wrapped her arms around
his neck. "An' I *know* you're not thinkin about how many *skips*
you can get from a rock."

Jacob looked into Rachael's eyes, half closed, beaming
green. Her lips parted slightly, trying to hold back a smile. Her
breath carried the hint of blueberries.

"Well, it ain't exactly *that* that I'm thinkin' about, either,
Denia."

"No?" She pulled him closer.

"I mean—what I mean is …"

"Don't talk," she whispered. She closed her eyes and
touched her lips on his. In a flash of bliss, Jacob forgot about the

cannons in Mumma's fields, the gathered armies on the eve of a great fight, his quest for a sparkling military rifle, his scheme to free Bigun—and the morning's killings.

Jacob pulled back, feigning resistance. "Rachael, I—my family's *Dunker*, an' I—"

"Shhh! I may not be a Dunker, but *you* ain't much of one yourself," she whispered. "Give your Daddy time. He'll get used to the idea once he sees how happy we are. Besides, the Iron Furnace will be hirin soon, if it's still *standin*. Most of the help's gone off to war. You'll have work there until your Daddy simmers down an' lets you come back to the wagon business, assumin you'll *want* to come back. As for where we'll live, well, there's a room over Shadwick's—"

"A *livery* stable? Rachael, I—"

"Shhh! I already got us dibs on it. Don't worry, it's clean. We can—"

"Hey, *boy*, whatchu got there?" shouted a voice from the bramble along the creek. Whispers followed.

Rachael and Jacob froze in surprise and looked.

"Hee, *heeee!* Now *that's* what I call a *fine*-lookin woman!" shouted another. "What say we come out for a chat, talk about the weather … an' stuff."

Rachael looked at Jacob. "Got your Remie?" she whispered.

"Left it on the porch."

Two Yankee soldiers, as frothy and disheveled as rabid animals, clothes wet to their necks, emerged from the trees and brush, rifles tilted barrel up. They approached the young couple. Jacob eyed the naked Bowies each carried under his belt.

"You like these here knives, boy?" one man asked as he pulled the blade and fingered its serrated edge. "Took 'em from a couple of Johnnies at South Mountain. Rip the guts from a bear, one stroke. Now, you don't wanna be no *bear*, do ya, boy?"

Jacob said nothing as he held Rachael behind him.

"Step aside, boy. Let some *real men* have a peek at your woman."

The other soldier reached for Rachael's breeze-swept hair. She smelled the pungency of his whiskey breath.

"Soft hair, little lady," one soldier said as strands of hair fell between his fingers. "*Real* soft. Whatchu doin with a woman like *this*, boy?" he asked, answering, "Not *much*, I'm guessin." He laughed.

Rachael had a mind to deliver a kick to his groin, an act Jacob fully expected. He wanted her to, yet dreaded her doing it.

"You—you can't …" Jacob started.

The other man pulled his Bowie and grabbed Jacob's arm. He placed the blade to Jacob's throat.

"Calm down, boy," he said. "We gonna whip us some Rebs t'morrow, but *first* we're gonna warm up. You don't wanna call no *attention*, now, do you?"

"Let's see now," said the soldier with Rachael, as he scanned her form head to foot, "I'm gonna venture a guess as to whether y'all are *Yankee* Marylanders or *Confederate* Marylanders. Hard to tell who's who anymore. But, if my guess is right, I win the *prize*," the soldier said, stroking Rachael's hair. "Right answers deserve prizes, don't you agree? And my guess *will* be right."

"Boy, ain't you out of uniform?" the other soldier teased, pulling on Jacob's collared shirt. "A fine reb such as you ought to *be* in uniform. Would you like one of these blue suits, maybe a rifle to go with it?"

Jacob did not answer.

"*Would you?* But, then, I suspect *cowards* don't wear no uniform." Both men laughed. "Say, I got me an *extra* uniform down by the creek bank, boy, that'll fit you right *good*. Come with me." The soldier grabbed Jacob's arm.

"You men!" shouted a horse-mounted officer, flanked by four infantrymen, atop the low ridge on the opposite side of the creek.

Surprised, the men released Rachael and stepped back at attention.

"Back to your posts! *Now!*"

The men scrambled through the neck-deep water, rifles lifted over their heads, and disappeared into the anonymity of hillside foliage.

"General McClellan's compliments, ma'am," said the officer, removing his hat. "Please forgive the insolence of my men. They've not seen the likes of you in well over a year, and I suspect as well that was the last time they had any use for manners."

"No harm done, sir," Rachael replied, flipping her hair.

"If the battle on the morrow doesn't kill them, they will be placed under arrest," the officer added. "A piece of advice, if I may?"

"You may," Rachael said.

"The indiscretions of my men aside, you are not on safe ground. I strongly urge that you leave the area."

"A piece of advice, if *I* may, sir?" Jacob finally spoke.

The officer nodded.

"I strongly urge *you* to control your men, sir!" Jacob offered. "Or they're liable to get some of *my* insolence."

"Again, ma'am, my apologies."

The officer saluted and vanished beyond the ridgeline, his mount spanking the ground into a flurry of sod and dirt.

Jacob and Rachael stared across the creek.

"And you wanted me to join *that* army?" Jacob asked.

"Hold me," Rachael begged.

Jacob cuddled Rachael, her resolve at once faltering, her head buried into the fold of his arms. The ground beyond their view across the creek bristled with lustful sounds, men uttering muffled obscenities.

"They were there all this time," Rachael said as if such were a surprise. "Yankee men *gawking* at me like I was somebody's *concubine*," she whined, eyes dancing at the thought.

Jacob picked up the basket. "Let's go home, Rachael. War's too close."

"Marry me, John Jacob," Rachael chimed, smiling, "or one of these Yankee boys'll scoop me up, just like *that*," she said with a snap of her fingers.

"I thought you wanted a *fittin* proposal, from *me*," Jacob replied. "Rachael, there's somethin you got to know."

"What do I 'got to know', John Jacob? That you *love* me as I love you, and that you want me to bear your children? That you dream of my embrace in a downy bed on cold winter nights? That your sky-blue eyes and the curls of your blonde hair just about turn me inside out? That you see a long future for us filled with life and children, surrounded by the fruits of our dreams?"

"What?" Jacob asked, putting an arm's length between him and Rachael. "Rachael, how can you see *any* of that?"

"The hair and eyes, well, they're as plain to see as your narrow little nose, John Jacob," Rachael said, touching his nose with the tip of a finger "The rest I already know."

Jacob sighed.

"We're a nation at *war*, for God's sake. No time for talk of marriage, not *now*." Jacob shook his head.

"And why *not* now?"

"*Listen* to me! Bigun an' me were down fishin at Rohrbach's bridge this mornin, an'—"

"Came home empty-handed, right?"

"Rachael, *quiet!* We ran into … some problems."

"What sort of *problems*, Jacob?"

"The kind of problems that get a man *hanged*."

"*Hanged?* Whatever are you *talkin* about?"

"I'm talkin about me an' Bigun' killed a man. Actually, it was more like *three men*."

Rachael smiled, thinking Jacob was teasing her. He did not return the smile. He stared at the dirt road for a moment and then glanced at Rachael.

"I don't like this, Jacob. You're talkin *foolishness*. Tell me you're teasin and then ask me to marry you."

"Learned somethin else about you today."

"What might that be?"

"Learned that when you're full of mischief an' play, I'm 'John Jacob'. When things get serious, I'm just Jacob."

"John Jacob … Just Jacob, either way I want to *marry* you! *Now!*"

"I can't marry you, Rachael, not now. Maybe never. I got me a real problem, me and Bigun both."

"A hangin problem?"

"Could be."

Jacob told Rachael the story.

"That's why we can't marry now. Bigun an' me's got to get *out* of here, least 'til this blows over. Rebs weren't the only ones seen us with those men. Can't say anybody recognized us or that they actually seen the acts. But what if they *did?* Could be the law's lookin for us right this minute. It's obvious a battle is about to bust out. If not today, for sure tomorrow, but it's comin. Soldiers are everywhere. Artillery's scattered in the fields. Could be those men will just blend in with the rest of the dead once the battle starts. That's a chance we can't take, though. Me an' Bigun are leavin tonight, late."

"*Leavin?* Goin where? What're you gonna tell your Daddy?"

"Nothin to tell. He ain't gonna know I'm gone until dinner, an' *you* ain't about to tell him *before!* I got my lucky piece."

"Your watch?"

"That, an' my Remie, on the porch. Coin, too, in my pocket. I still think I can buy me a rifle with it, maybe trade my watch *and* coin. Bigun's gonna need the Remie. Bound to be a rifle or two for sale around here by now.

"He'll be a *runaway.* Lots of soul drivers up here just lookin for the likes of Bigun."

"He'll be with me. Anyway, he can take care of himself."

"You'll be comin back."

"Don't know. Maybe so, but no tellin when."

Rachael's eyes welled with tears. "Between you and Ros, what's a girl to do? Why do you want the damn rifle so much anyway?"

"You think *that's* what this is all about?"

"Isn't it?"

"After all that's happened, you can ask that? Besides, ain't never had one, an' I see my chance."

"You've never had *me*, either. You still want *me*, Jacob? Now's your *chance.* I'm here for the takin."

"More'n a bee wants a honeysuckle, Denia," Jacob whispered, kissing Rachael's forehead, "I want you. But all that's gonna have to wait. Until it's safe to come home," he said. "One of those dead men was an acquaintance of Daddy's. Claggett Parker."

"Claggett Parker?"

"He's come around before lookin to buy Bigun. Furnace let him go some years back, an' so he took up slave-tradin. He made a few dandy offers for 'im, but Daddy wouldn't sell Bigun. Made Claggett madder than a penned hound.

"He made a few threats, threats Daddy brushed off, but I didn't brush 'em off. I told Claggett in front of some other townsfolk there'd be trouble if he tried to take Bigun. Claggett would have killed any other man for sayin such to his face, but he just laughed at me, like I was some starvin alley cat.

"Now he's dead. Dead in the woods near the bridge where everybody knew Bigun an' me were goin fishin, like we always do on Tuesdays. Dead with those other two."

"Folks have left town, Jacob," Rachael said. "Nobody's home, except a few brave souls aimin to protect what's theirs from hungry, scavengin soldiers, as if they *could*. You saw the roads this mornin. People're on their way to Hagerstown and Harpers Ferry. Some are headed to Killing's Cave to wait this thing out. My folks, too. Nobody cares about the likes of Claggett Parker, and nobody seen what happened at the bridge. If anything, folk's will be glad to learn Claggett's gone from here; you did the valley a favor."

"Can't be sure, Rachael, not when there's a black man involved. Bigun thinks there was somebody in the woods watchin us, an' last I heard, murder's still against the law. I'll check back with you in a few days. You can tell me then which way the wind's blowin."

"Isaac's gonna want to know where you've been those few days."

"Seems I got me an excuse just waitin to happen," Jacob said, war in the air. "If not, I'll think of somethin. Go on home now, Rachael."

"Can we at least take one more walk through the Hog Trough. We're so close and—"

"Come on," Jacob answered in frustration, grabbing Rachael's hand, hoping to satisfy her romantic inclinations.

The pair trudged through Mumma's fields, stumbling among the clods of soil, occasionally falling and rising, laughing, sashaying. Jacob picked up some loosely packed dirt, squeezed it tight and tossed it at Rachael, missing her by inches.

"Since when did *you* become so playful, John Jacob Hoffman?"

"Since you spanked me with sunflower plates!" Jacob replied.

Rachael dropped the picnic basket, its contents scattered forgotten across the ground. She reached for her ammunition of dirt, and the battle was on, balls lobbed, exploding on heads and backs. Shouts and laughter echoed across the field.

They reached Hog Trough Road and stopped. They stared at the stretch. Hog Trough was *their* road, *their* hideaway, *their* place for dream-making, *their* furnace for forging memories. Its trench-like appearance lent solitude and privacy, a barn without walls and doors. Here, time stood still. Here, Rachael had fallen in love. Jacob held Rachael.

Shadows stretched as the afternoon passed. Jacob and Rachael heard the unmistakable rumble of artillery fire coming from north of town. Sounds of soldiers' shouts rippled over the fields. Activity increased toward the Dunker Church and in its surrounding woods. Riders stretched their mounts in full gallop.

"Time to go," Jacob whispered. "Your family will be wondering where you've been off to." He kissed her cheek.

"I love you, John Jacob Hoffman. Marry me."

Jacob looked into Rachael's moistened eyes, their green glistened by the lowering sun. *She does love me*, he thought. *She does.* He hugged her, stroking her hair and pressing her face to his chest, and wondered if he might never see her again. Even now, his thoughts waged war. He wondered why he so needed the rifle. He wondered what he was running from, *really* running from, perhaps running *toward*. He loved Rachael, but the words remained locked within his soul, like a spirit chained between worlds. He released her and bolted toward the Hagerstown Pike and the fields of farmer Reel. Even his kiss remained chained.

Jacob ran smack through elements of Stephen Lee's artillery arrayed in a neat northeastward row in Mumma's fields. He passed units of Stonewall Jackson's infantry bivouacked in those same fields and among the trees surrounding the Dunker Church, a line of battle stretching north and south of the church for as far as he could see. Several pockets of restless soldiers called, "Run, boy, *run!*" And run he did.

Jacob's sprint slowed to a trot, the energy burst expended. He glanced back a time or two but saw nothing of Rachael. Ignoring the soldiers' jests, he turned and meandered back toward the Pike.

Rifles! he thought.

He felt his pockets for the gold coin and the pocket watch. He steps drifted in no certain direction as he gazed upon a scene as alien to his experience as freedom to the slave. He fought off feelings of detachment, as if he at once found himself awakened from a dream of a foreign land. He loitered along the pike, as one stunned with dispossession, belying his casual kick of stones, efforts to remain indifferent, as if the sights were as normal as farmers working their fields. He looked around from time to time, assessing the images of faces and the voices of attitudes, gathering the nerve to ask the absurd, for a rebel to sell his rifle.

"Find you a seat an' stay for the show!" shouted a lean Confederate propped against a fence rail.

"I spect not," Jacob replied.

"Suit yourself," the soldier said, puffing his pipe. "I reckon if I was you, I wouldn't be a-stayin either."

Jacob gave a smile of acknowledgement to the soldier. "I'll buy your rifle," Jacob blurted.

"The *hell* you say, boy?" another replied.

Jacob did not repeat the question. "Nothin, sir," he said, lowering his head. Jacob reached into his pocket, his fingers grasping the coin. "It's just that I got this—Nothin, sir. Just came to see."

"Well, you *seen.* Now *git!*"

The evening slipped into dusk as the last rays of light kissed the debatable ground.

Jacob's Baptism

Chapter 13

A horseman rode into Sharpsburg that
Tuesday evening, his sweat and dust inconspicuous among the
throng of Confederates and refugees moving through town. His
brother had failed to meet an expected rendezvous and was last
seen this morning milling about the saloons and streets of the
village.

The horseman, a soul-driver, knew the pickings were ripe for
runaways and contraband. Anxious planters in the coastal cotton
states awaited his return and were prepared to pay top dollar for
strong bodies. He had in mind a few prized specimens in the
western Maryland theatre. He needed Bronson's help for the
roundup.

The horseman dismounted and stretched his arms skyward.
A gust caught his duster, whipping it against his legs, freeing soil
gathered from countless miles of road and trail. He entered the
Sharpsburg House restaurant.

"Beefsteak, rare," he ordered as he ambled toward a table in
the middle of the room. "And milk." He pulled the chair back
with his spurred boot and sat. The man removed one revolver,
placing it in the middle of the table, its grip within quick reach.

"*Milk*, sir?" the waiter asked, surprised by the request. "Don't get much call for that. Hard to keep it fresh."

"Milk. White, and of cows," he replied with sarcastic clarity.

"I don't believe we—"

"Then best you find some," he said, his raspy monotone void of emotion. He stared out the window at the flurry of human traffic.

"Comin up, sir," replied the bow-tied waiter.

"I need some information," the horseman said.

"Help you if I can, sir."

"Take a look," the man said, lifting his face and looking straight into the waiter's eyes.

"Sir?"

"You hard of hearin? Take a *look*," the man repeated. "You seen another man that looks like me come through town in the past couple of days?" He removed his hat, swept his hand through the gloss of his black, shoulder-length hair. The waiter did as he was told.

"I seen *you*, sir," the waiter replied, scanning his face. "I seen you in here this morning. Why, you're … Claggett Parker. *Everybody* knows who you are. But, I ain't seen nobody else that looks *like* you."

The man replaced his hat. "What you seen this mornin was my brother," Claggett said, replacing his hat on his head.

"Your *brother?*"

"*Twin* brother. From Lawrence, Kansas. He's been ridin with Quantrill, but now I need 'im. You gonna get me that beefsteak and milk?"

The waiter knew of Quantrill and his band of renegades. He froze in recall of newspaper accounts of the war between anti-slavery Kansans and pro-slavery Missourians.

"Would you feel better if he was a *Jayhawker?*" Claggett asked, irritated with the gawking waiter. "Blood is blood, no matter who's sheddin it."

"I—I … *Quantrill?*" the waiter stammered.

"Hey!" reminded Claggett, snapping his fingers, "I give you an order."

"Right away, Mister Parker."

The waiter stumbled toward the kitchen, bumping tables and chairs, and disappeared through swinging doors. After several minutes, he returned with Claggett's order.

"Milk's a bit lukewarm, I'm afraid, Mr. Parker, but fresh as a June bug in May," the waiter said, smiling.

Claggett did not return the smile. He cut into his steak and nodded approval.

"Enjoy your meal, sir. Check back with you in a few minutes."

Claggett dropped his hat onto the table. He sensed the muffled buzz of conversation stirring across the half-empty diner. Word of his brother, a Confederate Partisan Raider and comrade of the notorious Quantrill, spread in the restaurant like a winter cold in an orphanage. He paused with a forkful of red beef at his opened mouth, and listened. Discerning nothing offensive, he shoved the meat into his mouth.

"There he is, Mr. Simpson!" shouted a small boy tugging the man's hand as both burst through the door.

Claggett chewed like a grazing cow, startled but unconcerned. "What can I do for you, Simpson?"

"Pardon our intrusion, Mr. Parker, sir, but this young lad seems to believe you are ... well ... *deceased*," Simpson said, extending his hand in a conciliatory handshake. Simpson cleared his throat. "Obviously, you are *alive* and well, and we shan't bother you further. A very good day to you, sir."

Mr. Simpson hustled the boy toward the door, speaking hushed admonishments.

"Just a minute, Simpson. You there, front and center," Claggett said, pointing to the boy.

The room took on the silence of a tomb as the boy paced cautiously toward Claggett. Pushing a chair out from his table, Claggett motioned with a head tilt for the boy to sit. Simpson stood motionless.

"Now then," Claggett said, "what gives rise to this *exaggeration* of my demise?"

The boy stared blankly, as if in the presence of divinity.

"Cat got your tongue, boy? What makes you think I'm dead?"

"I—I seen you *stabbed*, Mr. Claggett," the boy said, chest heaving. "With a knife longer'n my arm. Before that, I seen *you* kill two other men, down by the creek this mornin."

"Stabbed, you say? How interesting." Claggett pulled open his duster. "Now then, do I *look* stabbed?" He shoved a forkful into his mouth and glanced from his periphery at the eavesdropping diners. "Obviously, I'm *here*," he said in full chew. "Tell me more of what you saw … or *think* you saw."

"Well, me an' Stump took off fishin at the creek this mornin. We seen Jacob Hoffman and his Daddy's blacksmith, Bigun, comin towards the creek, poles on their shoulders. They come down there every Tuesday.

"Anyway, out of the bushes stepped two men. Couldn't hear what they was talkin about, but it didn't look all that friendly. Next thing we knew, them two men went down, shot. Then, you—that is, some man—rode down off the ridge. There was more talkin, then Jacob and Bigun buried the men creekside, and then you—him—tied Bigun's hands with a rope attached to your saddle and pulled him off to the woods. After a while, Jacob followed; so did we, from a distance. We happened upon Bigun an' you takin a piss. That's when Bigun up an' stabbed you—him."

Claggett fixed his eyes upon the boy's. "That man wearin a duster, like mine?"

"Looked to be. Anyway, that's what I seen," the boy said. "'Cept you're *here*, so that man must've been somebody else."

"Where on the creek?"

"Rohrbach's Bridge."

"Did you take notice of the man's horse?"

"Yes, sir. Brown, with a white blaze on his forehead. White on the forelegs."

Claggett looked up at Simpson. "You verify his story, the killings?"

"No sir, not yet. We just figured it to be a child's babble, what with a battle brewing and soldiers everywhere and all. And knowing you were in the Sharpsburg House for supper—"

"More'n child's babble," Claggett said, as he slurped the last swallow of milk. *"Milk!"*

The waiter dashed to Claggett's table with a fresh glass. The restaurant's few diners craned their necks in feigned disinterest.

"That man who looked like me was my brother. Name of Bronson." Claggett emptied the milk in one mighty gulp and slammed the glass on the table. "Reckon I'll be payin Isaac Hoffman a visit this evenin after all," he said under his breath.

Claggett pulled out four bits and dropped it to the table. He handed the boy two bits. "Much obliged, boy."

"Wow! Thank you, Mister Claggett!"

"Sir, your steak?" reminded the waiter.

"You eat it," Claggett said as he pushed through the restaurant doors. "I'm goin' after some *fresh* meat."

"Hmph!" the waiter sulked, out of earshot. "And no tip," he added, lifting the wadded napkin from the table.

"I'll check out the boy's story, Mr. Simpson," Claggett said as he spurred his mount down Chapline Street toward the Lower Bridge Road. "You'll be hearin from me."

Bronson Parker joined Quantrill's Raiders in June, 1862, in allegiance to his firm support of the Confederacy and to his belief the Kansas Territory's destiny was slave statehood. An expert marksman, Bronson had mastered the art of guerilla warfare, facts inconsistent with his killing at the hands of a slave.

The thirty-three-year-old Bronson had declined Claggett's invitation to participate in John Brown's raid on Harpers Ferry in 1859. His heart and sympathies were Southern. Had he known Claggett's intentions relative to the raid on Harpers Ferry, to lure unsuspecting blacks, his participation would have been energetic.

Claggett had delivered a load of muskets and pikes, under the deceptive crating of Antietam Iron Furnace nails, to Harpers Ferry the day of the raid. He intended to rendezvous with Brown during the predawn hours before the raid, but a broken wagon wheel delayed the delivery. Unwilling to risk capture and hanging, Claggett abandoned the load behind the armory and blended in with the citizenry.

The lure of profits from the slave trade trumped his hollow convictions and thirst for glory. Instead, he appeared no more than a curious bystander to the failure of Brown's raid and awaited his opportunity. His wait was short. There, he saw Bigun.

Jim "Bigun" Pemberton had been Isaac Hoffman's blacksmith since 1855, having fled a South Carolina plantation owned by Devereaux the year before. His dexterity with fashioning iron rims around the wood of wagon wheels, as an artist might create the perfect mix of lines and depth, earned favored status with Isaac. Bigun forged his virtual freedom and made himself indispensable to the success of Hoffman's wagon trade.

Isaac had won a lucrative contract with the Antietam Iron Furnace the following year to manufacture and deliver one hundred wagons in two years' time, a wagon every week. The wagons were used by the Furnace to transport iron ore offloaded from barges floated up the creek from the Potomac River, as well as the delivery of pig iron, nails, coke, and an occasional artillery tube.

During this period, Claggett worked at the Furnace as a filler, earning a promotion to supervisor, and had frequent contact with Isaac Hoffman and Bigun, a black man he had long coveted and had tried once to purchase.

As the melee of John Brown's raid unfolded, Claggett set his sights on Bigun, one of a handful of uninjured participants with Brown's raiders. The final assault by Colonel Robert E. Lee's men on the arsenal at Harpers Ferry ended the raid and put to rest any organized slave uprising east of the Mississippi.

Bigun, unknown to locals of Harpers Ferry, managed to evade his pursuers, with Claggett's help, across the Potomac into Maryland and back to Sharpsburg.

Tempted by the good fortune of events, Claggett instead returned Bigun to the Hoffman farm with the promise never to reveal Bigun's whereabouts and participation on that fateful day, for which, if found out, Bigun would surely hang. In return, Bigun agreed to "run away" into Claggett's possession three years after the raid, as long as he agreed never to send Bigun south. Claggett had come to collect on a debt Bigun had long forgotten.

Now a ten-year-old boy had linked Bigun and Isaac's son to Bronson's death. Claggett intended first to unravel the riddle of this turn of events.

Night fast approached. Claggett encountered Rebel soldiers preparing the lines for tomorrow's inevitability. As Claggett approached the Rohrbach Bridge, Confederate pickets stopped Claggett and turned him back before he could get across the bridge.

Frustrated, Claggett returned to Sharpsburg, an eerily quiet, darkened village. The town was tense, like a child quaking behind a banister while her parents argued. He walked the deserted streets looking for signs of Bronson, hoping the boy's account was indeed imagination.

Finding nothing and no one, Claggett sat his horse and pulled one at a time each of his three Colt revolvers, spinning the cylinders and confirming the loads. A Confederate battery thundered through town, toward the Hagerstown Pike, the dust of its wake shutting Claggett's eyes. Good fortune intervened once again. Distractions were bountiful; witnesses were nonexistent or unobservant. Giving a gentle kick to his mount's sides, Claggett trotted toward the Landing Road and the Hoffman residence.

Chapter 14

Twilight diffused through the valley
air like the satiny amber of spilt whiskey. Ole Whooey poked his
head out of a hole in a chestnut tree on the northeastern boundary
of Hog Trough Road and Piper's cornfield. His yellow eyes
surveyed a landscape split by the sunken road and its parallel
ruts, Hog Trough Road, a divider between the Piper and Roulette
farms and a shortcut connecting Hagerstown Pike to Boonsboro
Pike.

Rodents and rabbits scampered through rows of corn and
fields of grass. The owl jumped to a nearby branch. Silhouetted
against the western sky, the blood-red sun half-sunk, Ole
Whooey began his hunt. The melancholy of his call rolled on the
air like an omen. Cicadas and whippoorwills joined this
resonance of dusk.

Bats darted, defying physics, as if filled with the Spirit. Ole
Whooey sprang from his perch, the spread of his six-foot span in
full glide. Prey scattered like buckshot through the fields and
across the depths of Hog Trough Road. Escape was brief, futile.
Life and death exchanged bows, and so began the dance.

Sharp exchanges of artillery north of town, armies posturing
for the contest, probing the enemy's strength, gave notice that for

thousands their moments of truth were at hand. Jacob stopped to listen.

Residents, the few remaining, heard and waited.

The sky dimmed.

Lamplights lowered.

The flicker of candlelight dwindled.

Heads lay on pillows and crates, rocks and ground, but few slept.

Sharpsburg, one eye opened, wilted into the darkness. Jacob took a deep breath for the final sprint home.

Ole Whooey returned to the chestnut branch overlooking Hog Trough Road and peered with patience, as he had done night after night, the limp catch ensnared in his talons. He pecked the form's lifeless body, preparing it for consumption.

Jacob skidded to a halt on the dirt lawn at the foot of the porch steps. He bent over, hands on hips.

"Where you been?" Bigun asked. "Missuh Isaac come back a while ago. Prob'bly good you *was* gone. Said fo' us to come d'rectly over to Missuh Samuel's place."

"*Samuel's* place?"

"Said he needed to talk to you an' me 'bout somethin. Reckon ... he knows?"

Jacob considered Bigun's question.

"Dem rebs done run off Missuh Samuel and Miss Lizzy and all eight of dem young-uns. Missuh Samuel and a couple of his boys and yo' Daddy is goin back to de house dis evenin to try to salvage some food and valu'bles. I 'spect de house'll be all to'n up by den. Won't be a crumb of food lef'. Where you *been* to be all tuckered?"

"Had to—had to take a walk with—with Rachael," Jacob said, panting. "She can be a *dadgum* pain when she—she sets her mind to it. Where's the Mumma family stayin?"

"At the chu'ch, I reckon. Yo' daddy, too," answered Bigun. "He says it be de safest place. Don't know *how* he knows dat. I know he spectin us at Missuh Mumma's."

"Daddy's stayin at the *church?*" Jacob asked, surprised. "I seen the church, an' it ain't *no* place to be. Rebs *everywhere!* I spect even *God's* headin for the cave."

"Missuh Isaac sent Jesse an' the young-uns wit' dat Missy Rachael's mama over to Killin's Cave. What I gawn do now, Missuh Jacob?"

Jacob pondered this turn of events. Taking Bigun without his family was the sort of separation he wanted to avoid.

"We ain't goin."

"We ain't goin?" Bigun asked. "We's *stayin?*"

"No, not stayin, neither. We ain't goin to Mumma's, is all. Or the church."

"Ain't goin' to Mumma's? What yo' daddy gawn do when we don't show up?"

"I don't know," Jacob answered, "but we can't go worryin about that now. We got enough pigs in the slop as it is. We'll be back in a couple of days. By then, Rachael will know if word's out about Claggett and them other two. Meanwhile, I know where we can find us the best seats in the house for one dandy of a fight. Don't you *want* to see a battle?"

"I spect," Bigun said, his mind in remembrance of the indignity of days spent on auction blocks and years spent in fields, the jeers and prods of white men filleting his spirit, his hope. "Got me a mind to pick me up a rifle and shoot some Rebs myse'f."

"I don't reckon *that'd* be such a good idea, Bigun, if you want to see your family again." Jacob paused and smiled. "Maybe we ought to scoot on around this fight so you won't go gettin' *your* blood up."

"Missy Rachael's mama done lef' you some food in de kitchen."

"Bless her heart! I thought I smelled a slice of Farnsworth heaven. Let's go."

Jacob and Bigun made their way to the kitchen and sat. Bigun guzzled a goblet of milk and shoved a fat biscuit into his mouth. He hunkered over his plate, like a stray dog over a bone, before it occurred to him he was eating at a white man's table.

He stopped in mid-chew; his guilty eyes shifted toward Jacob's, as would a child caught with his hand in the cookie jar.

"Scuse me," he mumbled, crumbs spilling from his mouth to the floor.

"For *what? Eat*, man! Black man's gotta eat same as a white. If anybody deserves to eat from this table, *any* table, *you* do."

"Talkin 'bout my mannuhs, Missuh Jacob."

"Oh," Jacob said, noticing Bigun's hulking chest and shoulders shadowing his plate. "Apology accepted—*after* you drop the Missuh. I don't want to hear it anymore."

Jacob grabbed a biscuit, turning it in his fingers, and pressed it into his mouth, crumbs falling. He smiled.

Bigun prayed. "Thanky, Lawd, for de bounty of dis table. Be wit Missuh Hoffman as he he'ps dem in need. If dey's a battle on the morrow, be wit dem what's fightin fo' de cause of freedom. In de Blessed name of *Jesus*, Amen."

Both grinned and reached for heaping portions of biscuits, milk, corn on the cob, sidemeat and a tub of white gravy.

"Only thing missin is the fried chicken," Jacob said, chewing. "What's this?"

"A note from Missy Rachael. Her mama say to me it explains takin Jesse an' de chillun to de cave."

Jacob took the note, read it and tossed it onto the table.

"More of Rachael's gibberish. Weird, ain't it?" Jacob observed.

Bigun split a biscuit, bathed it with butter, and stacked on a few slices of sidemeat. "I don't rightly know whatchu mean, suh."

"This house; this valley; this *age*. A nation at war with itself, and here we are in the *thick* of it, a white man an' a black man eatin biscuits *side by side* from the same table.

"This war ain't just in the newspapers no more. It's right outside our doors. You an' me in this house, by ourselves, at night before a battle that we get to *witness*. We're on the edge of *history*, Bigun, literal *history!* I got me a *feelin* about all this. Don't this sorta make your skin stand up?"

"Makes a *white* man's skin stand up. Mine's still sweaty, an' it *will* be as long as I be a slave. No offense to you, Missuh Jacob. I appreciate what Missuh Isaac do fo' me an' my family. I appreciate what *you* about to do fo' me. It's jus' dat—it's jus' dat dawn never *comes* fo' a slave. As long as whip and shackle meet black skin, ain't *none* of us free, not even you."

"For the *last* time, it's *Jacob*. Not *Mister* Jacob; not *sir*. Just Jacob. No offense taken, Bigun. We're gettin you out of here, your family, too. Just gotta go fetch 'em. Funny, though. Daddy's gone; Rachael's gone; your family, *gone*. We're *here*. Ain't *we* the ones supposed to be gone?"

"My fam'ly, Missuh Jacob; what I gawn do?"

"They'll be fine, Bigun. If they're with Rachael, they're in good hands. Then again, sometimes I think bein thrown into a battle *naked and unarmed* would be a more pleasin experience than bein in the company of Den … Rachael Farnsworth. Least in a battle, a man can shoot back or play dead," Jacob said, smiling. "Gettin dark. Let's finish this and get ready.

"Whatever food's left, pack it," Jacob continued. "Wrap some of these melons in sheets, along with that ham and a couple of pounds each of sugar and beans. Heck, get anything edible we can carry. Yanks will take *all* this, sure as sunshine, unless it ain't here to take."

"Rebs, too," Bigun offered.

"Rebs *especially*."

"Yankee soldiers jus' as soon shoot me as look at me," Bigun observed, spreading a sheet for the melons and other provisions. "Who de *good* guys be?" Bigun asked.

"Ain't none, I reckon," Jacob said after a brief ponder. "Lincoln?"

"An' Missuh Douglass," answered Bigun.

"*Him* you can call Mister."

Jacob and Bigun spent the next few hours stuffing valuables into the cellar nooks and packing essentials for their journey.

Jacob deduced the positions of the armies, having seen considerable elements of both. In basic terms, the Union Army occupied ground on the east side of the Antietam; the Rebels, the west side. The Confederates, he believed, possessed material disadvantages in men and arms, but as Rachael had pointed out, they seemed to possess an unfaltering spirit, a sense of immortality impenetrable by the fastest bullets or the heaviest shells. The Potomac River snaked to their backs, not three miles from Sharpsburg. While safe behind Rebel lines now, perhaps, the Hoffman house lay in direct line of a Southern rout.

Guns of artillery rumbled on occasion north and east, feeler shells sent forth harassing Confederate efforts to gain a few precious hours of sleep. Spatters of distant small-arms fire suggested a bulge of tension ready for the breach. Jacob stopped, a load of silver in his arms, and listened. Amid the grumbles of frogs and the chirps of crickets, a gigantic eruption of flesh and fire simmered at the point of boil.

"We best get a move on, Bigun," Jacob urged. "If I'm gonna get me that rifle, I best be doin it before dawn. We got us a whole army to get around, maybe two. Besides, Daddy'll be sending after us soon."

Jacob shoved his Remie between his belt and pants. He patted his pocket for his coin, his adventure. Both picked up their laden packs and started out eastward on the Landing Road toward the Reel farm.

A shroud of clouds snuffed the light of the moon. Gunfire had died down. The nocturnal and the sleepless owned the fields now. Only Jacob's and Bigun's blind familiarity with the terrain prevented utter disorientation. Ahead, the sound of a galloping horse grew louder.

"Off the road, Bigun!" Jacob said.

The two slouched in brush along the roadside and waited.

"Rebs?" whispered Bigun.

"Could be."

"They seen us?"

"Not unless they got the vision of Ole Whooey."

The horse sprinted by, scattering rocks and dirt, and disappeared in the grainy gray. Jacob strained to make out its rider.

"That's one of Mumma's, I believe," said Jacob. "Daniel or Sam, Jr., likely. He's slowin down at the house. Daddy's sent somebody out to find us, all right. Let's keep movin."

Jacob thought about what might await them. Lee's army lay bivouacked along the Hagerstown Pike and in the woods behind the Dunker church and in Mumma's and Piper's fields. As they approached the farmhouse of farmer Reel, the chatter of a great volume of men grew clearer. They saw limbers of cannon and caissons facing due east, toward the church and ready for deployment, their silhouettes made clearer by torch lights.

Jacob guessed the time to be around 2:00 a.m., his pocket watch long stopped. Activity swirled as soldiers cooked and ate rations, played cards, wrote letters, sang songs, and conversed. Some soldiers, firm in their belief this was their last night on Earth, meandered about like lost children, pensive, thinking of home, of family, staring at the heavens, hands in pockets or clasped behind them, some among them weighing the consequence of desertion against the valor of battle.

A group of pickets stopped Jacob and Bigun at the intersection of Reel's farm lane and the Landing Road.

"You fellers civilians?" asked a soldier.

"Yes, sir," answered Jacob.

"Oooo," the soldier teased, "y'all hear that? *'Yes, sir.'* "Whatchu got in them packs, boy? Smells awful good fer a darkie to be a-totin around."

"Stuff," replied Jacob.

"Stuff? What … stuff?" the soldier pried, reaching for Jacob's pack.

Jacob pivoted to avoid his reach.

"Hmm. Where y'all off to this time o' night, anyhow? How do we know y'all ain't Yankee spies?"

"I live down this road, that way," Jacob said, pointing. "This here's Bigun. He's a blacksmith; fits wheel rims and tracks for my daddy's wagon business."

"A slave?" asked one of the soldiers.

"My daddy's," answered Jacob. "Not for long, though."

"Don't be sayin that around here. What you fixin to do with 'im, sell 'im?"

"No, we're—we're thinkin about … about *joinin up* … with *you* boys. Got any rifles?"

Bigun, eyes widened and jaw dropped at Jacob's words, whipped his head in disbelief.

"Joinin up?" the soldier asked. "Be a lie to say we couldn't use another man or two, but some of these boys been th'ough the devil an' back fightin for somebody's right to hang on to these darkies. Some rather kill the slave than fight alongside him. Others might welcome the support, though I'm pressed to know why *any* slave would want to fight *for* his bondage. Others, well, they don't give two turds about nothin 'cept killin Billies."

"Billies?"

"Yanks. Blue Bellies. Where y'all headed?"

Jacob and Bigun looked at each other, neither sure how to answer his query.

"That way," Jacob answered, pointing northeast toward the obscurity of darkness. "Right here. Don't much matter where."

"Whatchu figure on doin, *watchin* the fight? I reckon you'll have yourself a front-row seat if you head that way. Tell you what," the soldier suggested.

"We listenin," said Bigun.

"Gen'ral Lee wants Maryland boys to join the Army of Northern Virginia," the soldier continued. He eyed Bigun. "I 'spect he'd just as soon take slaves as scraggly white trash. All you need's a musket, some cartridges, and a heap o' luck. They's a couple of Georgia regiments up yonder short o' men. Hell, the whole *army's* short o' men. Cain't promise you anything beyond tomorrow, but I can promise you an adventure. Interested?"

Jacob heard the magic words: 'musket' and 'adventure'.

"A musket? For *free?*" Jacob asked like a schoolboy in a toyshop.

"Jacob," Bigun leaned and whispered, "we ain't here to fight."

Jacob cleared his throat.

"Right, well … Georgia regiments, you say?" he replied to the soldier as the pair turned and set off through the bramble of Reel's fields.

"They got some Enfields, I hear!" shouted the picket. "Don't take the shotguns." Soldiers resting in a cove let out cackles of laughter and hollered profanities, none of which, Jacob convinced himself, were directed at him and Bigun.

"Where you reckon the chu'ch be, Missuh Jacob?"

"'Bout a half mile or so through those trees," he replied, pointing, looking skyward. "Ain't but a smudge of light to go by. 'Spect they don't want the Yankee sharpshooters drawin no bead on 'em or findin cannon range.

"Dey lookin fo' mo'e soldiers, Jacob. Dey gawn take us in, like it or not, an' th'ow us a rifle, a bag of bullets, an'—"

"I know, I *know*." Jacob was now as certain of getting his rifle as a bird is of dropping dung on one's Sunday suit. He was prepared to give his five dollars gold, Remie and watch as well, if he had to, but the asking price of *enlistment* was a trifle more than he was willing to go. "Let's camp here."

"Here?" said Bigun, surprised by the sudden change of plans.

"I think we ought to camp right *here,* right where we're standin."

"You an' yo' senses has parted comp'ny!"

"Look, Bigun, if we go farther, we're bound to run across some soldier who'd just as soon cut our throats and take our food as look at us. Did you see the look in that soldier's face back yonder? We're lucky they didn't eat our food an' shoot us as spies. No, let's take our rest right here an' see what happens come light."

"You de boss, but I ain't likin dis one bit. Why don't we jus' go on over to Missuh Samuel's place, take our chances wit' Missuh Isaac."

"Same thing, Bigun. We'd have to cross as many Rebs that way as this way, more even. Let's just see what happens," Jacob decided, unpacking his bedroll and blanket.

Bigun sighed and followed suit.

"Too quiet," Jacob observed.

Jacob's Baptism

"Only 'cause you knows what's comin," Bigun replied.

"Reckon Ole Whooey knows what's comin?"

"Ole Whooey knowed before the armies knowed."

"He ain't no legend for nothin," Jacob added.

Bigun smiled, wiping sweat from his forehead. "Crickets ain't quiet."

Jacob sighed and adjusted his bedroll. "Crickets are *always* quiet. Just gotta know how to hear 'em, is all."

The two lay down on an earthen mattress, wadded shirts for pillows, and stared at the heavens. Jacob brushed a night crawler off his chest. Clouds had parted, leaving jagged, moving holes across the ranks of infinity. A falling star sliced across the northeastern sky, its trail etched into Jacob's brain. Two more streaks followed.

"You see that, Bigun?"

"Sho' did."

"Damn perty, them things, when you can *see* 'em. Sneaky as possums in daylight, though." Jacob exhaled a breath of misplaced contentment and smiled, his thoughts filled with Rachael and Roswell. And rifles.

"Or bullets in battle," added Bigun.

Jacob's smile receded. He closed his eyes and thought about the thousands of soldiers who had just seen the same shooting stars.

Chapter 15

The boy's story of Bronson's killing burned hot in Claggett's mind like embers under a branding iron. He held little doubt as to the story's veracity. He pondered what to do about it. Bronson was dead. Revenge was alive.

Barrel-chested and arms like oak stumps, Claggett carried the stench of sweat, layers upon layers of it, skunk-like in its power to repel, though no one dared accuse him of such. Claggett was the reigning arm-wrestling and bare-fist-fight champion of Maryland, a title shared alternately with Bronson, such skills he readily displayed at the slightest provocation. Few men dared challenge his physical prowess, and those who did never made the same mistake twice.

Claggett had been promised the robust sum of ten thousand dollars gold for the return of an alive-and-well Bigun to Gustav Devereaux, owner of vast tracts of rice, cotton, and cane sugar along the Cooper River of Charleston. Claggett knew he would have to take down Bigun, in order to *take* Bigun, one of few men possessed with the physique and stamina needed to go toe to toe with the likes of Claggett Parker. While Claggett did not doubt his ability to snag and deliver Bigun, the task had become corrupted by his equally strong desire to heap revenge upon him.

Jacob's Baptism

The countryside along the Landing Road was dark, foreboding, like a keg of black powder sitting upon a stove fire. Claggett cantered his mount past the Reel farm and, seeing the silhouette of a familiar structure, yanked the reigns left. Midnight had come and gone, transformed into the dead of night. The time was ripe for raiding the home of Isaac Hoffman, exacting his surrogate revenge upon Jacob and collecting his human debt.

Claggett stepped from his horse and into his eagerness for the ease of killing Isaac's son, perhaps Isaac as well. He had reason enough, so he believed, as if such mattered to Claggett. Isaac had snapped the rug out from under Claggett's attempt to buy Bigun those years ago, and now Bigun—accompanied by Jacob—had killed Bronson. Reason mattered little to Claggett.

Rationale, on the other hand, gave freedom to his decisions. The price of blood was *blood*, a personal code of conduct reduced to its simplest terms. He would put a bullet into Bigun if worse came to worst, figuring out later how to extract the gold bounty from Devereaux.

Revolver drawn, Claggett placed his ear to the front door and listened. Silence. Not one for subtly, he drew up his leg and smashed in the front door, knocking it clear off its hinges. Poised to shoot anything that moved, he waited, listened. Hearing nothing, he replaced his guns and scratched a match to a lantern found on the kitchen table.

Claggett searched every room, kicking in more doors. He found the remnants of a meal, still warm, the only evidence of recent occupation. He caught glimpse of a note on the kitchen table. He took a half-eaten biscuit in one hand and the note in the other. The note read:

'Dearest Jacob,

'Have taken Bigun's family with mine to Killing's Cave to wait out tomorrow's battle.

'Be careful, my sweet. This incident at the bridge will all blow over, as will tomorrow's fight, and I will have you in my arms again.

'In my heart, Jacob, I know you love me, though you struggle to say the words. No matter. I feel your heart speaking, as Poe wrote:

'But our Love it was stronger by far than the Love

Of those who were older than we

Of many far wiser than we

And neither the angels in Heaven above,

Nor the demons down under the sea,

Can ever dissever my soul from the soul

Of the beautiful Annabel Lee.

'Until I see you again, I remain your devoted Rachael.'

"So Jacob's got him a woman," Claggett said, as he wadded the note and dropped it to the floor. "Killing's Cave, eh? And Bigun's with Jacob. Let's see what a little bait can do to draw him back."

Kicking the wadded note, he grabbed three biscuits from the floor, sat, and penned his own note. When he finished, he folded it, shoved it into his buckskin pocket, and exited the house. He turned, thinking for a moment of torching the place. Rethinking, he mounted and set off for the cave by way of Snyder's Landing.

Claggett knew well the trail to the cave and could traverse it blind. A short while into his ride, he saw flickers of torches and the rising sparks of campfires and heard the muffled chatter of the assembled refugees. Firelight cast sputtering shadows onto the walls surrounding the cave's entrance, a broad arch overlooking the Potomac River and the Chesapeake and Ohio Canal.

Tying his horse to a branch protruding from the rock cliff, Claggett sat on a boulder, awaiting his prey like a spider in the recesses of its web, and observed the wandering masses.

"Excuse me, sir," said an elderly man, clutching a cane in one hand and a cigar in the other. "Spare a match?"

"S'pose I can, old man," answered Claggett, striking the match on the boulder and touching it to the cigar. "Gonna be a big-un."

"What say?" the old man asked, his cigar-holding hand cupped around an ear.

"The *battle*," Claggett replied. "It's going to be *big*."

"I spect. Can't ever tell about these things," the old man grumbled between draws. "Little Mac's got himself an army that ought to show ol' Lee exactly what Maryland thinks of secesh."

"You don't think Lee can take 'im, old man?"

The man drew heavy on his cigar. One eye closed, he surveyed Claggett's frame. "You're a perty big ol' boy, yourself. I reckon *you* could take Lee." The man wheezed a laugh. "Have you forgotten about Malvern Hill?"

"Malvern Hill was a fool's fight," Claggett answered. "Just ain't sure who was the bigger fool, Lee or McClellan. Lee ought to have known better, massing infantry assaults against artillery."

"Precisely why I believe Lee's risk-taking is his Achilles heal."

"Lee's *got* to take risks, if his army has *any* chance in this war. Have *you* forgotten about Manassas, old man?" Claggett countered, drawing his Bowie knife and grabbing a stick felled by a storm.

"Hmph! Pope proved a *bigger* fool than the lot of 'em," the man answered and ambled away toward the cave's entrance, pecking his cane upon the ground. "I reckon Lincoln learned his lesson, taking Little Mac out of the war. Now that he's back in his rightful role, McClellan will do to Lee what your Bowie's 'bout to do to that stick."

"Wait a second, old man!" Claggett called. "Let me ask you something."

The man stopped and turned, looking more like a smoldering bush than a spent human being, smoke rising from the cigar clinging to his lips.

"What is it now?"

"I'm lookin for somebody. Hopin you might be able to help."

"Help if I can."

"I'm lookin for Isaac Hoffman and that big ol' blacksmith of his."

"You mean Bigun? Ain't seen neither one of 'em goin on three days now. Jacob, neither. I figure they're stayin with the house or headed over to the Furnace. That's where most of Isaac's business is these days. That's about all the help I can give. What business you have with the Hoffmans?"

"Never you mind, old man," Claggett said, whittling his stick. "Go find yourself a comfortable place. You're gonna be here a day or two, maybe longer."

"Have seen *Bigun's* family," the old man revealed.

"Oh, yeah?" Claggett asked, shaving bark from the stick, pretending indifference.

"Yep. Up yonder by the cave entrance, next to that cook fire," the old man said, pointing. "They might help you."

Claggett glanced up the hill and discerned three forms huddled against the exterior cave wall. "Obliged," he told the old man.

"Glad I could help."

"Bait," Claggett muttered.

"What's that you say?" the old man asked.

"Nothing," Claggett said, sharpening the stick. "Thinkin out loud."

Claggett shoved the Bowie into its scabbard. He stood and approached the group of three blacks, a woman and two female children.

Rachael brought over two tin cups of water, drops scattered with each step, and a loaf of bread tucked under her arm. She handed the cups and bread to Jesse, who gave it to her children weary from the journey.

"Thanky, Missy Rachael," Jesse said, eyes reddened with tears of worry. "Reckon where my man be dis night. You s'pose dem Rebs got holt of 'im?" The prospect gave her pause, and she looked skyward. "Oh, *Lawd*, he'p 'im!"

"Calm yourself, Jesse," Rachael whispered, wrapping her arms around her. "Jesus has got Bigun right where He wants 'im. Jacob, too. They'll be *all right*, you'll see. Take your seat here. Tend to the girls. I'm going to go get us more bread and water. You'll be *fine* here, you'll see."

Rachael picked a torch planted in a hole next to the cook fire and set off for the riverbank. Congregations of townsfolk handed food and water and offered blankets and other assistance as needed.

Claggett approached Jesse, who had not yet noticed him.

"Miz Pemberton?" Claggett said with the gentleness of a preacher.

Jesse lowered her cup and looked up. "Yassuh?" she answered.

"Miz Pemberton, may I have a word with you, please?"

"'Bout what, suh?" Jesse asked, clutching her two children, wary of the white man's deceptively soft tone.

"About Bigun, ma'am."

Jesse's attention opened like flowers to a bee. "You know where my man be?"

"Indeed I know, Miz Pemberton, and I can take you to him."

"Where my man be, Missuh—?"

"Parker, ma'am. Gather your children and follow me. I'll take you to him."

"He okay? I mean, dey ain't *kilt* 'im, has dey?"

Claggett rested his palm on Jesse's shoulder. "He's fine, Miz Pemberton. This way, please."

Claggett extended his arm, gesturing for Jesse to precede him. He glanced toward the riverbank, watchful for a returning Rachael.

Claggett spotted the old man lounging on a stump near the cave entrance, the orange of his cigar stump burning its last.

"Wait here, ma'am," he told Jesse. "I'll just be a moment."

Trotting over to the old man, Claggett reached into his pocket and pulled out a folded piece of paper.

"Do me a small favor, old man?" he asked.

"If I can," he replied, "but it'll cost you three cigars."

Smiling, Claggett handed the man five cigars and some matches. "Give this note to the *prettiest* young lady you see here tonight."

"A strong, handsome man that you are, and you're *afraid* to give it to her *yourself?*" the old man teased.

"Not afraid, old man. Just busy. Here, take two more cigars," Claggett said, pointing to Rachael struggling up the hill, pressing foodstuffs and a torch against her body. "Yonder she comes now."

The old man looked, squinting his eyes. "Hmmm," he said, remembering younger years, "Picked yourself a *peach*, you did." He chuckled and turned toward Claggett, who had vanished.

Claggett, Jesse, and her children stepped past the cave entrance, the chattering townsfolk inattentive to their presence. Just then, Rachael returned with more bread and water. She noticed Jesse and her children walking toward the road with a mountain of a white man pulling the reigns of a horse, their shadows spreading in the torch glow like spilled molasses. Curious, Rachael took a few steps toward the departing group. The bouncing waves of the man's hair sealed his identification.

*Claggett? That's **Claggett Parker!*** She thought. *Jacob said Bigun had killed him, so how come—*

"Ma'am?" the old man said.

Rachael turned around. "Yes?"

"A man asked me to give this to you." The old man handed Rachael the note. "Big man. Make a fine husband to a filly like yourself."

"Take the torch, please?" Rachael asked.

The old man took the torch and propped it against the cave wall. Rachael set the bread and water on the ground and took the note. She turned, but Claggett and Jesse had melted into the darkness. She dared not pursue them now or announce their departure for fear of what Claggett might do to them. She unfolded the paper and read the scrawl.

> *"Have Jesse and children. Will exchange all for Bigun. Deliver to Rohrbach's Bridge noon of September 24. Tell no one. Bring no one. No weapons. If instructions not followed to the letter, all will die. – CP"*

Rachael crumpled the note and tucked it inside her dress. She scampered to the road, stopped, listened for voices, and stared into the sheet of black silence.

Chapter 16

"I got the guard," announced a private come to relieve Bull. "Grub's on the fire, down-ridge, behind a little white buildin yonder, church, I reckon. Ain't got no steeple. Some of Hood's boys killed three or four hogs and rounded up a mess of corn ears, sweet taters. Farmer's cussin like a plucked chicken, says he cain't whoop us hisself but them Yanks sho' nuff will." The private snickered and wiped his forehead with his backhand as he propped his smoothbore against a maple. "Madder'n a picked tick, he is. Best eatin I had since Selma. You better git on after them fixins."

"Obliged," the veteran acknowledged. Bull folded the notepaper as if he were turning a baby for its changing. He lowered the paper and the stub of a pencil into his pocket. The private watched with silent amazement Bull's patience with seating the items. Bull came to his feet and grabbed his rifle and haversack. He noticed the private's stare.

"Words from home," Bull said. "Might be the last time I get to take 'em in. So I was scribblin a few of my own, for them. I'll have 'em sent out before mornin light, unless this little tussle starts sooner."

"Where's home?"

"Little town in Georgia. Rome."

"They'll see 'em. An' you again, too," the private replied.

The two men stared across a fallow field toward a mass of woods some six hundred yards east northeast. The private nurtured images of glory, invincibility, as might a child reaching for the marvel of a hornet's nest, oblivious to the reality at hand. Bull pondered an outcome filled with realism, immediacy, finality.

"I hear Mac's ego's 'bout as big as his army?" the private observed, gazing into the black toward the few dots of light scattered like stars along and above the meander of the Antietam.

The action of an hour ago had sputtered to an occasional spurt of blind musketry from nervous pickets. The armies surrendered to the deceptive calm of darkness.

"Pride goeth b'fore a fall, my Mama always tol' me." The private sighed, continuing his thought, chin propped on hands cupped over the muzzle of his musket. "Bet them boys is eatin biscuits and gravy right about now, reckon? Laughin and singin and carryin on like they ain't got a care in this world." The private shook his head. "All I got to say is they best get their bellies full, 'cause t'morrow's the day we gawn kick some Yankee you-know-what. Gawn be quite a show. Yes sir, *quite* a show. Brockenbrough's done set up his guns in them trees yonder. Stephen Lee's batteries are down the line a piece, a whole bunch of 'em. We got the high ground *and* open fields of fire. The way I see it, *target practice*."

"Quite a show," echoed Bull in the stoic, faraway monotone of experience as he began his trek rearward. Bull stopped and turned toward the private. He opened his mouth to speak but hadn't the verve to dress down the private's simplistic view of battle. "This your first fight, boy?"

"Got here this mornin, part of the 6th Alabama," the private replied. "Don't know much about war, but I do know I can knock off a squirrel's head at two hundred yards. Fact is, I can load and shoot this here rifle four or five times a minute, *six* if they make me mad."

Bull nodded, impressed. "At that rate of fire, you better have yourself quick access to an ammo chest," Bull said. "Or to your dead comrades' boxes."

The private laughed until Bull's meaning sank in. He cleared his throat.

"Funny thing, though," the private noted. "They keep tellin me them Yanks got *elephants* in their ranks. I seen me a picture of one once, elephant, that is. I figure that *alone* was worth joinin the ruckus. I come to see them elephants."

Bull just stared at the boy. The private would find out soon enough about 'elephants' and in images far more stark and lurid than Bull could articulate. Besides, the boy was *here*, and not a rifle *here* could be spared, especially those firing at six rounds per minute.

Bull waved and continued down the road. The pork, corn, and sweet potatoes, a feast by Rebel standards, fed a fantasy of plenty and was, itself, payment in advance for the coming fight. Bull was off to get his, mindful to shoot any man, Rebel or Yank, who tried to stop him.

The private, meanwhile, with whom Bull had parted company just minutes prior, fingered the two and one half pounds of lead in his cartridge box. *Thirty-seven, thirty-eight, thirty-nine,* he thought. *Number forty's in my rifle. Forty rounds ought to be plenty. Whoop 'em b'fore breakfast.*

Flush with a sense of immortality born of his enthusiasm, or perhaps with the euphoria that comes from blind ignorance, the private removed his cap and mopped the slime of sweat and dirt from his hairline and smiled toward the unseen enemy. He sighed. Crickets chirped nearby, inducing the private's doze. An owl swooped low over head, startling the soldier, causing him to level his rifle and fire into the darkness, which triggered the sporadic *pop, pop, pop* of muskets down the line and across the fields, awakening soldiers who had dared sleep.

Thirty-nine cartridges.

Bull had fought off sleep for three days and had no patience for it now. He scuffed his blistered, shoeless feet along a farm lane across the Hagerstown Pike, south of a corn field. Most of the day had been spent marching the seventeen miles of hills, rocks, and roots from Harpers Ferry, a march forced by Lee's desperate call for troops. The Pike swarmed with clusters of stragglers searching for their command, their leisure interrupted by the staccato of the probing musketry of skirmishers and the thunder of couriers galloping past. Bull paused and watched the urgency of the individual pockets of preparation. He had seen it before. Like crazed ants, officers scurried men and equipment from point to point past men who had found their points.

Rebel cook fires dotted the depths of woods and ridge lines as far as Bull could strain his waterless eyes to see. Rations, those not long consumed, disappeared like carrion before the coyote, the men knowing this chance to know the pleasures of a filled belly might be their last. Many soldiers of Lee's army had not eaten for days.

Company commanders shouted orders ignored. The men had come to fight, to die, not to take minutia from officers. Men lay down their heads on the damp cotton of bedrolls. Bull made his way between a white rectangular building atop a knoll alongside the Pike and a line of artillery stretching along a rise, pointed northeastward, Stephen Lee's guns. Regiments teemed around and behind the structure, each soldier searching for spot to call his own, to take care of pressing pre-battle business, to scribe quick entries in diaries or to scrawl letters home, to eat morsels scavenged during the day, to make peace with his God.

Must be that church, Bull thought, taking a long look at the white rectangular building. "Sixth Alabama?" he shouted above the din of chatter and the clanking of arms and accouterments echoing through the trees.

"Down yonder!" a man replied, pointing southward. "Five or six hundred yards you'll see two roads to the left. Take the second one. The Sixth is bivouacked in some corn and apples, damn lucky dogs. Prob'ly done et 'em every last one of 'em by now. You'll see the fires an' the colors."

"Appreciate it," Bull said.

Bull Stokes found the Sixth, and Sergeant Teaseley, bivouacked with Rodes' brigade in the cornfield of Henry Piper. Relative quiet enveloped this sector of the line. Against orders, men killed, cooked, carved, and ate pigs taken from Piper's stock. Satisfaction was hunger's only commander. Soldiers plucked and roasted dried corn left on the stalks for cattle feed.

Some of the troops, veterans, slept like newborns. They'd survived the charge of the elephant during the Seven Days and again at Second Manassas. They'd learned the worth of sleep, along with the ability to command it.

Others wandered the ground fueled by their restlessness, destined never again to know the peace of earthly sleep. Strains of "Bonnie Blue Flag" carried the music of home to ears of these restless.

Clouds gathered after midnight, and a chilling sprinkle commenced. Bull reported for duty.

"Stokes," Teaseley said, smiling at the unflappable veteran, "where the *hell* you been? Fill your belly and get some sleep."

Bull nodded as he eased the rifle strap from his shoulder, placing the weapon against the wheel of a caisson. He saw a group of men standing around a pit fire, reflections of the flames dancing across their bodies, their laughter rising with the smoke. He stretched and massaged his cracked, blistered toes before setting his feet upon a carpet of corn stalks and dampened earth. Bull released a sigh acknowledging appreciation for the pettiest of luxuries. He ambled toward the group of men, the coolness surging between his toes, tamping down the raw burn.

"Mind if I join you men, have me a bite or two?" Bull asked as a matter of courtesy.

"He'p yourse'f, soldier," replied a stringy boy no more than sixteen. "Plenty left, thanks to our Maryland friends."

"Coffee's hot," said another soldier. "Ain't had this kind of eatin since the knapsacks of Manassas. Likely won't again after tonight."

"Speak for yourse'f, boy!" shouted a voice among the men. "One of the spoils of war is eatin the *enemy's* food, the reason *I'm* fightin."

"Or pilferin the *locals'* food," said another.

Bull sliced a few strips of pork and laid them on a warming plate he had picked off a dead officer at the battle of Second Manassas. He poured the coffee, sniffed his steaming cup, and raised his eyebrows in contentment.

"Yep, it's real coffee," Bull said between sips. "*Yankee* coffee, the one thing them bluebellies do right."

"*Another* reason I'm fightin!"

"It's Maryland coffee," said the stringy soldier.

"Yankee enough for me," Bull replied, taking another sip, "and it sure beats the Dickens out of mealy bugs and ragweed."

"Got some sugar here, if you'd care to take some," said the stringy soldier. "Yankee sugar, too, complements of the 125th Pennsylvania Reserves."

"Obliged," Bull said, smiling at the unexpected bounty. "What's your name, soldier?"

"Pilchard. Avery Pilchard. Folks call me Spider."

"I can see why … Spider," Bull said, smiling as he studied the skeletal limbs of the underfed, over-marched lad. "Stokes is my name. Friends call me Bull. Where you from, Spider?"

"See why they call you Bull," Spider acknowledged with a smile, his teeth as white as moonlight. "Tuscaloosa, Alabama. We gawn see that elephant t'morrow, ain't we?" Spider's anxious, proud grip tightened around the barrel of his rifle.

Bull thought about the private who relieved him of picket duty. "Reckon so," Bull replied, dipping a spoon into the sugar.

"Ain't never seen the elephant b'fore," Spider revealed, apprehension evident in his confession. "Oh, I seen a *real* elephant, just not the battle kind. What's—what's it like?"

Bull stared at the cloudy sky for a moment, a few sprinkles of rain tapping his face, and turned to Spider.

"You'll do fine, soldier."

"I reckon I will, but …"

"But what?" Bull folded a strip of pork between two hardtack crackers. "Simple thing, really. They shoot at us; we shoot back. Aim low, an' don't make yourself a target."

"Nerves, I s'pose. Sergeant says the whole Yankee army's right through them woods yonder."

"Lee's got his whole army ready to say 'hello'," Bull replied with a smile of reassurance, fully aware Lee's army could almost take a night swim in the Potomac. "Get yourself a few hours' sleep."

"Cain't sleep." Spider said, pacing the ground like a caged dog.

"Then find a spot off by yourself and write your folks a letter." Bull advised. "You got folks, ain't you?"

"I got folks. Ain't got no *paper*. Pencil neither."

Bull stared at the boy, seeing himself from not too many months ago. "Here," he said, reaching into his pocket and retrieving a neatly creased paper, "use mine." He tore off the bottom half, handing it and the stubbed pencil to Spider.

Spider took the paper and pencil from Bull's hand. "I can see why they call you Bull," Spider repeated as the pit fire painted Bull's forearm and hand in shadow and light, revealing lean crevices of muscle, tendon, and bone. "Give the pencil back to you directly, Bull."

Bull nodded and, with a sigh, lay on a bed of stalks.

Just as Bull drifted into the realm of sleep, the familiar shrill of an artillery shell slapped him to consciousness. Instincts wide awake, he scrambled for the cover of a supply wagon. The shell burst overhead, sending shards of sharp, white-hot metal hissing and howling amid the men, striking several. Stephen D. Lee's batteries replied, all sixteen guns, and for a few moments the uneasy thought of a night-shielded Union assault gripped the soldiers.

The shell served its purpose. Relaxation became effort. Sleep became futile. Soldiers knelt in battle formation, lines of infantry dressed, watchful for any movement in their front. Skirmishers were sent forward into the fields. Bull sat and rested his back against the supply wagon and pulled out his unfinished letter. He read silently:

Dearest Caroline,

It is early predawn of 17 September, and we have crossed the Potomac River into Maryland. Plenty of beautiful countryside up here. Mountains, streams – makes me feel like I brought home with me. We hope to find more than enough food to fill our stomachs, shoes to cover our feet. Have not seen many smiling faces amongst the locals. Union loyalists, most of them.

A fight like none other awaits us in a few hours. General Robert wants to take the fighting north. The men are excited and yet seem less nervous than usual, and even in the absence of provisions, laughter and song fill their mouths. The thought of injury or death looms as always, but something about this fight has the men distant of mind, almost spellbound, as if thrust into another world, a world filled with promise. Maybe they realize there's no arguing with death.

I write you, my dearest Caroline, to tell you to abandon all worry. I am in God's hands, and I have no fear of what the enemy might bring. If I am killed, know that I loved you as supremely as any man could and that my spirit will accompany your every breath.

Your Beloved Timothy, the "Bull"

Bull looked up and noticed the flurry of activity by the pit fire. Stretcher bearers stumbled to and from points near the site. He saw a man on his back, the light of fire revealing his blood-soaked shirt. He walked over and stared at the man. Bull had witnessed this scenario with somber frequency.

Alive one minute, dead the next. The Lord giveth; the Lord taketh away. Bull bent down and took the pencil gripped in the man's frozen hand. Paper, scribbled with the sentiment of frightened uncertainty, speckled with blood, rested on the man's chest.

Bull saw it coming. Just sooner than he'd expected.

"I'll get your letter home, Spider," Bull whispered.

Chapter 17

Yesterday, the roads out of Sharpsburg
choked with the traffic of human refugees. The moment feared
had arrived. The question of a great battle in western Maryland
no longer dominated the hearths of homes and the tables of
meeting places. The question of battle asked was now answered.
The combatants had taken their positions, displacing families
seeking relative safety. The valley of the Antietam awaited its
turn with war.

Rachael and Jacob had made the journey to and from
Killing's Cave, a moniker they innocently applied to Killiansburg
Cave, as often as they had traversed the length of Hog Trough
Road. The cave was a frequent subject of Rachael's artwork and
a cozy seclusion for the smitten teens. Now Rachael pressed the
damp, dark road from the cave to Jacob's home. Claggett was
alive, in possession of Bigun's family, despite Jacob's account of
his gory demise.

Taking advantage of darkness and the swirl of pre-battle
activity, Claggett had shuffled Bigun's family from the cave, its
significance unnoticed by everyone except Rachael. She raced to
find Jacob, or his father, and tell the news.

Jacob's Baptism

Her darkness-adjusted eyes perceived the muted outline of the Hoffman home just ahead. She saw no lamplight from its quarters. The night lay quiet, the occasional cricket its only keeper. The land slept in its pretense of serenity.

Rachael stepped onto the porch. Her easel stood where she had left it, the paint brush on the floor beneath it. She noticed the shattered door. She listened, then made her way into the abandoned house, stepping over shards of boards and broken kitchenware. She kept a watchful guard, eyes shifting left to right, scanning the gray air for movement, mindful of Claggett.

She knew as well as Jacob the layout of the home and the location of its contents. Finding a box of matches on the mantle, she scraped a match head along the stone hearth, its flame bursting to life, and lit the wick of an oil lantern. The light threw distorted shadows as she moved from room to room. Objects seemed to swell and recede in the moving light like the waves of stormy seas. The floors dispensed groans with her every step, as if hell itself were waking.

Bedroom doors showed signs of damage. Household articles had been scattered. Someone had eaten the food she prepared for Jacob and Bigun. She picked up a wadded scrap of paper, the note she had left for Jacob, from atop a shard of a shattered platter. The kitchen had been sacked, dishes broken, anything edible taken. She placed the lantern on the floor, dimmed its light, and settled into a parlor chair. Rachael decided it best to wait for Isaac's return.

The early morning calm exploded, stirring Rachael from her sleep. She gasped and opened her eyes.

"*Jacob!*"

Artillery pounded to the northeast. Rachael snapped to consciousness and raced to the porch. Hints of yellows and grays spread their tentacles along the eastern horizon. The great battle was on, its roar rising all around, and somewhere, Jacob was out there. Rachael grabbed a straw broom from its corner perch, as if a house-cleaning would distract her, and swept with the vigor and haste of one expecting company.

Try as she may, Rachael's busyness did not quell the battle's insistent rage. Volleys of musketry and salvos of artillery shattered the peace of the valley, as if someone had taken sledgehammers to a vast pane of glass.

Rachael stopped sweeping. She stepped off the porch and detected through the sliver of a misplaced lull the faint pierce of yipping yells, wordless shouts, soldiers in the throes of a charge. The intensity grew, more voices giving it monstrous form. Then, as if its presence were shunned, the lull vanished in the roar of sweeping musketry and consuming cannon blasts, swallowing men. Their yells evaporated, blasted from existence almost as quickly as they began. She resumed her sweeping, as did the exchange of lulls and yells and the patter of musketry. For three hours she swept.

The battle's woods-muffled roar subsided, for now. Between bursts, Rachael detected the monotone of rattles and squeaks, distant at first but drawing steadily nearer. She continued sweeping, her effort little more than hollow waves of the broom on the air. She dodged bursts of dust shaken from shelves by the percussive vibrations of exploding shells. Then came a different sound, peculiar utterances growing louder and more frequent. Rachael cupped her ear.

She thought of the familiar high pitch of pig squeals and the mournful bellows of sunning cattle. *Strange*, she thought, aware any such animals had been taken by foraging soldiers. She stepped onto the porch, cautious of stray projectiles, some of which had pecked the house earlier, one passing through her painting. She peeked down the road.

Wagons pulled by piteous horses streamed up Landing Road toward the house like a parade of the damned, their cargo of shot men stabbed further with each rise and fall of the rolling wheels over rocks and holes, arms and legs the dangles of stringless puppets.

Rachael gasped. She saw no end to the train of wagons. Wounded men, their bodies torn in every conceivable place, awash in blood and dirt, wailed for water, some for merciful releases from life. The first of the battle's consequences arrived.

Orderlies hauled men to the shelter of a stand of hardwoods and grouped the wounded according to the severity of wounds, quick neglect given those shot through the torso, those wounds considered mortal. For most of the wounded—those cursed with consciousness—searing, unspeakable pain had replaced the numbness of shock. Men able strained to lift arms high enough for notice, begging for relief from the agony swept upon them. Screams cut through the air. Rachael set the broom against a porch post, along with her thoughts of Jacob and Isaac and Claggett, and waded, dazed, into the rising sea of anguish.

"Need water, ma'am, and linens, food, anything you got," a Confederate soldier said with the calm urgency. "Need this house. Need you, too, ma'am."

Rachael nodded.

"You men unhinge the doors; search the grounds for boards, logs, tables, anything to make places for the sawbones. Ma'am, we need hay and space for the wounded."

Space for the wounded. Rachael stared, frozen by the unimaginable, as men were taken from wagons and placed on the ground. "Barn around back," she managed to say, "plenty of hay, too. I'll—I'll fetch some water."

Chapter 18

Late summer insects found a human
feast in the fallow field. Jacob and Bigun dozed intermittently,
neither of them mindful they might never again know the peace
of sleep. Bigun slapped a mosquito on his arm and glimpsed the
smear of first light. He nudged Jacob's shoulder.

"Jacob. *Jacob!*"

"Hmmm? *What!*" Jacob mumbled, jerking back his
shoulder as he stirred. He lifted his arms and stretched, his mind
swimming in blissful oblivion.

Then, like a mighty wind, the abruptness of reality rushed
over him. His eyes opened. "Damn! Get *up*, Bigun! What time
is it?"

"I be up, Missuh Jacob. Been up. I figguh it to be five, six
o'clock. Hear dat?"

The first rays of morning had lit the fuse. The tension was
breached. Artillery salvos exploded toward the northeast,
signaling the battle's beginning.

"Dadgumit! I was havin a *fine* dream. Me an' Rachael were
walkin down the Hog Trough Road when lightnin struck Ole
Whooey's tree, just as we passed, scatterin that ol' bird, an' *us*
with 'im," Jacob said, a chuckle on his lips. "Rachael an' me fell

to the ground and … an' then a God-awful racket of thunder …
Come on, Bigun!"

Jacob was determined to get another glimpse of the mighty
Army of Northern Virginia, Lee's legions that had whipped Pope
just three weeks earlier at Manassas. He thought of the soldier
they had met during the night, the one who had suggested he join
the Georgia regiment short of men. To join Lee's army—leave
home and march and drill and slog through the miseries of
camp—was one thing. But to have battle delivered to his home,
that was another altogether. He patted his pocket and felt the
reassurance of his coin. Today, though, was not the day for
buying adventures. After all, none was for sale. Glory, on the
other hand, was something Jacob could earn.

Jacob and Bigun hastily gathered their belongings and trotted
through the drops of a morning sprinkle toward the sounds. They
exited a patch of woods and stopped at the post-and-rail fence
spanning the length of the Hagerstown Pike, a hundred yards
south of a white square of a building the Dunkers called church.
Jacob wondered if his daddy and the Mummas had spent the
night there.

The area teemed with rebel souls marching in line of battle
through the treeless fields and countless others held in reserve
sheltered by woods. Northward, beyond Smoketown Road,
Jacob and Bigun saw clouds of smoke and debris swirling around
the blurred forms of shouting, screaming men. Jacob stared at
this other-worldly sight, flinching as Stephen Lee's guns blasted
from the field opposite the church.

The Dunker Church sat on ground given for such purpose by
Samuel Mumma. The structure looked like a roofed,
whitewashed box. No steeple. No house of God given to
pretension. No immodesty.

The church was built on a rise of ground at the intersection
of the Hagerstown Pike and the Smoketown Road. It was an
unassuming feature bordered on the east by open ground and
fields of corn, stalks higher than the tallest man and fat with ears
ready for harvest. To the west and north of the church, a stand of
woods lent the pretense of protection to those occupying it. This

church, this ordinary spot of antiwar holiness, soon would quake within the grasp of mighty armies, desperate individual struggles for survival and conquest.

Ignoring stray, spent projectiles clipping leaves and nicking fence rails, Jacob grabbed a rail and pulled atop the fence to gain a clearer view of the calamity of human emotions playing out in fields familiar. Cannon and caissons rumbled up the Pike and across fields, spitting dirt and rocks in their wake, scattering groups of walking wounded before them. Lee's guns, the wheels of their 12-pounder Howitzers leaping off the ground with each thunderous belch of iron and flame, continued their uninterrupted barrage on the approaching Union lines. Jacob pressed his palms against his ears, his eyes twitching with each sound. Bigun stared.

Horses swept over the undulation of fields, riders urging their mounts with frenzied lashings of the reigns. Lines of smoke from countless breakfast fires, abandoned to burn themselves out, drifted straight into the air and dissipated above the trees behind the church, comingling with the expanding blanket of battle haze. A mass of Confederates double-quicked past Jacob as he straddled the fence and stumbled, dazed, onto the Hagerstown Pike.

The battle exploded again a few hundred yards in front of them. North of the church, in David Miller's corn, volleys of musketry crashed back and forth, waves of charging men enveloped in the violence, lives swept away as quickly as dirt from a floor.

Artillery shells exploded over the heads of men, raining shards of indiscriminate metal hissing, spinning, its hot edges piercing and severing flesh with seeming randomness, the reasons for those chosen understood only by God.

Bullets by the thousands, conical creations of lead, spun through the air unseen, save the results of their devastating power. They pinged and thudded, buzzed and crunched, playing a relentless symphony of death delivered by desperate men. Bodies jerked, limbs flailed, as if pulled by puppeteers, lifeblood gushing from ghastly holes. Men shouted, laughed, screamed, cursed, defiant as long as life allowed.

Soldiers did not look like soldiers, not as Jacob had imagined soldiers might look going into battle. These were energetic, confident, eager men ready to accomplish their duty and move on. Their experienced steps were quick to the drummer's tap-tap-tap. Their chins were high, eyes forward, resolve firm. Rifles rested erect against their right shoulders. Officers gripped sabers, raised high and mirror-clean, orders of "Forward!" shouted. Pockets of men counted time singing "Yellow Rose of Texas". Laughter spilled from the mouths of these tanned, leathered men. Expletives and oaths rolled freely off tongues like water through a downspout.

These men marching in front of Jacob and Bigun, led by Colonel William Wofford, had only glory to lose, their lives all but sacrificed the moment they mustered in. Their colors boldly announced the single white star of the Texas Brigade, a blending of troops from Texas, Georgia and South Carolina. Red banners of the Southern Cross snapped with the brigade's optimism and to the beat of the breeze.

Ahead, up the Pike and beyond the church, in Miller's corn, men simply disappeared in the face of canister, blades of lead scything through what corn remained and cutting to shreds all flesh in its path. Eyes, moments earlier seething with a lust to kill, lay frozen, freed of enmity, in their moment of truth.

The quest for glory, for adventure, ended in the obscurity of somebody's cornfield far from everybody's home. Boys from Georgia, Mississippi, Louisiana, and Texas, Pennsylvania, New York, Wisconsin and Rhode Island fell, their bodies slammed to the ground in exclamation, futures silenced.

The screams and wails of desperate wounded, many trampled by the charges and counter-charges, begged for relief, for the only hope of glory left—death. The ground itself seemed to writhe, its wounded trying in desperate disbelief to undo what had been done.

"Come on, Bigun," shouted Jacob, "this way!"

Jacob pulled on Bigun's shirt, trying to shake the big man free from his trance of shock. Remnants of regiments and walking wounded streamed rearward to the safety of the trees behind the church, their proud colors shell-torn and bullet-riddled, clawed and ripped by the blue lions.

"Hey, boy!" shouted a laughing voice above a throng of voices, "take up a rifle and come on!" Others chuckled at the unlikely notion.

"A black man and a skinny white boy," shouted another. "Ya'll wanderin around like dazed kids at a carnival. They's some elephants in that big circus out yonder if you care to see." Chuckles turned to laughter in spite of the carnage, perhaps because of it.

Front-row seat.

Jacob's Baptism

Chapter 19

How old are you, boy?" a soldier asked, his arm shattered above the elbow, hanging numb by threads of flesh.

Jacob stared at the arm and the blood that dripped from it. "S-seventeen," he said.

The soldier laughed as he walked past Jacob, eyes glazed with shock. "Prime dyin age, boy."

"See that lad over there?" another soldier asked Jacob, pointing to the corner of the Dunker Church. "He claims he's sixteen, but hell, we *all* know he's thirteen, maybe *twelve*. His *musket's* taller than he is!"

Indeed, the boy was an ear of corn among cornstalks, and Jacob wondered how he handled the unwieldy weapon.

"Damn good shot, he is," the soldier said. "*Damn* good. Sharpshooter with Ripley's command. He can handle a nine-pound musket better'n most grown men. Cain't afford to send 'im out into this melee. Too damn valu'ble."

"How good a shot?" asked Jacob.

"Didn't you hear me say *damn* good, boy?" the soldier repeated. "He can plug an acorn from a squirrel's mouth at two hundred paces.

"How old are *you?*" Jacob asked.

"Just turned nineteen, an' I'm fixin to kill me some Yankees. Where'd you git this here nigger?"

"He ain't no … *that!* He's a *man*, just like you an' me."

"Maybe so," the soldier replied, scanning Bigun head to toe. "Bet he wouldn't have no problem holdin a *cannon*."

Jacob smiled.

"Yours?"

Jacob looked at Bigun. "My daddy's," Jacob replied.

"Good as yours. Git him a rifle, too. Let 'im *fight* for his freedom" the soldier shouted as he scampered up the Pike to catch up with his unit. "We need *bodies!* All blood's the same color."

"You're exactly where I want to be," Jacob said.

"What the *hell* are you talkin about?" another passing soldier asked in amazement, forgetting that he, too, once was filled with this same naiveté.

"I'm talkin about you're a Confederate soldier fightin with the Robert E. Lee. Don't that mean somethin to you?"

The young soldier laughed. "What's your name, buck?"

"Jacob Hoffman. An' yours?"

"Rushin. Sergeant T.J. Rushin, 12th Georgia."

Sergeant Rushin stood six feet-four inches, hair like wheat and eyes of hazel. Blood stained the bandage wrapped around his left forearm. Jacob stared at the wound and suspected a bullet had done this work but dared not venture into so private an issue. This was a man headed *toward* the fray, not away from it.

"This?" Rushin said, touching his elbow and sensing Jacob's curiosity. "Hell, boy, this ain't *nothin*. I been hurt worse plowin with Sister Sara back home. Damn mule would kick a man for breathin." He lifted his arm. "Yanks gonna have to do a lot better'n this if they want *me* out of the fight."

"What's the T.J. stand for," Jacob pried.

"Thomas Jefferson, but it's a damn might easier to just call me T.J." Rushin looked straight into Jacob's eyes. "Or, in your case, 'sir'."

"Yes, sir."

"Aw, heck, boy, I'm just *joshin* you. Now, you asked me if bein a Confederate soldier fightin with the Robert E. Lee meant somethin. Depends."

"On what?"

"On if I get to sit in the tent with 'im whilst these boys fight."

Jacob stared speechless.

"See that officer over yonder standin next to the 12-pounder?" he asked, pointing to Captain William Parker barking orders and pacing the battery poised on the low ridge across the Hagerstown Pike from the Dunker Church.

Jacob didn't know a 12-pounder from a siege mortar but figured the officer to whom T.J. referred must be the man gesturing in every direction.

"I see 'im."

"Got a wife at home pregnant with a baby he'll prob'ly never see. Looks like a pile of Yankees in those fields yonder—an' a pile of 'em dead, too—but Little Mac's got most of his boys over on the other side of the Antietam. What you see up yonder's just a taste of what's to come. They gonna give us all we care to take," said Rushin as he shifted his musket strap to a less worn part of his shoulder. "A whole mess of these boys, gray an' blue, seen their last sunrise this mornin. Some are gone; others'll be gone before the sun sets. I'd give my sweet mother to be in your shoes now. I spect the Cap'n would too."

"Where're you from, Sergeant Rushin?" Jacob asked.

"A slice of heaven in South Georgia called Buena Vista," Rushin replied. "Reckon you don't know where that is."

"Reckon I don't," Jacob said, filled with wonder at what a land Georgia must be.

"It don't matter. Home for now is wherever I can find me some ripe roastin ears for my belly an' a pillow of straw for my head. I got me a little lady down there, eighteen years old and ready, if you know what I mean. Course, I don't reckon you *do* know what I mean, do you, boy?"

Jacob's Baptism

Jacob thought about Rachael. "Oh yeah. I got me a good idea what you're talkin about, sir," he said, a grin spreading across his face.

Rushin chuckled as he put fire to his pipe and sucked. Smoke snaked out his mouth. "She's worth dodgin bullets for, if I can just figure me out a way," he said, lifting his wounded arm. "Right now, we gotta keep these Yankees from comin south. Virginia's had her share. Tennessee's getting hers now. Georgia ain't far behind."

"By headin *north?*" Jacob asked.

"An' by takin McClellan *with* us, by keepin them bluebellies from sackin our food, terrorizin our citizens. But if you got a *better* idea, I reckon General Lee will lend you his ear."

"No, sir, I ain't got a better—"

"I think the plan was to get this army between McClellan and Washington. Seems we got ourselves between McClellan and the *Potomac*. Least the ground here's to our likin. Lee's tryin to force Lincoln to settle. All we need is one more like Manassas, just *one* more, an' England *might* just be willin to run the blockade for cotton, help supply us with guns, food."

"Lookin awful bad up there," Jacob said, observing the fighting in David Miller's cornfield, "for both sides."

"We were hopin Little Mac might step aside, like Pope done, so we could put a quick end to this war. Reckon we'll take care of that part for 'im, like we done with Pope."

"You believe you can do that?"

Sergeant Rushin gazed at the smoke of battle. Regiments of soldiers rushed toward the front.

"Yeah," he said softly. "I spect so. Gonna take an awful lot more killin, I'm afraid."

"Don't you *want* to kill Yankees?" Jacob asked.

Rushin took another draw on his pipe and blew the smoke. "Yeah, I reckon I do wanna kill 'em. Same as they want to kill me. Trouble with battle ain't the killin. It's the noise. Fills your ears, that racket. Bullets whistlin by, puncturin flesh and bone of your comrades, shells screamin through the air. An' never knowin which bullet or shell is meant for *you*, never knowin which soldier has his rifle trained on *your* chest." Rushin cradled his wounded forearm. "Men shoutin, dyin. Noisy affair, battle."

Jacob tuned out the cacophony, the racket, to his north and listened to the words of Sergeant Rushin.

"The noise I can take, I reckon, the more I think about it. It's the noise I *cain't* hear that scares me. You never hear the bullet that's meant for you. It'll come out the barrel of a rifle held by a man you ain't *never* met, and, except for circumstances, never *would*. It'll cut the air like lightnin, a beeline for your body, before the noise reaches your ears. You won't hear it. Bullet hits you before the sound does."

The wounded and the expended streamed rearward.

"Just trustin the Lord the bullet takes me right off. I don't want to linger on the field gut-shot or limb-shattered, bleedin, unable to move, no water, no relief, no hope. If I'm meant to die in this war, this battle, I want to die *right off*," Rushin said with a sweep of his unwounded arm. "I don't want to be shot by some *lamebrained* green Yankee, his eyes closed every time he pulls the trigger, hopin he hits *somethin*. If I'm to be shot, I want to be shot by a soldier who *wants* to kill me as bad as I want kill him."

Jacob said nothing; the words forming in his mind felt puny, insignificant.

"Move 'em out, Sergeant!" a captain yelled.

"Sir!" Rushin acknowledged, giving salute. "Well," he said, his voice firm with the acceptance of his fate, "Time to see the elephant. Again."

"See *what?*" Jacob asked.

"We're headin into that jungle yonder, takin our boys to victory. *That's* where you'll find the elephant. If you got a hankerin for glory, then get yourself a rifle an' a cartridge box. Get one for your friend, too. Plenty of rifles an' glory to go around. Dead men earned their glory and won't be needin their rifles. But my boys sure as sassafras need y'all."

Jacob's eyes spanned the open fields as he walked with Rushin. Columns of men marched north on the Hagerstown Pike. Others, awaiting orders, lingered in the woods behind the church.

Jacob's Baptism

Jacob stopped as he heard shouts of "Into battery!" Platoons of guns unlimbered and caissons of ammunition chests deployed. No more were the socials that filled the fields of Sharpsburg and the valley of the Antietam Creek in early autumn. Hundreds of holed shoes and bare feet, covered with little more than dirt and blood, marched northward, their shuffle muffled by the consuming calamity.

"Can I get me a couple of them muskets stacked over there?" Jacob asked a soldier. "Pay for 'em, that is, with gold." Jacob patted his pocket.

"*Pay* fer 'em?" Rushin shouted, overhearing Jacob's request while redressing his wound. "Boy, the only tender we'll take for them rifles is your *service*. This ain't no dry goods store. We're not arms merchants. If you want to take up a rifle, it comes with an *elephant*. Now get to it!"

"Sorry, boy," the soldier said, shaking his head, "but your gold wouldn't do us no good. Give you my rifle for free, if I could."

The soldier, face grimed with black powder thick around his mouth, hair clingy and curled, wet with sweat, gathered his cartridge box and rifle and fell into ranks with the rest of the slim body of men. The unit, depleted further by the morning's first round of service, had taken losses as well at Second Manassas and South Mountain.

Jacob watched Rushin's men toss haversacks and bedrolls, canteens and tin cups, in a pile to the roadside. Such would only hinder them now, as mobility assumed a premium. Soldiers needed only the equipment for waging the surrealism of war, buoyed by letters and photographs from home, mementos of a slice of reality far removed, its sweet reminders tucked inside hats or pockets. The men marched in a right oblique maneuver across Mumma's grass, just south of the Smoketown Road and east of the Hagerstown Pike, eyes forward, clothing glued by sweat to sticky skin, minds grasping the enormity of what lay ahead. Rushin ignored his wound, numb to his chances of surviving another round.

"Soldier?" Jacob started.

"Cain't talk now," the soldier blurted, his words more prophetic than he intended.

"Come on, Bigun!" Jacob said as he trotted toward the stack of arms.

"Missuh Jacob, you ain't about to do what I *think* you's about to do, is you?"

"Bigun, I'm just gonna get me a rifle, a *Yankee* rifle," Jacob said, "one of them Springfields. Ain't nobody usin 'em. An' I get to keep my five dollars gold! Can't beat *that* at the cockfights! Don't you want one of them rifles?"

"Dem rifles is fo' *fightin*. You ain't gawn f*ight*, is you?"

"I ain't gonna fight. Come on, Bigun! You can get you one, too."

"A black man, a *slave* whether you say so or not, behind Rebel lines, with a *weapon*? Missuh Jacob, I might as well draw me a red bulls eye on dis white shirt."

"Come *on*, Bigun! They're payin about as much attention to us as a glass of milk in a saloon."

Jacob and Bigun neared the glistening rifles, a shambled stack on the Pike side of the Dunker church. Bullets bore holes into the church walls.

The area of ground a few hundred yards north of the church and toward a patch of woods east of what yesterday was farmer Miller's field of harvest-ready corn took on a reddish-yellow tint of metal-torn bodies, some aligned in neat rows, others heaped atop comrades and enemy alike. Solid shot plowed the soil, digging long furrows, bouncing with a quickness to which soldiers could not react, ripping torsos from men. The field reaped a harvest of a different sort this day.

Jacob watched the fight in full view of a regiment of Yankee troops forming on a low rise in Mummas field across the road from the church. Bullets pattered the walls of the church, each strike sending a small explosion of dust, paint, and splinters into the air. Jacob's standup posture presented an irresistible target for target-hungry soldiers.

Jacob's Baptism

"Look, Bigun!" Jacob shouted. *"Yankee Springfields!* Every dang one of 'em." His face shone like child's on Christmas morning.

Jacob made a beeline for the bounty when a blue form caught his eye. A Union soldier lay on his back, near the Pike, one of his legs bent, his lifeless body riddled with bullets. Jacob stared, the man's eyes and mouth wide-open, shock frozen into his glare. Flies appeared and vanished around the Yankee's mouth and eyes, buzzing in a rising and receding constant.

The soldier held in his powder-stained fingers a musket, a Springfield, as if he were clinging to the security of a child's bedtime toy. Jacob gently wrenched the rifle from the man's curled fingers. Bullets puffed the dirt around him. He wiped the splatters of blood from the stock and barrel. He sighed and stared at the prize, blood-freed, its ownership duly transferred. He picked up the cartridge box, refilling it with scattered cartridges, and looked once more at the corpse.

Bigun stooped, paused, then reached and snapped up one of the Springfields from the stack. "Got a few of dem cartridges fo' me?" Bigun asked.

"Here," Jacob replied, handing Bigun a handful.

Both walked a quick pace south on the Hagerstown Pike, away from the action northward and eastward.

"Did you see that poor bastard back there?" Jacob asked.

"I seen 'im. He had at least five new holes in 'im. A frightful sight."

"I'm talkin about that look in his eye, that expression. Wonder what he felt, what he was thinkin, when he was hit."

"Dem eyes looked like he realized he'd walked into somethin he had no chance of gettin away from, like Claggett dis mo'nin," Bigun observed. "Don't spect he had a chance to feel much of nothin."

"Okay you two, let's go, let's *move* it! Now!" shouted a Confederate, his sleeves adorned with chevrons.

"Hey, we ain't—"

"Boy, I don't repeat myself. Don't make me shoot you and the darkie right here in this road. Now git on over there, in that road yonder, that sunken road!" the soldier shouted, pointing in the direction of Hog Trough Road.

Jacob and Bigun obeyed, seeing no alternative but bullets in their backs. They trotted with other Rebels through Piper's orchard and corn toward the road. They saw a battery of Confederate guns deploying to their left. Up ahead, through Piper's corn, they saw a mass of men and arms squirming within the confines of Hog Trough Road.

"Jesus, my *Jesus!*" Jacob said, gasping. "Hog Trough!"

"Jacob, you don't reckon dey's about to put *us* in dis fight, do you? Don't dey know we *ain't* soldiers?"

"I reckon they know *you* ain't no soldier, Bigun, but they need bodies, an' for that you're as guilty as me. I guess we found our hideaway for now."

"It done found *us*," Bigun said. "Think I'd rather face the hangman than what I fear's ahead fo' us.

Jacob's Baptism

Chapter 20

"Right here, boys!" instructed a sergeant
from the Sixth Alabama. "Squeeze in right here … and over here
… make room, boys … there! Check your rifles! Get 'em ready.
Ramrods in the ground! Get them fence rails stacked proper!
Lily-lickin bastards are just over that ridge."

Men filled every inch in the road. Ramrods were pressed
inside barrels, men confirming bullets already loaded. Others
rested rifles on fence rails, making sure their line of sight was
clear. Others stacked rails in ways that offered better protection,
eliminating gaps and elevating their positions. The road seethed
with the preparation of thousands of men, the center of Lee's thin
line.

"But *we* ain't soldiers!" Jacob protested to the sergeant.

"You're soldiers now, today. Have you boys home in time
for supper."

"But sergeant—"

"Look here, boy," the sergeant said, pulling his revolver and
pointing it at Jacob's face, "this ain't no debate. Get your butt in
that line and ready your weapon."

Jacob's Baptism

Jacob looked at his weapon, its stewardship bequeathed to him minutes earlier by the passing of a man known only to God. In an instant, possessing a Springfield lost all its luster.

"Wait a minute, you two," the sergeant shouted. Jacob and Bigun stopped. "Maybe you ain't soldiers after all."

Jacob smiled. "We tried to tell—"

"Open your mouths."

"Why do you want—"

The sergeant grabbed Jacob's cheeks, forcing open his mouth, revealing his teeth. The sergeant examined Jacob's top and bottom incisors. After a slight nod, he repeated the process on Bigun.

"You're soldiers. Fall in."

"I don't understand," Jacob said.

"As long as your teeth are strong enough to rip paper off cartridges, you're soldiers."

Men in position glanced back at the approach of the pair. They peered at Bigun, instincts in response to his bulk causing some to squeeze closer, making room for the armed black man. He slumped to his knees, giving one short nod of acknowledgement as he propped his Springfield against the fence-rail breastwork. Mindful of the eyes upon him, Bigun kept his gaze forward.

"Dang fine rifle for a darkie," noted a private, sitting, a stem of rye between his lips and his back against the fence.

"Here, you take it," Bigun replied. "I jus' as soon walk down dat road an' nevuh look back."

"Walk down that road an' never look back? Boy, if suicide's what you're hankerin for, go right ahead. You'll end up crow fodder in that corn or chained to a wagon bound for South Carolina. You're better off stayin here, defendin yourself, defendin your honor."

"Where's de honor fightin alongside white men who jus' as soon see me as crow fodder?"

"Ain't no man on this line got anything agin a Negro defendin hisse'f, not when he's shootin at Yankees. If you live, ain't a man on this line gawn stand in your way, boy."

"I'd like to see 'em try to stand in his way *now*," Jacob whispered, unheard.

"I be free *now*, on my way to Philadelphia."

"Philadelphia!" The soldier looked at Jacob. "This slave yours?"

"It's like he told you; he's *free*," Jacob said.

"You a Marylander, boy?"

"I am."

"I don't know about free, but I do know about *black*," the private said, "and there's plenty of scruff out there willin to take you as their own, sell you for the first good offer, or just kill you where you stand. I know your chances of makin it to … Philadelphia … are better if we see you shootin at them Yanks a-comin. You know how to fire that weapon, boy?"

"I learned the musket long b'fo you was a pup on the tit. I can take wings off a bee wit' a *rock*," Bigun boasted, ripping the paper off a cartridge and pouring its powder into the barrel. "I can *sho'* knock somethin down with dis."

Jacob smiled, proud of Bigun's fearless stand amid a sea of white.

The private grinned with uneasiness, mindful the enemy might have knelt among him.

"Well, then," the private said, clearing his throat, "see to it … soldier."

The sunken lane—Hog Trough Road—was not so much a road as it was a wagon-worn passage, in spots four feet below the bordering ground of surrounding fields. Etched into the earth over three generations, the lane was a Sharpsburg bypass, spurring east from the Hagerstown Pike, then southeast to a zigzagged rendezvous with Piper's Lane and the Boonsboro Road. Post-and-rail fences, splintered and broken by age and neglect, lined the lengths of both embankments.

The morning awoke under a shroud of clouds and to the thunder of battle. Hog Trough Road hung suspended between heaven and hell, destiny awaiting its turn, as General Lee fed unit after unit from his center to shore up the onslaught of the Union's First Corps through Miller's corn, three quarters of a mile north of Hog Trough Road. The center of Lee's line stretched along a thousand yards of the sunken lane, scratched into the bucolic landscape like a mass grave filled with the living.

Wayward rabbits and mice were crushed under the weight of waiting humans. Anxious men cast wagers for the privilege of bayoneting these field animals. Men exchanged fantastic bets in card games believed their last. Cards dotted the ground as men forsook their sinful ways, grasping again their last measure of repentance. The fury of the fight that came in early morning was no stranger to these veterans. Nor was the fury to come.

South of Hog Trough Road was Henry Piper's cornfield, Ole Whooey's domain, stalks of tan and green standing like silent sentinels. The north and northeast sides of the road bordered an expanse of grass and corn extending well beyond the farms of Mumma's and Roulette's. The undulation of the ground, its dips and rises, swales and knolls, offered to Yankees precious moments of rest from the march, of cover from the fire—and the realization of the horror that waited atop each crest.

The fight near Sharpsburg was barely two hours old and already the serene fields a mile north of town were choked with debris, the blood and flesh and shattered materiel, of unparalled violence. Union General George Greene's Second Division, Twelfth Corps, had penetrated Confederate lines into the woods surrounding the Dunker Church west of the Hagerstown Pike. This attack, characteristic of all Union thrusts of the morning, was isolated and unsupported, Georgians and Virginians pushing Greene's men back east of the Hagerstown Pike.

Then came General John Sedgwick's turn. Sedgwick's Second Corps division, line after blue line of infantry, trod over the open ground, and the cornfield, north of Smoketown Road. The Union objective, the whitewashed speck of a church set against the dark green of woods, was the same as it had been since the battle's first shot.

Confederate divisions commanded by McLaws and Walker, concealed in the woods behind the church, turned Sedgwick's left flank, pouring coordinated volleys of musketry into the Union front, left, and rear. Panicked soldiers streamed north and east, mindless of dead and wounded comrades over which they trampled and the blood through which they splashed.

The battle raged in the Dunker Church sector for two hours. The Rebels holding Lee's center in the Hog Trough Road, just south of the church, sat and listened with growing apprehension as the storm of battle swirled to a crescendo several hundred yards to their north. The rattle of musketry and intermittent shrill of artillery died down, indications the battle near the church had spent its energy and was shifting elsewhere. Greene and Sedgwick thus repulsed, the battered Rebel left flank held. For the men occupying Hog Trough Road, their turn was minutes away.

The sickening carpet of death, the ooze of blood, replaced the lush green of corn and grass. Since the break of light, fire had fallen from the sun and ascended from hell, squeezing the battlefield and its occupants in its pinch, its inferno of carnage. Thousands of bodies, stilled and writhing, dotted the countryside.

The day—and the killing—had just begun.

Chapter 21

A macabre lull, the Grim Reaper taking a
breath, settled over the northern end of the battlefield. Countless
wounded, many trapped in the mangle of their gore, sprawled
across the smoke-shrouded fields and fences and trees and
bramble, like scattered debris of a tornado, let loose a wail of
agony, its continuity of sound displacing the intermittent roar of
cannon and the zing of bullets. The fearless had become the
helpless.

McClellan sent General William French, commander of the
Second Corps's third division, splashing across Antietam Creek
to support the Union left flank at the woods near the church.
Instead, unable to find Sedgwick's shattered, scattered division
through the shield of smoke, French's command drifted left
oblique southwestwardly, in the direction of Lee's center at the
Hog Trough Road.

Confederate artillerists on high ground had not failed to
notice the Federal movement. Rebel shells shrieked overhead
ripping branches from trees, showering anxious men with leaves
and limbs, giving notice the elephant lurked just ahead.
Inexperienced soldiers in regiments from obscure villages of
Pennsylvania, New York, Ohio, Delaware, and Maryland pressed

forward over farmer Roulette's land and around his farmhouse, disturbing stacked crates of honeybees and tasting their first sting of battle.

More Rebels, under the division command of Daniel Harvey Hill, spilled into Hog Trough Road in answer to the approaching Union threat, giving support to the defense of the thousand-yard, boomerang-shaped span.

Desperation replaced the ephemeral swagger of success earned moments earlier from having ambushed Sedgwick's thrust into the woods north and west of Dunker Church.

Lee's left flank, many of its soldiers borrowed from other sectors of the line, had held against McClellan's staccato, broken advances since the early morning. McClellan's predictable caution was Lee's salvation, allowing Lee to focus resources where needed in lieu of defending an entire line of battle against a coordinated assault.

As if prepared by the gods of war, Hog Trough Road served a position advantageous for its Confederate possessors. The protection provided by terrain and fence; the security of unbroken numbers; the strength of leadership; the courage of hardened flesh and blood; a sense of invulnerability earned from a summer of fighting—and winning; all of this was immutable in the minds of Southern soldiers searching for a foothold in the psychology of advantage.

Yet, beneath the pretense of relative advantage, reality reared, stark in its punch of truth. The time was now. Nowhere to run. Nowhere to advance. Nowhere to hide. Reserves, if not spent, were scarce. The stand for the Confederacy was here in the once-quaint farm lane of Hog Trough Road. Turn the enemy here or die in the attempt. Ole Whooey clung to his branch and watched the strange dance, head tilted.

The legacies of ordinary humans, their countless memories and hopes on the brink of the extraordinary, melded into a mighty bond of unity at this singular moment in the timeline of eternity. Officers paced the line, shouting their pep talks, encouraging men to heights of valor, assuring them their cause resided on the side of God, imploring souls to stand fast. When words of magnanimity were spent, practical advice followed. "Aim low!"

The last breath of summer rustled across the valley, a cooling respite from the sizzle of the September sun. The sky teased, exchanging its intermittent ripples of heat with the occasional relief of the shadow of clouds. Rain might fall; it might not; either way, lightning and thunder were certainties.

Rifles rested on fence rails, pointed toward an enemy unseen but no less present. Orders barked. Men obeyed. Flags snapped. Runners carried messages. Flies buzzed. Sweat rolled. Eyes squinted. Stomachs growled; for some, they heaved. Grasshoppers sprang in all directions tending to their instincts for survival, oblivious to the universe of battle surrounding them. Homes beckoned in the minds of men, and hearts sank with the suddenness of truth, as if the lead of enemy bullets had already found their marks.

Men in regiments from Alabama and North Carolina and remnants of Colquitt's Georgia brigade, all under the command of Generals Rodes and Anderson, occupied the rutted stretch. To take Sharpsburg, McClellan's Yankees had to pierce Lee's center, the attempts of the early morning on Lee's left dismal failures of miscommunication. McClellan had to take Hog Trough Road. Ole Whooey peered, still and unblinking, an ignorant sage to the folly unfolding.

Jacob turned toward the rear. Lines of infantry stretched in both directions behind him, ready to fill the front-line gaps sure to form. The sergeant that had confiscated the services of him and Bigun stared through field glasses. Jacob sighed and turned back, yanking the paper tip off a cartridge with his teeth, bits of black powder scattering through the air and into his mouth. He spat the bitter grains from his tongue, its taste of sulfur as repulsive as week-old coffee. He shoved the remaining propellant down the barrel, eyes fixed upon the crest of a low ridge seventy-five yards forward. He hadn't the relief of shade. No one did. He wiped away ranks of sweat assaulting his skin wherever gravity took them. He looked right and left, then right again.

Is this really happening? he thought.

Hundreds of human lives, shoulder upon shoulder, crouched still behind a breastwork of fence rails, mouthed words of prayer for deliverance. Butterflies, bees, and grasshoppers fluttered, buzzed, and jumped from the green of the sloping field facing the soldiers, as if nothing were happening, like a breath of contradiction.

Some men stared into space, forming a mind's-eye image of the do-or-die fight to come, telling themselves what they would do given the situation. Others craned peeks in the direction of the invisible enemy, wondering when the blue sea would rise.

Some laughed, telling tired jokes, to conceal their fear.

Some lounged, hats over eyes, veterans these, awaiting orders they had heard before, the whole experience the drudgery of repetition.

Some sang songs of home.

Some broke teeth on bites of plundered hardtack.

Some drank the last from their canteens, tossing the obtrusive vessels aside.

Some lit pipes and sucked fires that never caught.

Some shouted obscenities.

Some penned hastened letters to loved ones and stuffed the scribblings into pockets.

Others prayed without ceasing, for forgiveness, for their lives spared.

All were scared, though not one admitted it.

A few soldiers scattered to take up positions as skirmishers along the ridgeline.

Near the point in the line where Hog Trough Road intersected Roulette's lane—the apex of the boomerang—a man of the 2nd North Carolina rested his rifle, raised his head, and let loose:

"Whenever I turn to view the place, the tears doth fall and blind

  me;

"When I think of the charming grace, of the girl I left behind me.

"My mind her image full retains; whether asleep or awakened;

"I hope to see my jewel again; for her my heart is breaking."

Soldiers looked toward the source of the melody. A short, vacuous silence gripped the line, followed piecemeal by others joining the singing of the somber, solemn song. Soon, the entire line joined in singing the mournful words. As if to say goodbye to loved ones, men mouthed the tune with one eye toward home, unable to spill the sounds without pouring their tears, resigned that fate might well give them a new home.

Jacob, ignorant of the song and its meaning, dropped the .58-caliber projectile down the muzzle of his U.S. Springfield, a possession prized in the steady hands of a veteran, taken from the frozen hands of a swollen Yankee at the woods near the Dunker Church. He stuffed ball and powder home, removed the ramrod and plunged it within quick reach into the rain-softened embankment, an act born more of common sense than the advice of officers. Only the wait remained.

"Bigun, you loaded up?" Jacob asked.

"I done it, but I don't know what fo'. To kill the ones come to liberate me? I be sittin on the wrong side of dis fight, Jacob."

"Bigun, them soldiers ain't come to liberate *nobody!* Those soldiers are here because somebody convinced 'em of the glory and adventure of war, same as Roswell. And the meals, the uniform, a rifle, an' thirteen dollars a month. Their officers are here because Lee's here. Ain't no politicians here, least not the ones who'll take a bullet. You think those men give a *rat's patoot* about your *freedom*?"

"Frederick Douglass give a rat's patoot," Bigun replied. "John Brown give a rat's patoot. Missuh Lincoln be the Patoot-Givuh in Chief, an' he done sent dem soldiers to give a little *mo'e* patoot. That's all I need to know."

"Bigun, if you *don't* fight, if you walk away, *these* soldiers are liable to put a bullet in *your* patoot, maybe your skull," Jacob whispered into Bigun's ear. "You wanna bullet in your skull?

Mister Lincoln wants to free you, but don't let *these* boys take that chance away from you."

Bigun thought a moment. "Rock an' a hard place," he answered.

"Rock an' a hard place," Jacob acknowledged.

"You here 'cause you want to be?" Bigun asked.

"Not at all. Not at first, anyway" Jacob answered after some thought. "That sergeant there convinced me. All I wanted was a rifle, *this* rifle, an' some distance 'tween us an' Claggett. But what I seen yesterday in Sharpsburg an' back yonder at the church, well, it set me to thinkin."

"About what?"

"About these rebs. They look like hell's stepchildren, but they got a *spark* in their eyes I ain't seen on *any* Yankee."

"When has you seen a *Yankee's* eyes 'cept the eyes of a *dead* one?" Bigun asked, propping his head against a fence rail.

"Rachael said these rebs ain't out-spirited. She's right. I bet there ain't many of these men that's even *seen* a slave, much less *owned* one. They're just defendin their homes, their honor, same as you an' me an' anybody else worth takin a breath."

"By comin' up *here*, up north?"

"I reckon they got a right to push Lincoln's army out of their country."

"*Their* country? Sounds to me like maybe you has had a change of heart, Jacob."

"There now, that wasn't so hard, was it?" Jacob asked, a smile spanning his face.

"What wasn't so hard? Your change of heart?"

"You called me Jacob."

"Ain't dat what I *always* call you?" Bigun spat onto his shirt sleeve and with it wiped smudges off his rifle barrel.

Jacob tilted his head, the smile intact.

"My change of heart ain't about slavery, Bigun. I loathe it more than ever, an' I know you deserve as much freedom as any human."

"But, Jacob, if de South wins—"

"I know, Bigun, I *know*."

"Ain't we he'pin the enemy win?"

"It don't make sense to me, neither. Maybe I'm here because of *Roswell*. Maybe I'm here for *Rachael*. Maybe it's because Hog Trough is *our* road, mine an' Rachael's. Heck, maybe I'm here 'cause Daddy don't *want* me here, who knows. Maybe I'm just afraid to turn tail, afraid that *sergeant* will shoot me. All I know is here I am, an' I believe God had *somethin* to do with that."

"God?" Bigun stared at Jacob. He shook his head and pulled the hammer on his musket to half-cock. "You ain't been baptized yet, has you?"

"I'll get around to it."

Veteran soldiers of Lee's army peered across the expanse of ground. The growing tension exacerbated personal discomforts of diarrhea, toothaches, hunger, mosquito bites, and the unquenchable longing to be somewhere else.

Sweat mixed with the black of powder and the filth of soldiering and gave to the line of men the appearance of a great scaled serpent, the red of battle flags writhing in the wind like festering wounds, the glint of steel dancing to the cadence of twenty-five hundred pulses.

Pools of perspiration formed in the crevices of foreheads, which on occasion spilled forth, pushed by floods of longings for home.

Bare feet, bruised, blistered, and cut, had now a chance for rest. Most of these men, mere boys three Christmases ago, came to Sharpsburg as husbands; daddies; farmers; craftsmen and proprietors, all busy once upon a time with taming their corners of the world, each scantly attentive to the orations of men bent on forging history and carving a new country. Men wiggled their contorted toes in the cool soil, mindlessly aware of this fleeting luxury, fighters focused on doing their duty and returning to their corners.

They were veterans now, survivors of a war bellowed in the beginning to be little more than a ninety-day distraction, a glorious excursion to faraway places. Home by August, they were promised. That was over a year ago. Then, last April, the war for Southern independence took an ugly turn at Shiloh. All hope for a quick end dissolved.

Since their muster, they had experienced the bloodlettings at First and Second Manassas and the Seven Days and South Mountain, and now Sharpsburg. These were grizzled rebels bearing arms against a teetering union, fighting more because "they're down here" than for any pretense of forming a nation of their own, as the politicians saw fit to do, as their kin had done nearly a century prior. The desire to hold another man as chattel seemed a laughable reason to kill one another, especially to these men whose calloused hands themselves were now all but property of the Confederacy.

Chapter 22

"**Them Yanks** *ain't* **gonna** take this road!" Jacob shouted, turning his head side to side as he spoke, standing in defiance, anxious energy getting the better of him.

"Git on this ground, jackass!" said a soldier, grabbing Jacob's pants and pulling him down. "Them Yankees are about to give us the devil's own, but first they gawn give you his *pitchfork!*

"*Look* at this place!" Jacob said, knowing the road better than anyone. "Jesus *himself* couldn't take this road!"

"Jesus hisse'f ain't *got* to take this road," replied a whiskered soldier crouched next to Jacob. "Tha's what He's got them Irish fellers fer," he said, pointing northward and referring to the assumed presence of General Thomas Meagher's Irish Brigade. "Them boys'll wade through hell, drag it with 'em, an' throw it our laps."

"Yeah. Well. *Let* them Irish come, is all I got to say," boasted the transformed Jacob, imbibed by the spirit of a veteran fighter, eager to engage his newfound enemy. He spat lingering specks of gunpowder to the ground. "We'll throw it back at 'em. It don't matter a lick *who* comes! A Hoffman can whip an Irish just as easy."

Jacob's Baptism

The man chuckled at Jacob's ignorance.

"Careful, boy," said the whiskered soldier. "Lord knows we need your enthusiasm. Know this, too. We got some Irish lads among us who just as soon put a bullet in you as shoot a Yankee. They're hungry; they're tired; and they're mad. Don't give 'em another excuse.

"Anyway, they'll be on soon enough, boy. Best you have a little talk with your Jesus, make your peace, scrawl your name on a piece of paper an' shove it in your pocket. An' for God's sake put your damn *head* down lest you attract the twitchins of a nervous Yankee finger!"

"Make my *peace?* I got my *peace* in the barrel of this here rifle," Jacob declared, ducking for a moment behind the relative cover of a hewn fence rail. He patted the barrel like a pet hound. "An' I intend on givin them Yanks a little taste of … peace."

Bigun glared at Jacob, astonished with the abrupt bravado. He reasoned Jacob acted fearless because he had never known fear. Not real fear. Not the sort of fear that gripped a man's mind like the jaws of a grizzly. Not the sort of fear that crept into a man's soul, like rot into a fruit, unyielding, unforgiving in its course.

Jacob's naiveté was his best friend—and his worst enemy. His mind's inability to grasp the magnitude of the approaching violence, the coming killing, was a measure of innocence long ago ripped from the true veterans that filled Hog Trough Road. A collision loomed between the brutality of battle and the fantasy of youth, a convergence of divergent wills, a pivotal struggle between his delusions of immortality and the deadening fury of war.

Colonel Charles Tew, commander of the 2nd North Carolina regiment, paced the line and gazed across the rolling fields to his front, anger and determination in the slits of his eyes, the look of a fear aged and pounded, like molten iron, into a defiant respect for his foe. Death stared back, unblinking.

Colonel John Gordon commanded the 6th Alabama regiment, holders of the apex of Hog Tough Road, where Jacob and Bigun were posted. His men occupied the road to the immediate left of Tew's North Carolinians. Gordon turned to see a general, right arm in a sling, canter with Generals D.H. Hill and Robert Rodes to a dirt-slung stop a few paces to the rear of the line. The commanders saluted and exchanged pleasantries.

Jacob turned, his attention drawn by the shuffle of hooves and the chatter of men. He noticed the meeting, the graveness of their expressions.

Jacob's companion rolled onto his side and propped his right leg and rifle against a fence rail and took up a strip of rye between his teeth.

"Officers and politicians," another soldier observed, a blade of grass bobbing between his lips like a wagging finger. "We're better off without 'em."

The soldiers on this day, at this moment, understood the gravity of their predicament. They were less disposed to dispense with the spontaneity of cheers for their beloved commander. The matter of repulsing an entire Federal division, maybe two, gripped their thoughts. The matter of sudden death, far from family and home, held more sway. A personal visit to the center-front lines by the Commander of the Army of Northern Virginia meant one thing only—desperation.

The bulk of Lee's army still engaged the enemy several hundred yards north, around the church and in the fields east. As such, companies had been pulled from the ranks in the sunken road to augment that engagement, to ensure that Lee's left held. The looming task in the sunken lane took on a feeling of futility.

Men sat on the road's slope, heads rested on hands pressed against the muzzles of rifle barrels. Their eyes stared at nothing. Their minds pondered everything.

"Boy," the soldier said, removing the blade of grass from his mouth, "that there's Marse Robert and General Daniel Harvey Hill."

"Robert E. *Lee?*" Jacob asked in full surprise. *The* Robert E. Lee?" Jacob asked again as if confirming the Second Coming.

"Well, don't go wetchur britches, boy! He's a damn good general, but he *ain't* the Almighty," the whiskered soldier said as he spat. "He pisses on the ground, same as you an' me."

"I'll be *cursed!*" Jacob said. "I'll be *chewed an' spit!* Robert E. Lee *himself.*"

Soldiers within earshot strained to hear their commander's words. Lee gazed through binoculars toward the north and northeast, his right arm in a sling.

"Hold this line, Colonel," Lee said as he handed the binoculars to General Rodes. "Hold it at all peril, and do not let it go."

Lee's mount shuffled and danced, sensing with impatience the serpent approaching beyond the ridge. Indeed, the snake was at its hooves.

"We will *stay* here until the sun goes down or victory is *won!*" Colonel Gordon promised.

"God be with you, Colonel," Lee replied with a salute.

Those who heard Gordon's pledge knew well it was a metaphor for a fight to the death. These men of proud southern stock were resolute in their determination to quell the Union storm approaching. The soldiers knew they had honor going in; the task now was to hold on to honor going out, dead or alive. Most preferred the plunge into the uncertainty of battle than the surrender of honor. These men, Jacob excluded, had seen mayhem enough to render their consciences as numb as bare skin in a January blow. A cold acceptance enveloped their spirit.

"Heh, heh. Ain't I heard *that* a hunnerd times!" said the whiskered soldier. "I give Gordon his due, though. He's a man among officers and fights as good as any soldier I ever seen. This your first fight, boy?" asked the soldier, swatting a sweat bee.

"*No!*" lied Jacob. "What I mean is … it ain't like I don't know what to do! My daddy taught me how to shoot two, maybe three, rounds a minute. Let's see Billy top *that.*"

"*Billy?* Where's your *respect*, boy?" the whiskered soldier said with a laugh. "Two rounds a minute, eh. That's about what I thought. What's your name, anyhow?"

"Maybe *three!* Jacob Hoffman. Yours?"

"Stokes. Friends call me Bull. S'pose you can, too. Here, take you a swallow," he said, handing Jacob his canteen.

"Tellin me you can do better?" Jacob asked, removing the canteen's cork.

"First off, boy, you better hope them Yankees don't pick this stretch right off to bring their shootin. See where this road bends right over there? From where you an' me are sittin to right over yonder on the other side of that bend is the 6th Alabama. That's where they'll push the issue, if not sooner, then later. When you see what you're in for, the wave of rifles comin at you over that ridge, you might just find yourself skedaddlin right up that bank," Bull said, gesturing with his head to the cornfield behind them. "You might just find yourself shakin under your mama's quilt before we get started good.

"See there?" Bull said, pointing. "Steep bank to skedaddle over, ain't it? They'll charge this line a time or two, try to scare us off. Only way they can get us outa this road, though, is to *flank* us, somethin even them mule-headed Irish'll figure out in due time.

"Then things'll get hot, an' I mean *hot*. An' when things *do* get hot, you should know for a fact that at *two rounds* a minute … shaw, boy, you might as well be a turkey on a whiskey barrel."

"Mister, I ain't runnin *nowhere!* Look at this line! There're enough rifles pointed towards them Yanks to stop the Almighty had *He* a mind to charge." Jacob stood, again exposing his head and chest above the breastworks of fence rails.

"Get your scrawny butt *down,* boy!" shouted another rebel.

Bull looked at Jacob and measured him as a farmer would a milking cow.

"You cain't be no more'n thirteen, fourteen maybe. What's your unit? How'd you hook up with the Sixth?"

"I'm *eighteen!*" Jacob insisted.

Bull squinted with doubtful eyes at Jacob.

"Well … *next* September, anyhow. Me an' Bigun here come up from Sharpsburg this mornin, over off Landing Road, saw y'all marching through. Y'all looked a might scraggly, an' I said to Bigun, 'these boys need some *help!* ' an', well … help has arrived."

"Sharpsburg?" asked Bull. "Over that ridge yonder?"

"Yep."

"Does Sharpsburg have a right fine restaurant on Main Street, with a maplewood bar polished to the hilt, finest slab of beefsteak east of the Mississip?"

"That's *right!*"

"An' a general store with a balding man, about forty-five, loves to talk, an' people come from far an' near to play checkers, yak awhile, just to get away from life?"

"Yeah! You *know* Sharpsburg?"

"Never heard of it. Sounds like every small town I've been through since spring of '61."

Jacob sank to the ground and stared through an opening in the fence rails. Bigun grinned.

"Just havin some fun with you, boy. I thought you Marylanders didn't want anything to do with us rebs," Bull said, locking his blue eyes onto Jacob's. "We splashed across the Potomac expectin a rousin welcome. Instead, we got nothin but waggin fingers and shakin heads. Ain't never heard such cussin."

Jacob said nothing.

"You know what y'all in for, boy?" Bull probed.

"You mean the fightin," Jacob replied. "I reckon we do. They shoot at us; we shoot at them. Only they're out in the open, while we—"

"Boy, hear me good," Bull said, shifting his weight from a prone to a kneeling position, his upper body now fully exposed, ignoring his own advice to keep low. "In ten minutes, you gonna wish you kept your curiosity home milkin cows an' shuckin corn. This ain't no *game*. We need every man, true, but this *ain't* no boy's fight. Not yet, anyway. Let me tell you a thing or two 'bout this war, an' you best take a good listen whilst you got the chance to do somethin about it."

Bigun perked up. Jacob stared at the field. Dragonflies hovered over ground. Devil's darning needles.

"You see that ridge out yonder?" Bull asked Jacob, pointing toward the rolling pinnacle of meadow grass waving on the breeze. He spat his rye stem to the ground.

"I see it."

"Soon enough, an army bigger than any you'll *ever* see is going to march right over that rise, anxious and scared as we are. Some want to see the elephant, just like you. But, like you, a lot of 'em don't know what the hell that means, what it *really* means. Their colors'll be flappin faster than a thirsty dog's tongue, an' their heads'll be low to the ground, as if that makes 'em less a target, an' soon they'll come on the double-quick, each one of 'em fearin their last breath might be but a short step away, but most of 'em not knowin what that *really* means.

"They won't stop, though. They'll come on because they've been told dyin's the lesser of the two evils of war, dishonor bein the other."

Bull paused, snapping off another rye stem. He stared straight over the waving grass, waiting for his thoughts to catch up with his words.

"Darn mosquitoes!" Jacob said, slapping his arm.

"Love fresh blood, I reckon. What blood the Yanks ain't took, skeeters *have*," Bull said, sniffing his body. "Skeeters ignore me. I don't know whether I'm blessed or insulted. They smell me an' run, like scared Yankees. A good omen, I'm hopin."

The two shared a chuckle and a moment of silence.

"Dyin's easier than runnin, boy," Bull continued, his voice scratched by the maniacal shouts of battles prior. "That's a lesson you'll learn if you survive this little scrape. Once that lesson's learned, there ain't no turnin back. Easier to stay an' fight it out. Sounds strange, but a man's gotta have the courage of Job to up an' run." Bull squeezed the barrel of his rifle, extracting a measure of security, like a child coddling a doll. "Ain't *no man* got that kind of courage."

Bull wiped the sweat of his palms on the sides of his trousers and adjusted his hat to better deflect the blast of the morning sun. He checked his musket, seating a percussion cap as he watched skirmishers fan out over the field. Bull Stokes said no more, knowing words now were a waste of breath.

Chapter 23

"Thirty-one, thirty-two …"

The soldier with the blade of grass hanging between his lips, like a thirsty green tongue, settled to Jacob's left. He finished counting his remaining cartridges.

"Gawn need me more'n thirty-six," he said, looking at Jacob's supply.

"Well, don't look at *me!*" Jacob said. "Mine's for a rifle. You got a smoothbore, different caliber."

"Not just *any* smoothbore. Bessie's her name, an' like me she's seen her share of the elephant." The soldier lay on his belly, rifle propped against rails. "It's all the same, them elephants."

"Elephants?" Jacob asked.

"When they get close enough, right around twenty paces, we're gawn make that first rank wish they's never born," he said, experience his guide. "But they's another wave right behind the first-un, and another wave after that. An' then some. Before long, they'll be too many of 'em. Yessiree, we can hold 'em off fer a spell, maybe long enough fer A.P. Hill to come up from Harper's Ferry, but you can bet your Sweet Jesus ol' McClellan's sendin a whole division, maybe two, right at this Godforsaken spit of ground, an' then ... well, then, it's just a matter of time."

"What do mean, a ... matter of time?"

"A matter of time's what I mean, boy! Before they kill us *all*. *That* you can count on! You best be ready for the long sleep, boy, or run like an ol' hare through that cornfield yonder whilst you got the notion."

Captain John Gorman and Colonel Charles Tew, alerted by rebel spotters forward in the fields, trotted the few dozen yards to the crest of the ridge in front of the fence line bordering Hog Trough Road. The enemy was advancing at intervals through farmer Roulette's field, three lines deep and a half-mile wide. The silence of the Confederate officers told the waiting rebels all that needed saying.

The blue waves rolled forward, straight and precise, echoes of orders bouncing across the air. Flags snapped. Soldiers in blue marched, lips tight, preparing their bodies as best they could for the impact. The odor of spent powder, the scent of death, drifted through the ranks.

"What's it mean, anyway, seein the elephant?" asked Jacob, familiar now with the idea, but wanting as many perspectives as possible. "To you, that is."

"Ain't you ever wanted to see a circus elephant?"

"Circus ... yeah, but—"

"It's a *manner of speakin*, boy. Goin into battle is like facing an elephant, sort of; except this elephant shoots back. It's an *awesome* sight to behold, that elephant, the adventure of a lifetime comin straight at you at the charge. Bullets singin; shells whistlin; men cussin; hearts stoppin at the sheer sight an' sound of it all." The soldier shook his head. "Ain't *never* felt more alive than when I see the elephant. Every battle, I live another lifetime." The soldier laughed, biting off a chunk of tobacco, chewing it like cattle chew cud. He counted his cartridges again.

Jacob turned to Bull, the tilt of his torn hat a measure of his experience and wisdom. *Adventure of a lifetime*, Jacob thought.

"Seems like *you've* done perty good so far," Jacob observed. "Why you still doin' it, Bull, seein the elephant, that is? Why take the risk over an' over of gettin killed?"

Bull pried off, then pressed back on, the percussion cap and turned to Jacob. He smiled.

"I got me a wife an' two kids, a boy an' a girl, back home outside Rome, Georgia. Used to be I wanted more than anything to see that ol' elephant, to revel in the glory everyone told me about. I loved seein the wave of a lady's handkerchief, hearin the cheers of homefolk wherever we marched. Whippin them Yanks at Manassas, twice to boot, felt good—felt *real* good—but it set my mind straight."

Bull's eyes narrowed as he clutched a cartridge between his fingers, grains of powder falling into his palm.

"I've seen these damned Minies do things to a man I never thought possible to do. I've heard the zing and buzz of bullets flyin through the air like bees at a flower show. I've felt the vibrations of their spin on my temple. I've heard the crunch, like snowballs on a barn door, bullets striking flesh an' bone of men no more than a hand's length away, beside me, in front of me, an' I've wondered *how on God's sweet earth* was *I* spared. I was surely no saint an' not one ounce more deservin to live than they.

"I've seen legs an' arms ripped away from men who a second before were yellin with all the vigor of boys showin off in a school yard.

"I've seen blood pour out of men's necks and heads and chests like red floods.

"I've seen desperate men, *doomed* men, eyes big as harvest moons, tryin to salvage their guts—their *guts*—from the ground and tuck 'em back inside, tryin to live, *desperate* to live, some laughin with embarrassment, like a woman who spilled her laundry, as if he'd somehow done it to himself.

"I've seen men cryin like *babies* for their mamas' cuddles, men filled with terror as death came.

"I've seen a shell tear a man in two, torso from legs. I've smelled the dung that come out of men as they took their last breath, an' I've smelled the rottin bodies of men bloated by the sun an' half eaten by maggots, an' I've smelled the vomit of survivors changed forever by the sights. That's the elephant no recruiters or politicians want to talk about.

"See, boy, I don't care a wit about seein the elephant no more. I'm fightin for my family's name an' my honor. I ain't gonna run from no Yankee, 'cause I know he ain't gonna run from *me*. Duty and country is one thing. Personal honor is why I'm on this line, rifle pointed that way. I don't care about slaves or States' rights. A colored's as much a man as me an' has as much a God-given right to—"

THULCH.

Jacob reeled.

A bullet finished Bull's thought, smashing into his forehead, splattering blood, bone, and brain onto Jacob's face and shirt. Bull teetered on his knees, his life shot away, gravity unsure which way to take him.

THULCH.

Another bullet followed, tearing through the middle of his chest. Bull slumped over Jacob's chest, the flame of life snuffed in an instant.

Trapped by the weight of Bull, Jacob stared a moment, his eyes widened with shock at the lifeless form. He thought of the words spoken seconds earlier, now echoes in Jacob's mind.

"Damn!" Bigun shouted.

With a realization as sudden as Bull's death, Jacob frantically shoved the body down the embankment behind him as if he were shaking off a spider.

Two folded pieces of paper, one scrawled with the name 'Caroline', an amber-tinged hole burned through them both, slipped from Bull's shirt pocket and flitted in the breeze among the crouched men. It bounced and tumbled along the dirt and grass until it settled somewhere in Piper's corn, safe for the moment from further sacrilege.

Jacob resumed his position, eyes at ground level, finger on his rifle's trigger, lungs panting, as he scanned the distance for the source of the killing shots.

Soldiers who had neglected to do so pressed percussion caps into place and pulled back the hammers of their muskets, a sound which resonated down the line like sleet off a tin roof. The moment, the adventure, the elephant, had arrived.

"Steady, boys! *Aim low!*" barked the command repeated down the line.

Ole Whooey lowered his beak and nudged his breast feathers, unable to sleep amid the clamor. His eyes opened full and yellow.

The fighting in the Sunken Road, aka Hog Trough Road
9:30 a.m. – 1:00 p.m., September 17, 1862
Confederates from Alabama, North Carolina, and Georgia faced
two divisions of Union troops under the commands of Generals
French and Richardson. Jacob and Bigun find themselves thrust
into line of battle with the 6th Alabama at the apex of the Sunken
Road.

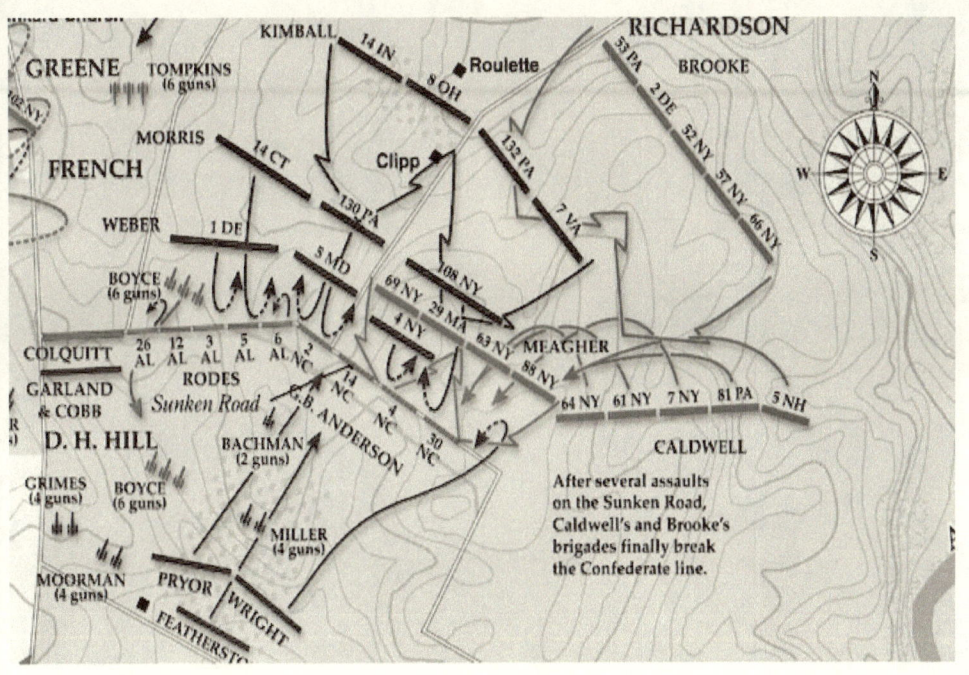

After several assaults
on the Sunken Road,
Caldwell's and Brooke's
brigades finally break
the Confederate line.

Jacob's Baptism

Chapter 24

Jacob scraped his cotton-dry tongue
across his lips. He listened, hearing distinctly the clatter of steel
grow louder, the shuffle of troops draw nearer, beyond the
ridgeline, a blue curtain lifting for an act he had rehearsed only in
the harbors of his imagination. Voices along the line fell as silent
as death, the men's final thoughts swirling trapped within, their
moment of truth upon them.

Soldiers from Delaware; Connecticut; Pennsylvania; New
York; and Maryland, regiments of Weber's brigade of Brigadier
General William French's Third Division, Second Corps,
marched through Mumma's gardens and around his farm
buildings, parade-like columns on their way to Hog Trough Road
and the waiting Confederates. Bullets meant to stop them rested
quietly within the Rebels' long barrels. On the way, troops
dismantled fences to clear the way for those who followed. They
dodged tree limbs severed by artillery shells. They beat a hasty
advance away from knocked-down crates of honeybees. Men
grumbled about their sticky trousers and shoes, soaked from their
wading of the Antietam moments earlier. Soon, the voices of
these men faded as they realized what they were required to do.

Unlike men who with zeal and commitment had joined the ranks of the combatants, a Tuesday morning routine of fishing had set off a chain of events giving thrust to Jacob's insertion into the heart of a major battle, with men he shared little common ground, save the dirt they now occupied. The veteran who had offered Jacob advice, introspection, lay in a dead clump behind him. Jacob's and Rachael's beloved Hog Trough prepared to receive its new purpose, its destiny.

He patted his pocket for his gold coin. Still there. Watch, too.

"This adventure's *free*, Grandpa," he whispered, thinking how clever he must be for still possessing the coin, while failing to consider that the coin did not have to be spent, physically exchanged, in order to fulfill its purpose for adventure.

Jacob pulled two dried flowers of gardenia, wrapped in vellum, from his pocket, gave them a sniff and a kiss, and returned them, one flower falling unnoticed to the dirt.

"Don't rightly know what's gonna happen here, Denia, but if I'm gonna return to you, so I can *marry* you ... well, I'll be needin your luck." Jacob sighed. "I love you, Rachael." Jacob issued a chuckle of surprise for his vocal acknowledgment of love for Rachael.

Detached, literally, from the antiwar tenets of his daddy's Dunker faith, the non-baptized Jacob considered the idea that men were *born* for war, that great proving ground of manhood, that lair for the intrepid and the bane of cowards. Though tender of age and lacking maturity in reason, he believed above all else that his life's duty was to utilize circumstances, whether of his making or otherwise, to carve his path to manhood. War and manhood, the circumstances no longer debatable, beckoned.

Jacob laid low in this line of rebel fighters, Bigun beside him, facing perhaps the *very man* who had killed Roswell. Maybe this was the opportunity to avenge his friend's death. Maybe God had placed him here for that reason. An eagerness to avenge surged in his blood. He felt Roswell's tug.

Such complex thoughts of theory and retribution and manhood melted, the likelihood of death looming nearer. Jacob's abrupt thirst for manhood was quenched just as suddenly by a swell of fear. Maybe the boundary of the remainder of his life stretched only minutes ahead. Maybe manhood could wait. Bull's life ended, picked off by a sharpshooter, before fighting in this sector began. Jacob had little reason to believe things would be different for him.

Jacob *wanted* to serve, if only he knew—knew with *certainty*—*whom* to serve and why. He wanted to flee, but to where? He wanted time to prepare his mind and spirit for such heights of commitment. What he did not want was to die. He shifted his leg, giving the dropped gardenia flower an unknowing push into the dirt. The sun's blinding glares off the barrel of his Springfield suggested to Jacob that the familiarity of routine had ended.

Unfinished thoughts churned in his brain, each one cutting off the other, running together, like stampedes of thunder-scattered cattle. One thing he knew. Claggett and those other two dead men no longer mattered. Springfield rifles did not matter. The luster of vengeance was losing its shine. Returning to Rachael mattered. Living mattered. On came the blue lines.

Whom to fight against, whom to fight for—to fight at all— the matter for Jacob had taken a turn for the personal, and the rationale felt valid for either choice. He and Bigun were here. The option of running long stripped, the two waited. Jacob would be his friend's surrogate, for now, while fighting the battle of self-defense. He was not fighting for ideology or against it. He felt no hate for the enemy. His fight was for life, to walk away with the only possession that mattered. He suspected every soldier, when the water was boiled away, was left with the fight for self-preservation, to return to family, to home, to routine, to all that mattered.

Jacob pulled the hammer to full cock. God had chosen sides for him. He glanced left and right, affirming the focus of the long string of soldiers.

"Here it comes, Bigun. Like a storm you can't run from."

Jacob leveled his eye, eyelid aquiver, down the sight of the steel-blue barrel of his rifle and fixed his focus upon the middle of some poor bastard's chest pounding with the cadence of a thousand heartbeats, a thousand longings to be elsewhere, *anywhere*, carried by legs edging closer to the precipice.

Jacob had never engaged in a schoolyard scuffle or so much as killed a crow. Before him now marched, and beside him now waited, whole armies of living, feeling, thinking beings, souls far from the securities of home, souls in a spot well past the point of no return. Jacob believed hope for tomorrow was carried by the notion death waited, tucked deep inside a pigeonhole, denied daily for another day. The pigeonhole spilled.

He thought of the conical gray ounce of lead cradled inanimate in the breech of his rifle, forged from raw material taken from the dust of the earth, destined from the dawn of time to snuff the future of a man with whom he had no tiff, no grudge.

Maybe the man to Jacob's right or left, Bigun perhaps, had placed aim against the same poor bastard. His guilt eased a bit.

Ole Whooey stared at the distant incoming blue mass, strange invaders of Jacob's and Rachael's courting grounds. Spotting a mouse, he swooped, grabbing it, killing it.

General William French's division, Second Corps, Army of the Potomac, swept aside the nuisance of rebel skirmish lines. Light of the mid-morning sun flickered off rifles and the array of clanking metallic objects attached to the belts and backs of the approaching troops, moving like wildfire pushed by the wind. Bluecoats marched with the steadiness of drill, precision preceding tumult.

Again, soldiers in Hog Trough were ordered prone, as stupidity of the curious betrayed common sense. Still, some ignored orders and stood, watching in amazement the parade-like scene advancing before them. Rebels took long draws from their canteens, holding the vessels high in gestures of respect for fellow soldiers across the way, soldiers who, like themselves, were on the cusp of an experience that would be their last. This, if nothing else, they shared. They wiped their mouths and brows with rolled sleeves, for many their final measure of physical comfort.

Others derided the blue lines with verbal stones of discouragement, quests for advantages coming in such forms.

Men in the Union ranks flung flasks of whiskey to the ground, by doing so perhaps gaining some measure of Godly favor, adding a chance or two to the credit side of Divine bookkeeping. The rebels had already done so.

Opportunists, veterans who knew the value of a flask, raked up the scattered treasures and stuffed them into trouser pockets, anticipating an outcome worthy of celebration. More men than did not lifted their heads in prayer and kissed photographs of homefolk.

"Get us reinforcements; for God's sake, *do it now!*" shouted a Confederate colonel to an aide. The aide bolted rearward. "God be with us," the officer whispered, gazing through field glasses at the approaching blue tide.

The front line of Confederate infantry was supported by secondary lines, in the road and along the southern side of Hog Trough Road, Piper's cornfield to their backs. Their primary purpose was to load rifles, hand them to the front rank, helping ensure a continuous rate of fire.

"Hold your fire until you see their breastplates!" shouted another colonel, standing as an example of defiance atop the rear slope of the southeast-running sector of Hog Trough Road, occupied by regiments from North Carolina. Again came the advice, "And aim low!"

Jacob looked at Bigun, who lay resolute of purpose, rifle sight fixed upon those who would free him. He believed Southern soldiers would spare him as long as he fought beside them, or gave the appearance of such. He knew as well that his color offered no shield to a Yankee bullet.

Jacob turned his head to the serenity of the field behind. Piper's corn beckoned his flight. He thought of the notion Bull spoke about. Hell was about to erupt. If he were going to run, now was the time.

The battle, the war, was ended for Bull, blood covering his face and torso like a crimson sheet. No more traipsing around the house and yard with his daughter on his shoulders. No more snug winter nights cuddled close with his beloved under quilts of goose down. No more Sunday picnics in the shaded coves of Oostanaula River. No more dreams. No more disappointments. No more winters of ravaging illness. No more spring plowings and summer droughts. No more autumn harvests. No more cackling of children's laughter. No more Christmas. No more struggles. No more contentment. No more strife. No more life. Now only peace. If life made little sense for Bull, afterlife perhaps provided the explanation.

"We—we stayin, Bigun?" Jacob stuttered, shifting his weight from leg to leg, the question already answered.

"Got no choice," Bigun replied, glancing left and right. "If we run, somebody'll shoot us—shoot *me*. I ain't hankerin fo' no bullet in my back. If dis be my time, I gawn die a man."

"That's—that sure is a passel of bluecoats out yonder," observed Jacob. "Reckon we can whip 'em?"

Bigun glared at Jacob, as if Jacob had traded his senses for that rifle.

"It ain't about *whippin* nobody," Bigun replied. "If I has to kill me a Yankee standin over me with a bayonet to my throat, dat's one thing. But for me, I gawn do all I can to stay outa dis fight, even if I has to lie still under one of dese dead rebs, play dead myse'f, while y'all kill each other. I'm fightin for *my* survival, for gettin back to my family."

Jacob watched the incoming blue and let Bigun's words take root.

"I want to live, too," Jacob said. "Only dog I got in this hunt is the one that sergeant done tied to us. I do know that this line is all that's between them Union boys an' my daddy's farm. An' Rachael. Ain't that worth me fightin for?"

Bigun turned and looked at Jacob. He gave a smile. "See you when it's over," Bigun said after a thoughtful pause. The pair shook hands. "Keep low."

Steady veterans, no strangers to tight fixes, honed the aims of their muskets as best they could. Pounding pulses resonated through the hands of untested recruits, their rifles trembling with uncertainty.

Bluecoats in the forward ranks, exposed, eyed one another, wondering who might break first. No words were spoken, each step forward an expression of resolution. These were McClellan's green troops, fresh from their sit-down coffees with the glory-speak of silk-tongued recruiters. These soldiers were barely accustomed to the skill of cleaning oneself with leaves. Now they were required to fire and load their long guns in the face of flashing muskets, sheets of invisible metal, an enemy determined to destroy them. These were the expendable ones, their purpose to absorb volleys and buy time between enemy loadings, time enough for the veterans to gain a foothold of ground and close on the enemy, inch by inch. Few in these front waves of green troops possessed the witness of gore, of shredded men, chaos in the churning maelstrom, the fury of flying debris, cursing men, and screaming souls.

They marched upon the debatable ground, onward they marched, for some the bliss of ignorance their only friend, for others their thumping hearts bursting with the knowledge that the coming flash of twenty-six hundred muskets might be the last sight they saw on this earth. Anxiety had a way of pushing some legs faster than others. The lines bulged and bent, the S-curves crushing the grass like a blue wheel.

"Steady, boys!" Colonel John Gordon of the Sixth Alabama barked, his tone as firm and strong as his countenance. "Alabamans never waver!"

"He looks like one mean cooter," Jacob observed, "like an army of one! No wonder ain't nobody runnin'."

"He just another casualty waitin to happen," Bigun said with a spit. "Look at 'im walkin dat line like Jesus. Yankees got their bead on 'im, you can be sho' o' dat."

Gordon had come to embody an air of invincibility, not only for his command, but also for the Army of Northern Virginia. He had taken seven bullets through his clothing at the Battle of Seven Pines, none of which pricked his flesh. His men were willing to face any odds as long as Colonel John Gordon held command.

Jacob and Bigun braced for the attack. Features on the faces of Yankees were as clear as the blue sky. Men up and down the lane glanced impatiently at their commanding officers and squirmed to receive the order to let loose their loads. Rodes' Alabamans, Anderson's North Carolinians, Colquitt's Georgians, others of patchwork units, all readied for the firestorm. Fingers caressed triggers, a disquiet rising in men desperate to blow backwards the rolling tide.

Yankee banners of green and gold and red and blue, each emblazoned with the stitched names of prior engagements, appeared to rise out of the grass on the crest of the ridge, like Satan's legions.

The soldiers in the road, set for the shoot, gazed with awe at the uniformity and precision of the advance and with respect for the courage upon which they would soon lay waste. A spontaneous cheer arose from the Rebel line. Men again stood and waved hats, honoring the approaching men, honoring themselves.

Standard-bearers of the Second Corp waved their proud regimental colors. Onward came the 130th and 132nd Pennsylvania, the 8th Ohio, the 5th Maryland, the 14th Indiana, the 1st Delaware, the 4th New York, and others in the vanguard, all roosters scratching the soil, girding for the fight.

These young boys, many at the pinnacle of their first grand adventure, dipped into a swale of temporary safety, out of sight; a few minutes later they topped the crest of a rise and saw clearly before them countless holes of shining barrels resting on fence rails, rifles aimed low, pointed motionless at them. Each barrel held a message from the Reaper. A sudden, collective shudder gripped the blue ranks, the realization full, now a fatal thirty yards away, each man aware his moment of truth had arrived.

"Fire!" Colonel Gordon shouted, the veins of his neck bulging with blood.

The din of discharging rifles again shattered the valley air like the collapse of a glass city. Muskets spat their flaming tongues, an unbroken line of fire and smoke. Bullets carved paths through the thick air, spitting dirt and grass, pinging canteens and rifles, and smashing into chests and foreheads and arms and necks and stomachs and knees and thighs and shoulders and faces. Walls of lead lifted men and slammed them in contortions to the ground. Blood surged from hundreds of wounds, coloring the grass and soil with a red sludge.

Jacob held his breath as he handed his rifle to the line behind him, receiving a loaded rifle in return, careful to keep his body low. He looked around. Yankee bullets thunked the wood rails and kicked puffs of dirt in the eyes of Confederate faces. Dead bodies absorbed rounds. Rebels tore paper off cartridges and spat, pouring the powder into muzzles, shoving home the rounds. The road filled with sounds of scraping, clinking ramrods, like sandpaper and nails. The blue tide receded, for now.

Chapter 25

"Name's *Tucker!* Tucker McGavin! Second North Carolina!" the teenager shouted, his voice scarcely audible above the roar. He rammed a ball down the barrel of his .69 caliber smoothbore. "We in a *fight* now, you 'spect?" He held out his bloodstained left hand, not as introduction but as demonstration. "Damn ball took away half my middle finger, jus' as I was given 'em what for! Ain't much on dressin wounds under fire. They're hittin us left, right, and front. Looks like a *million* of 'em. They'll be in our rear 'fore long. What's your name, soldier?"

Jacob hesitated to return his name, giving Tucker a glance, realizing that on this day names meant nothing except distractions. Conversation was suicidal. Jacob leveled his rifle and pulled its trigger.

Who the heck can think about talkin now? thought Jacob, as he glanced again at Tucker, then forward to the new assault. He plunged powder and ball into his Springfield, loading his own rifle. *This ain't no church social!*

Tucker spread on the ground, like a Sunday picnic, rifle propped against the breastwork, tending his nagging wound.

Bullets thunked into rails and posts, sending splinters of wood flying. He ignored them.

"It's Jacob!" he relented as he planted a percussion cap onto his rifle's nipple, yanked back the hammer, and fired low and level between the stacked fence rails into the smoke-shielded enemy. He winced as the rifle's butt recoiled into his bruised shoulder.

"Welcome to the circus, Jacob," Tucker replied. "Man, I'd *love* to get my hands one of them Sons of Erin flags," he said, pointing, referring to the 69th New York of the Irish Brigade. "Just about pulled out of line an' run after it when I seen it fall. If them boys weren't so far down the line. Reckon one of them Carolina boys'll go for it."

Like a slashing monster with invisible teeth, bullets shattered fence, spit dust, splattered flesh, and crunched bone, sending pieces of debris spinning through the air like seeds in a spring storm. This vortex of violence filled with screams, orders, pleas, curses, leaden smoke, lead and iron. How anyone remained unscathed was no less than a miracle. As long as hands could hold them, regimental colors waved side to side, daring the enemy to advance. The enemy obliged. Bullets slapped buntings and thumped bodies.

"They comin at us from over yonder," shouted Tucker, pointing front-left towards a knoll adjacent to Roulette's lane, "an' directly yonder; an' they's artill'ry somewhere over that rise there, lobbin shells, knockin the *slap* out of us!

A soldier next to Tucker turned right, his attention grabbed by events at the right of the line of battle toward the Fourth and Thirtieth North Carolina regiments. As he pointed, a ball slammed into his throat, ripping away half his neck. Blood gurgled, then gushed, like a torrent through a downspout. A flash of terror, truth, crossed the man's face, and then he was gone. For him, and thousands more, the debate was over.

"Goddamn flankin fire!" erupted Tucker, wiping away splotches of the man's blood. "Here they come!"

Tucker licked his thumb, cocked the hammer, stood and delivered a shot into the ranks of the 64th New York, part of

Francis Barlow's command bearing down on the right flank of the beleaguered Confederate line. Tucker stood firm, erect in defiance of the enemy, precious seconds robbed by the arduous process of reloading. Men reeled, jerked, dropped into the sea of carnage. Tucker did not flinch.

Jacob yelled, "What them fellas *yonder* cheerin about?" referring to a mass of waving blue caps on the ridge to the road's front.

"God knows what! Hell, they prob'ly jus' glad they's *able*," Tucker grunted, lifting his rifle and firing.

Bullets zinged and zipped past Jacob's ears, and he marveled at his good fortune for having avoided blocking their path. Jacob felt surrounded by a vacuum of immortality, a sensation of audacity that suggested point-blank shots were as peas against his shield of Thor. Perhaps today was *not* Jacob's day to die. Perhaps his survival was sheer birthright, prosperity granted by the gods of war.

He looked behind him and saw Colonel Gordon, bleeding from his right leg and left shoulder, hobbling back and forth, spurring his men to hold the line, ignoring his perilous injuries as best he could, standing not only for his men as an example of courage but as a distraction for Yankee rifles.

"Jesus, *look* at that man!" shouted Jacob, pointing to Gordon.

"He's taken two or three bullets otherwise meant for *you*, Jacob," Tucker replied. "You ain't got time to be a-lookin! Be grateful for 'im an' load up!"

Colonel Gordon hobbled. He stopped and glanced at the noon sun and wiped his brow. His body drained blood faster than the day drained sunlight.

Jacob saw the sunken road filling with bodies and parts of bodies. He smelled the stench, the gut-wrenching contents of dead and dying men, the sulfur of countless rounds. He heard the laughter of maniacs, the screams of men burning with pain unthinkable, each comforted once upon a time by the song and sunshine of the Potomac crossing and the thought that when battle came, death would find the *other* man.

Now men flailed to fend off the inevitable, as one might spin and dance and curse in the repulse of hornet swarms. Jacob heard coming from within the cacophony the agony of voices pleading for mamas and girlfriends, desperate cries for security beyond all reach, yet well within the forefront of fading consciousness.

He watched the cheering enemy. They kept coming, falling, coming. Coming still, a blue flood, all but drowning the rebel defenses. In this fight of attrition, the numbers favored the Federals. Men gasped with terror, pillaged cartridge boxes for ammunition and the ground for stones, savage quests to cannibalize anything worth flinging at the coming hordes. The rebel gods of battle raked their hands across empty scabbards, their fingers inside arrowless quivers, desperate for miracles. Even the supernatural had no answer.

"Shoot your Goddamned gun!" Tucker roared.

Musket fire pattered all around as men hugged the soil and pulled dead comrades close to rest their rifles upon, to absorb incoming rounds. The air was furious, a stained, sulfuric sarcophagus.

Oblivious to his pause, Jacob rested his head against a pockmarked fence post. Smoke shrouded him like a specter. He stared blankly at the madness, dazed, given over to his newfound sense of invulnerability, willing no more to resist. Bullets pinged rifle barrels, clipped wooden posts, and ripped through loose clothing. Men were lifted off the ground by simultaneous impacts, their bodies shredded to pulp. These were the lucky ones, the killed-outright ones. Tucker grabbed Jacob's weapon and pulled the hammer.

"Gimme a cap," Tucker shouted.

His motion mechanical, Jacob handed Tucker a percussion cap. Tucker pressed the cap onto the nipple and shoved the rifle back to Jacob.

"Best you git back in this fight, boy. Might as well take as many of them yankity-yanks with us as we can, 'cause sure as the sun is high, this road's our *grave!*"

Tucker loaded and fired like a madman possessed. The firing lines of Gaines Mill, Malvern Hill, and Manassas had taught him to keep the enemy as pinned as possible. Seldom came opportunities for picking targets, for casual aims. Anything that appeared through the smoke was a target. The direction of enemy movements, the sounds of enemy rifles, often little better than guesses, were the targets.

Hog Trough Road presented a damning twist. The enemy had thrown two divisions at the sunken farm lane, the center of Lee's line. The road bent in its center, like a boomerang, exposing the rebel line to enfilading crossfire from either side of the angle.

Now the Yankees were firing up the right flank of the road as well. Caldwell's brigade, shooting down-slope of the road, blistered the reeling line of rebels. Bullets smacked Confederates from three directions. Bodies falling in one direction were at once jerked to another. The situation worsened to the point of panic. Still, the rebels held.

Colonel Gordon's head snapped back. A fifth ball struck under his left eye, exiting out the right side of his neck. He slammed to the ground, face down inside his hat.

Jacob glanced to either side in search of Bigun. He noticed an object moving in his periphery, lifted his rifle, and fired at the blue blur hurdling the fence breastwork. The soldier tumbled to the lane, dead, atop the mounting stack. Jacob felt a sting punch his left chest, staggering him. Gasping for breath, he brushed his hand over the area. Finding no blood, consciousness intact, he reached for a cartridge.

As he loaded his rifle, Jacob noticed the brown skin of a man's leg protruding from under a stack of bodies. "Bigun!" he shouted. *"Bigun!"*

Jacob knew. His first instinct was to pull away the bodies. He thought better, realizing a dead man was beyond help.

As had been the case all morning for the rebels, officers ordered men from the strongest positions to relieve the severest points of stress along the firing line. Such luxury was no longer available. These Confederates had no choice but to hold or die in the attempt, even as Barlow's 64th/61st New York and Caldwell's 5th New Hampshire applied untenable pressure on the Confederate right in the sunken road. The Yankees had breached Hog Trough; the rebels were being flanked. Ole Whooey watched it all, picking at his field kill.

Orders were shouted to men of the 6th Alabama to meet the new Union threat. In the tumult, this order was mistaken for a call to *abandon* the road for the safety of Piper's corn and the Piper's Lane beyond. Other regiments noticed men streaming rearward, and in their desperation to live, they followed. Rebel defenses crumbled in Hog Trough Road.

"Everybody's *skedaddlin*, Tucker! *Look!*" Jacob said, grabbing Tucker's elbow.

"Jacob! *Look out!*" Tucker shouted as he raised his musket to a near vertical point, the barrel wedged under the chin of a charging Yankee. The bluecoat pointed a revolver at Jacob's head, but before he could pull the trigger, Tucker pulled his, sending the officer's head over the breastwork.

Jacob looked at Tucker and managed a quivering smile of gratitude just as another officer's sword impaled Tucker from mid-back through the belly. Tucker's eyes widened with shock as he fell to his knees, hands gripping the blade. Blood rushed from the wound and trickled out his mouth.

The officer pushed Tucker to the ground with his boot, yanking the sword from Tucker's body. He raised his sword to repeat the process on Jacob but was met with the thrust of a bayonet into his chest. Tucker released the bayonet's handle. He gave Jacob a wink as he fell face down atop his killer.

Rebels raced through Piper's cornfield, a mad rush from the killing in the road. Some men ran backwards, afraid of the dishonor of a bullet in the back. Others knelt and managed to fire a round or two before falling back. Lee's center, as it existed in Hog Trough Road, had collapsed.

Yankees poured into the road, stepping on bridges of corpses and wounded. Jacob wanted to run but could not muster the nerve to chance it. He lay prone on his belly, frozen in the ice of indecision. He watched soldiers strain to scramble up the steep southern embankment of Hog Trough, desperate to escape the onslaught. Many did not make it. As he reached for his Springfield, a bullet zipped though his body just below his left shoulder. Jacob fell amid heaps of dead Confederates, next to Tucker.

Chapter 26

Ole Whooey stood perched atop his tree on the southern bank of the sunken road, pecking flesh off his fresh kill. In the Hog Trough below, and in the fronting meadows, wounded covered the ground, groans of desperation filled the air, each a plea to reverse the misery. Men writhed, hit in every conceivable point on their bodies. Pierced lungs gasped for air. Ripped skulls exposed brains; jaws were shot away; flesh blown open beyond any notion of repair; parched throats rasped for water. Voices of torn bodies, lives hanging by threads of pain seething, begged for merciful ends to consciousness. Men locked in the throes of death sought one last frantic measure of comfort, a swallow of water, anything to curb the hell of their reality. Others sprawled on the ground or atop comrades, unable to lift themselves, chests heaving with disbelief of the unthinkable butchery. Men in full awareness clutched abdomens gashed open, intestines slithering from their holds; holes the size of silver dollars shot through chests, revealing beating hearts and other vitals; limbs shattered, clinging to their hosts by strips of flesh and shards of bone, some shot clean away; futures of thousands riding the swift flow of blood to the soil.

Jacob's Baptism

Hog Trough Road squirmed like a hacked snake. The open ground fronting the sunken road took on a sickening blend of uniform-blue, grass-green, and blood-red, it too wringing with the movement of soldiers trapped in their misery. The bulk of the fighting shifted to discordant attacks in Mumma's fields two hundred yards north-northeast of the road and to Piper's corn a few hundred yards south of the road.

Soldiers of the Seventh Maine screamed with the voice of victory as they leapt over the bridge of bodies in the road. Their objective was a mob of fleeing Confederates regrouping in the orchards of Piper's farm, survivors from Anderson's and Rode's brigades thrown together in desperate haste to stem the hurl from Hog Trough Road and to save Lee's center, his army, the Confederacy itself.

Jacob raked his hands across his torso in a feverish search for his wound. He found the warm squish of his blood-soaked shirt. Beside him lay a standard-bearer of the Sixth Alabama, who minutes before waved the battle banner side to side in a frantic attempt to rally the panicked retreaters, the unclaimed prize now draped like a sheet over his bullet-splattered body.

Jacob managed to wriggle the banner free of its shaft. He wadded the cloth and pressed it inside his shirt, against the ooze. The flag's field of red mingled with Jacob's blood. He laid his head upon a dead soldier's thigh and waited for death to still dreams still vivid, dreams born of innocence, tarnished of battle.

Little attention was given the injured Rebels in the road aside from the occasional sympathetic Union soldier who lowered his canteen to the enemy's lips. No one noticed the prize of Jacob's wound dressing, indistinguishable now from a bloodstained shirt. No one, except Bigun.

Bigun emerged from beneath the cover of dead soldiers. He pushed aside legs, arms, boots, heads with eyes frozen open in their moment of death. Covered by the stench, he was unscathed nonetheless and intended to remain so. The last of the pursuing Yankees scampered across the road. Bigun rose to his knees and scanned the horror surrounding him. Bullets meant for other targets zipped through the air, crunching the dead and doubling the misery of wounded mounded in the road.

"Jacob!" he shouted.

He glanced around in search of Jacob. The pools of blood and mangle of flesh made recognition of human features and individuals next to impossible. Eyes stared heavenward. Mouths gaped in their realization. Bigun counted sixteen bullet holes in the body of the standard-bearer. Those were the wounds he could see. He noticed the shaft stripped of its flag, undoubtedly now a Yankee trophy.

The cacophony of misery rang in Bigun's ears like the peal of Hell's bells. He noticed a lumpy blotch of red and blue tucked sloppily under a man's shirt. The man turned his face toward Bigun.

Bigun gasped. "Jacob!"

Bigun scrambled over a few corpses and reached Jacob. He touched the sticky flag and gently peeled it back. He saw Jacob's eyes blink, his chest rise and fall slightly, evidence his friend was alive. Bigun lifted the flag and viewed the wound. He wiped away thick blood and dabbed the flow of fresh blood. The wound was silver-dollar sized. Bigun ignored the dash of a squad of Yankees scrambling past, and they ignored him, each soldier distracted by the chore of maneuvering the body-strewn road and catching up with the division's advance.

"Lawd have mercy," Bigun said repeatedly.

"How bad, Bigun?" Jacob mumbled.

"Bad," Bigun replied, reaching his fingers under Jacob's back searching for an exit wound. "You lost a lot of blood, but least it ain't comin oucha mouth, so I reckon your lungs ain't hit. Bullet went clean th'ough."

Jacob smiled. "One heck of an elephant. You—you get hit?"

"Naw. I found me a body to—" Bigun checked his answer and changed the subject. "Jacob, I got to gitchu out from here. I got to gitchu home!"

"How you … mmmph … gonna do *that*, Bigun? Fightin ain't stopped."

The sounds of battle rattled loud. Home was about a mile west of the apex of Hog Trough Road, a beeline beyond the Hagerstown Pike across the stubble and grass of the Reel farm and then the Landing Road.

Bigun hesitated amid the melee but concluded no one would shoot a man helping the wounded off the field. He perused the immediate ground for a swatch of white cloth. Finding nothing of so innocent a color, he ripped a piece from his sweat-stained shirt, tied the cloth around a broken ramrod, and tucked the ramrod behind the belt of his pants. The cloth flittered in the breeze.

He reached down and lifted Jacob, praying aloud the Lord to deflect the stream of stray bullets whizzing like flies. He began a westward trot across no-man's-land toward the Hagerstown Pike.

Bigun bent forward, shielding Jacob and minimizing his profile, as he stepped over bodies, some issuing with the lift of limp hands pitiful pleas for water. He made it across the field toward the Pike. To his left, Rebel artillery sprayed canister, stalling the enemy's advance.

The patchwork line of Rebels along the Pike stood and raised their caps and hats, cheering the approaching pair to the relative safety of a waist-high stone wall. Bigun stepped over the wall and passed through the line of soldiers, all blackened with powder and sweat, some tending wounds with tourniquets or cornhusks. He felt scarcely safer behind the new Rebel line, given the carnage in the relative protection of Hog Trough Road and the likelihood the Yankees would resume the full measure of assault.

"What—whatchu gonna tell my daddy?" Jacob asked Bigun.

"Reckon I won't have to *do* much tellin," Bigun said between quick breaths. "Missuh Isaac got eyes an' ears. He knows dey's a battle in dese fields, but I spect once he sees dis reb flag dressin up yo' wound, he gawn ask a few questions. Course, then, he might jus' go ahead an' put *another* bullet in you once he hears whatchu got to say.

"Question is, what*chu* gonna tell 'im?" Bigun asked. "He gawn know you been *in* the fight, not jus' a innocent boy who happened to stop a bullet. B'sides, you got enough powder on yo' face to pass as my kin. From the looks of things, you all sent a passel of dem Yankee boys to their glory."

Bigun laughed as they swished through the grass. Jacob tried laughing, the movement exacerbating his pain.

"Yeah, I reckon we did that," Jacob replied. "Where's … where's my rifle?"

"Where's yo' rifle?" Bigun asked, the question seeming anything but pertinent. "Whatchu *mean*, where's yo' rifle? Boy, you lucky to have yo' *life*. Ax me sump'n else."

"What we gonna do with this reb flag, Bigun?"

"You want me to th'ow it away?"

"No!" Jacob replied. He coughed. "I took a *bullet* for the South, for Roswell, an' I aim to keep my payment."

"But, Missuh Isaac, he'll—"

"I don't give a rat's cheese what my daddy thinks of this war, of me, of Rachael, anymore. I've made *my* decisions. But I do reckon he'd burn this flag if he got hold of it." Jacob pondered the problem. "Bigun, you got to hide it for me. You got to take—"

"*Me? Me* hide a *rebel* flag? Lemme check yo' *head* for wounds. Whatchu think my people'll do to me if dey finds dis here flag in my possession? Shoot, I might as well pluck de feathers an' stir up dat tar pot myse'f."

Jacob chuckled. "You're right, you're right. Still, I don't want to lose this flag. What's it say on it?"

"You *has* lost a lot of blood! How on God's sweet earth you spect me to *read* it when ain't nobody *teached* me?"

"How's the bleedin?" Jacob asked.

Bigun set Jacob against a tree stump and gently removed the flag from the wound.

"Stopped, fo' now," he replied.

"Good. Hurts like a son of—"

"Hold on!" Bigun said. "Ainchu got no respec' fo' yo' mama, for mamas *everywhere*?"

"How'd you know what I was about to say, anyhow? Seems to me I've earned the right."

"Not around *me*, you ain't!"

"Okay, okay. Hurts like *the devil*. Can you take the flag off, spread it on the ground?"

Bigun heard blasts of artillery and the shatter of musketry east of the Pike. He believed it only a matter of a short while before their spot was overrun by retreating Confederates, none of whom would offer a smidgeon of sympathy for Jacob's possession of so solemn a symbol. Looking over his shoulder, Bigun spread the flag on the ground. Jacob gazed, stunned by the volume of blood, most of it his, covering the flag. He felt spells of dizziness as he read sites of battles painted along the edges of the banner, evidence of the regiment's prior engagements.

Dozens of gray-rimmed holes pierced this flag, jagged points of red and blue cloth flitting in the breeze, confirmation that an army's soul, its will, was its colors. Kill the standard-bearer, pierce the soul. Pierce the soul, wither the will. Unarmed men, hoisting in the savage midst the symbol of all the reasons worth fighting for, had fallen, their only defense a shield of flesh and an unwithering will.

Jacob had spent the past three hours in a quagmire of violence. But his blood painted this flag with a searing bond of commitment. Once more, his thoughts turned to Roswell. He had seen the elephant, ridden it standing up, just as Roswell had yearned to do. And Jacob lived.

Chapter 27

Bigun's trot across the Reel fields ebbed to a quickened walk. Jacob's weight seemed to grow with each step. Bigun ignored his cramping muscles and dared not set down his cargo again. The thunder of artillery rolled across the fields and through the trees, drifting from the southeast, toward Rohrbach's Bridge. The gray haze of battle covered the valley, hiding the sun and choking memories of peace. The countryside festered in a hellish brew of bodies and debris.

Jacob said nothing. Blood loss had sapped his energy. Bigun noticed Jacob's unconsciousness, a good thing, he believed, given the severity of his wound. The bleeding had subsided, despite the shaking of the trot over uneven terrain.

As Bigun approached the Reel farm, shells fell, rolled, and exploded in fields around the barn and surrounding buildings. Federal artillery, perhaps their long-range pieces across the Antietam, had a bead on the structures. Forward-bent stretcher-bearers performed their dismal work entering and exiting the barn, ferrying their wounded loads to overburdened surgeons, then returning to the canvas of carnage, to reload.

Officers barked orders. Companies of soldiers formed ranks. Shells screamed, exploded. Regiments hastened from this staging area to the woods bordering the Dunker Church and to fields abandoned by Bigun moments earlier.

Bigun stopped to catch his breath. He had considered taking Jacob to Reel's barn but thought better of it, considering the volume of wounded now occupying it. No patch of earth seemed out of harm's reach. He filled his lungs with air and started his trot toward home. The crunch of timbers and an explosion rocked his cadence as he reached the fence along the Landing Road.

Turning toward the sound, he saw the barn ravaged by fast-spreading flames, its mobile living in full flight. He heard screams within, punctuation to the injuries by so grievous an insult. While some managed to remove a few of the helpless, the fire raced through the dry, hay-filled barn like wolves through carrion.

Military traffic filled Landing Road. Reserves of infantry, what few remained, headed east toward the Hagerstown Pike. A moving barrier of wounded, stragglers, and deserters slowed the fresh troops. Bigun maneuvered his way through the human tide, holding firm his friend.

Bigun stopped and stared as he approached the Hoffman property. The house was awash with activity, bloodied men hauled within its walls, dead men carried out. Aides hurried with the removal of doors from their hinges. These they placed atop barrels and sawhorses for service as operating tables for the surgeons. Men rushed buckets of water inside. Red water tossed through opened windows sloshed to the ground.

Surgeons wiped scalpels on their aprons, accumulating ghastly smears of blood. Calls for linens, water, mamas, and home rose above the groans of those who could no more than groan.

Stunned in disbelief, Bigun approached Jacob's home, *his* home. Scores of wounded carpeted the yard. Those gut-shot and chest-shot were set aside, arid of hope, their deaths imminent. Soldiers wounded in their extremities were assigned priority.

"Put 'im down here, boy, and get out of my way!" said one of the attendants preparing the wounded.

Bigun stooped and placed his friend against the trunk of a sycamore. Jacob stirred.

An orderly stooped and lifted the flag dressing, ignored its significance, and took a cursory glance at Jacob's wound. Releasing the dressing, he scampered to a wagon to help offload a fresh group of injured.

"Wh-where am— *Bigun?*"

"I'm right here, Jacob. We come home," he said with a reassuring grin.

"Home?" Jacob said, reaching to rise. "*My* home? "Where's Isaac? *Rachael.*"

"Be *still* now. Ain't nobody here but doctors and wounded. We're lucky we got *dem*. They done turned yo' house into a hospital."

"Hospital?"

"Ain't no place like home to heal a man's hurt."

Jacob smiled, followed by a grimace. "Hurts like *damnation*."

Bigun returned a smile. "You rest now. You gawn be fine."

"Where you reckon Isaac is?" Jacob asked. "When he sees what the rebs have done to his—"

"I spect he skedaddled once the fightin started," Bigun answered, wondering the same about his family. "Couldn't stay in dat chu'ch like he said him an' Missuh Samuel was gawn do."

"No, not Isaac," Jacob asserted. "He vowed never to let this place fall into Rebel hands, lest he died first." Jacob paused. "Reckon they killed him?"

"Shaw, no!" Bigun replied. "Even yo' daddy cain't hold off the whole Rebel army, an' he ain't fool enough to try. I reckon he went down to Otto's or maybe even to Boonsboro, to wait dis out. He'll be along after while."

"You think them three men dead at the bridge are amongst the dead soldiers?"

Bigun gazed transfixed by the horror swirling about him. An arm sailed out a window, followed by a leg thrown from the porch, falling amid piles of other severed limbs. Men begged their desperate defiance into the ears of doctors. Surgeons' aides held down the wounded as best they could.   Screams met the sight of surgeons' knives and the inevitability of amputations. Chloroform silenced a lucky few, until the supplies ran dry, replaced by swallows of whiskey, vice grips of teeth on sticks, new horizons of pain thresholds.

The dreadful work began again. Aides winced as the surgeon, grim-faced and bloodied, bent over a patient and cut flaps into the flesh. The surgeon gripped the amputation knife between his teeth and took up a saw, pulling it fore and aft across the bone with feverish efficiency, the destroyed limb falling to the floor in a matter of seconds.

"Bigun?" Jacob said.

"Wha-? Oh, dem men. You talkin 'bout Claggett and dem other two? I reckon ain't nobody gawn know 'em from any other dead man out there. Don't worry yo'self about dat no mo'."

"How bad?" Jacob asked again. "My wound."

Bigun lifted the blood-red banner, careful not to disturb coagulated bleeders.

"It ain't lookin all dat bad," Bigun lied. "Fact is, you is alive and talkin. Dem doctors'll clean you up, slap on a bandage, and you'll be shootin pumpkins off fence posts befo' you know it." Bigun looked about the grounds. "You in a lot better way dan most of dese men."

Jacob smiled. "Liar."

"Whatchu want me to do wit' dis flag, Jacob?"

"Tuck it under your shirt, *quick,* before somebody realizes what it is. Take it—take it across the road to that big cedar down the road a piece, the one with the lightnin strike. You know the one I'm talkin about. The one with the hollow at the base."

Bigun thought a moment. "I know it."

"Put it there, down deep in that hollow. Don't you say *nothin* to *nobody* about it, you hear me?"

Bigun bent over Jacob to conceal his actions. He took the flag, fashioned a disheveled fold and stuffed it under his shirt.

"Step aside," shouted an aide. Bigun froze, his hands pressed against his shirt. "Lemme look at you, boy," the soldier said, peeling back Jacob's shirt.

Bigun stood. He slowly stepped his way over and around bodies, making his way toward Landing Road. Jacob closed his eyes as the attendant splashed a water-soaked sponge on his chest. He lifted Jacob onto his right side.

"Went clean through you, soldier. Count yourse'f among the lucky. Most of these boys here caught bullets in an arm or leg. Docs cain't do much for them fellers except saw the blame things off. Most of them fellers over yonder are just too damn hurt, an' well—hey, you cain't be more'n thirteen, fourteen years old."

"Seventeen," Jacob corrected. "Why I do look so young to everybody?"

"Hey, you!" the aide shouted toward two stretcher-bearers. "He'p me git this boy upstairs!" The aide dabbed the holes with more water. "Bleedin's stopped, I spect. You're one we can save. Wound's near enough to your shoulder, an' it don't appear to have shattered any bone, not that I can tell, anyhow. I got jus' the place for ya. Hurtin much?"

"Like *damnation*," Jacob said through a pained smile, feeling a battle-won freedom of expression coursing through his torn body.

The soldiers lifted Jacob and carried him through the congestion and squalor of the parlor, the sounds of dying men, suffering men in each room, covering every inch of usable floor space, surgeons and attendants scurrying about like insects. Jacob recognized the shadowed contours of the house as his, its contents either removed in return for the space they once occupied or dismantled for their medical use.

"Get that body off that bed! *Now!*" the aide shouted like a colonel in the field.

The soldiers placed Jacob on the stained bed, Jacob's bed. Jacob gave a quick glance toward the chest of drawers. The wooden trinket box had not been disturbed. An aide washed the wound of its jelled blood, revealing a hole two inches in diameter opened between the left shoulder and breast.

"Whew! I can just about see right through you," the aide said. "Got to close them holes, boy."

Jacob looked at the aide, a mere boy himself.

"That's right. Me. I'll be doin the closin."

"But you ain't—"

"I know, but all the sawbones are downstairs tendin to the amputations." The aide pulled a flask of brandy from his pocket and with his teeth yanked the cork. "Take a swaller or two of this. Ain't got no opium to spare you."

Jacob turned the flask up, this his first taste of spirits, and drew the contents into his mouth like water. He lurched and coughed, spraying brandy and saliva. Fresh blood oozed from his wound.

"Damn, boy, go *easy!*" the aide scorned, grabbing the flask and taking a swallow. "What I mean is, we ain't got much of that whiskey to go 'round." The aide cleared Jacob's wound of bits of clothing and dabbed it with water. "Where you from, soldier?"

"'Round here," Jacob answered.

Jacob felt a pinch as the aide inserted a sewing needle into Jacob's shock-numbed wound. He coursed saliva-moistened thread through the eyelet, knotted it and pulled it through Jacob's skin. He repeated the crude process, narrowing the opening with each tug.

"Sharpsburg? Heck, boy, you're *home!* If a soldier's gonna be shot in this godforsaken war, ain't no better place to be, home."

"*This* is my home, right *here!* You're *standin* on its floors," Jacob said, the numbness subsiding, the pain growing.

"Yeah, *sure*, an'—hold *still!*—an' Marse Robert's my Daddy!" the aide replied dryly. He placed strips of cloth on the sewn holes and wrapped Jacob's chest and back with linen bandages. "Daddy Robert'll be by directly with some buttermilk biscuits an' gravy, bacon, some hot coffee," the aide said, counting off the items on his fingers, pleased with his sarcasm. "I'll be sure to bring you some up. Heck, Daddy Robert hisse'f will bring it up to you."

"You don't understand. This house *is*—"

"I understand *plenty*, soldier. Ain't a one of us that don't wish we was home. Just you rest up an' maybe some of that *delirium* will clear up. I got more wounded than a hive's got bees, an' judgin from the sound of things," the aide observed, pulling back a curtain and glancing outside, "we might soon be behind Union lines."

"But—"

"No 'buts'! *Rest.*" the aide insisted as he wrenched the cork off his flask of whiskey. "A drink for the living," he boasted, gesturing the flask toward Jacob and gulping the liquid. He paused, wiping his mouth. "And a toast to the dead." He took another swallow and left the room.

Jacob stared at the ceiling. The pain worsened, but he had learned to adapt. He imagined the agony of the men downstairs, hearing their utterances, most with arms and legs shot away, bones splintered beyond repair, wounded in places inconceivable, facing the shock of amputation and worse. Shouts and screams drowned out the occasional patter of spent musket balls and the whine overhead of hot shells. Men no longer fought for any cause except personal relief, the glory of secession forgotten.

Wounded men spotted the floor around him. Some appeared dead. A few hummed unrecognizable tunes, their eyes shut tight and chins uplifted, images of another time their only comfort. Jacob closed his eyes and tried to sleep. He was startled by a voice, a familiar female voice, coming from the hallway outside his room.

"Rachael?"

Delirium.

Chapter 28

"Ma'am? We need water." the orderly
repeated, his hand on her shoulder.

"Sir?" Rachael replied. "Oh, *yes*, right away." She lifted the
hem of her dress, enough to clear the bodies, and scuttled to the
house.

Rachael returned with an urn of water and a tin cup.

"Ma'am," the orderly said, softly at first, his voice rising,
"they gawn need you to make bandages. Any clothes in that
house, get 'em. Rip 'em in shreds, *fast*. All sizes. Do it *now*."

Without a word, Rachael raced back inside and pulled from a
downstairs closet clothes belonging to Jacob's deceased mother.
Isaac had set them aside after her death and demanded they
remain hanging in the event, as he had believed, "Mama should
need them." Rachael once thought the gesture romantic. She
looked at the wardrobe for a reflective moment, then pulled the
clothes down and began the shredding. *Perhaps not she*, Rachael
thought, *but others do.*

Arms cuddled around bundles of stripped cloth, pieces
falling to the floor, Rachael scurried up the stairs, stopping along
the way, her back pressing the wall to allow passage of dead men
taken outside for burial. She half-heard the sound of her name

coming from an upstairs room, its call not clicking in her consciousness. More pressing concerns demanded her attention as she shuffled down the stairs and back again. Then she stopped straight up, with the yank of an epiphany, body stilled and eyes wide. She turned.

"Jacob?" she whispered.

She listened for the call to come again, her mind silencing the cacophony of madness around her. She heard nothing. Shaking her head, she continued down the stairs and toward a surgeon standing over the breakfast table.

In a corner propped a man barely conscious, shot through his abdomen and groin. Next to him sprawled a soldier with two bullet holes in his abdomen, entrails exposed. He mumbled words unintelligible, tears streaming down his face.

Overcome, Rachael knelt before him, dropping the strips of cloth. She turned her head, ear to the man's mouth and strained to discern his gibberish. The man's condition, his prognosis, were obvious. Her eyes filled with sadness for the man. She wondered what he believed he was telling her, his eyes fixed upon hers, his limp fingers reaching for her lips, her voice. His whiskered expression, sad, lonely, resigned, gripped Rachael. She felt desperate to learn the man's thoughts, to understand his feelings, in these final moments of life.

The man reached into his pocket, pulling out a photograph. He held it for Rachael to see. Two girls, three or four years old, Rachael believed. She took the picture. The man returned a proud smile, closed his eyes, and died. Rachael touched the man's cheek and gently slid the picture back into his pocket.

Another man complained of his inability to clamber out of the hole in which he stood—until he was told both his legs had been shot away.

Still another had no jaw, eyes darting side to side like a child peering over a red wall.

A bullet had carved a groove through the side of a man's skull, exposing his brain.

The home of the peaceful Dunker family now echoed the horrors of war, the chords of discord.

"Sir, what are you saying? I'm here," Rachael whispered to another gut-shot man. "Shhh. It's going to be all right. Tell me. I'm listening."

"Virginia? Virginia, is that—is that you, Virginia?" the man, hearing Rachael's voice, replied with an effort swamped in agony. He pressed his hand against the air.

"No, sir, I'm Rach—yes, *yes*, it's *Virginia*. Tell me what you're feeling. What's happening to you, this minute?" Rachael begged, torn between pity for the man's fate and her need to know the essence of the transition from life to death.

The man touched Rachael's cheek, softly stroking it.

"I smell bread, Virginia," he whispered. "Thank you for your bread … Virginia." He sniffed the memory of bread and exhaled, his last breath pushing aside Rachael's bangs.

"You there! *Bandages!*" shouted a surgeon's assistant.

Rachael set the man's stilled hand upon his chest, over his heart. She scooped the strips of cloth from the floor and rushed to the table.

Atop the breakfast table sprawled a Union soldier, a corporal. The surgeon's aid removed the soldier's forage cap, its green blades of grass falling to the floor and trampled underfoot. An assistant finished shearing the soldier's pants to his waist, the shreds of blue trouser quivering with the bustle of activity. His left leg hung like a red pulp, a jagged hole through his knee. His right hand lay half-clenched on the table, shattered at the wrist. Barely conscious, he muttered, "Faugh-a-Ballagh! Faugh-a-Ballagh!"

"What's he saying?" Rachael asked, sweeping aside the soldier's sweat-drenched black hair and dabbing his forehead.

The surgeon reached into his medical bag, hands smeared with blood, and removed a vial of chloroform. He gave it to his aid. "Irish expression," the surgeon explained. "Means 'Clear the way!'". Appropriate words, I must say, under these circumstances."

The aide dripped some chloroform onto a cloth cone and held it to the soldier's nose.

"Faugh-a-Ballagh! Faugh-a-Ballagh!" he shouted again, thrashing, slinging blood and bits of bone onto Rachael's dress. He attempted standing, an out-of-mind reaction to the sleep-inducing chemical. Two assistants restrained him.

"He's still in the fight," said the surgeon, scanning the scores of Confederate wounded on the floor and grounds. "I know how this Yankee feels. What part of the field was he brought from?"

"Came in on a wagon from across the Hagerstown Pike, out of some cornfield. Ain't much of a cornfield *now*, I'm told. Hell of a fight over yonder, they say. Said blue and gray littered the ground like autumn leaves."

"Don't our boys know a Yankee when they see one?"

"Some of the men said he was givin' water to our wounded when he was shot. Thought it only fittin to bring him in. Don't spect he'll mind a Confederate doctor savin his life."

"I reckon not," confirmed the surgeon. "Got him under?"

The aid lifted the soldier's eyelids. "Like a baby, sir. Flap?"

The surgeon nodded agreement for the procedure. "Let me have the long knife."

"Barton ... somebody," Rachael said. "Can't make out his last name. 27th Indiana."

"What?" asked the distracted surgeon.

"His name. Barton. Pinned to his blouse. Regiment's sewn on his cap."

"He's lucky. At least this one's *got* a name."

The soldier slid his uninjured hand until it touched Rachael's. He held two of her fingers as she stared at his closed eyes.

Barton, she thought. Her eyes flew open. *Barton? 27th Indiana?*

Rachael dipped a shred of cloth into the urn of water. She wiped away the grime of battle from his face. Then she knew, his features peeling back the translucence of her memory. She squeezed his hand and looked at the surgeon.

"He's under," the surgeon said, noticing the soldier's grip. "Reflex, that's all. He would have grabbed a snake had it been there."

The surgeon pinched the skin and muscle of the soldier's thigh and guided the amputation knife through the leg until he struck bone. He checked the soldier for reaction to the cut. Tap, tap. Rachael winced at the gruesome sight, turning her head but keeping her eyes on the procedure. Blood streamed onto the table and dripped to the floor, broadening the slick coverage of red slime. The surgeon sliced through the muscle in an upward angle, producing a flap of flesh with which to wrap the stump upon removal of the bone. The surgeon repeated the procedure on the underside of the thigh.

"God help him!" Rachael whispered, suppressing as best she could her rising nausea.

Minutes passed. Both flaps were lifted back revealing the bone. An aide handed the surgeon a capital saw. He began the crunching, gnawing process of the amputation, arm racing fore and aft like a lumberjack, the indifference of repetition washing over his face. The leg fell free, the ghastly stump more frightful in its separation than the mangled knee moments earlier. Aids cleaned the stump, sutured the flaps, and applied adhesive plaster.

The surgeon wiped wet blood from his hands onto his apron, sighed, and then removed the soldier's right hand with the swift, practiced stroke of perfection.

He listened to the shifting decibels of battle and checked the endless exodus of wounded carted up the Landing Road toward the Hoffman home.

"My God," he said, shrieks of hellish agony filling his ears, "what have we *done?*" He sighed. No time for questions or regrets. "Next!"

The soldier's leg and hand were tossed out the window, like meal scraps, falling atop heaps of other anonymous limbs, their usefulness destroyed.

"Get him upstairs, out of the way," shouted an aide. "Doc needs this table."

"May I come?" Rachael asked the soldiers.

"You don't have to ask, ma'am," a soldier answered. "Bring some water with you. This boy'll be comin to directly, an' he'll be wantin water to wash his throat and a perty face to fill his eyes."

Rachael applied a wet compress on Barton's forehead as soldiers carried the corporal on three planks of lumber stripped from the house and nailed into a makeshift transport. She smiled. Despite the necessity of surgery, he rested, oblivious to the pain sure to come. Rachael dabbed sweat rising from his forehead and the straight slope of his nose, some rolling to his dimpled chin.

Barton, she thought, pushing back strands of his hair. *You can't be more than eighteen, nineteen.* She chuckled, releasing a gush of air, and shook her head. *Look at the trouble we caused with Lee's lost order.*

"In here! On the floor, under this window," said a soldier, directing placement. "Careful. Watch your step."

"Watch over these boys, ma'am. We got us some of Hood's Texans in here, Gordon's Alabamans, too. Texans took a thrashin up near Miller's place this morning. Alabamans caught it in some little sunken road. Hog Trough, I think, was its name. Maybe you can hum somethin to lift their spirits. Know any Yankee song?"

"A *Yankee* song?" asked a surprised Rachael.

"Got us a Yankee, too, remember?" the soldier said, pointing to the corporal. "How 'bout 'Dixie'?"

"'Dixie'? I thought that was a—"

"Confederate song? True, but it was written by a Yankee, an' it's one of Abe's favorites. Loved by *both* sides, ma'am. Can't go wrong with it." The soldier scanned the room, its space covered with men clinging to life. "I reckon most of these boys done seen their last sunrise anyhow. They gonna need a beauty like you to look upon and listen to, put 'em to mind of home. Spect you'll be needin fresh water, ma'am."

"Yes, of course," Rachael acknowledged as she turned to retrieve a pitcher.

"Rachael," came a voice across the room.

Rachael turned toward the sound, an array of men, all of whom looked unconscious. She gasped in surprise upon the sight of Jacob on his own bed, a blood-soaked bandage wrapped around his chest and shoulder.

"Jacob? My God, *Jacob!* It *is* you!" Rachael rushed to his side. "What on earth has *happened* to you?"

Jacob managed a smile and a chuckle. "Stepped in the way of a Yankee bullet. Didn't stop it, but I reckon I slowed it down."

"Jacob, your *chest!*"

"You should see the *other* fellow!"

I've seen the other fellow, Rachael thought. "But *how?* Where? How'd you get caught up in this God-forsaken fight?

"Long story, Denia. Right now, I just need—I just need some rest. Sip of water wouldn't hurt."

"Got it right here," Rachael said, shocked with her discovery.

Rachael dipped a porcelain cup into the basin of water and placed it against Jacob's lips. She tipped it slightly, her other hand tilting his head forward, allowing a steady trickle into his mouth. Jacob reached with both hands for the cup before withdrawing in pain.

"Ahhh! Son of a *biscuit!*"

"See you haven't lost your sense of humor. Slowly, now."

"But I'm just so dang *thirsty*."

"I know." Rachael gave Jacob the half the cup's contents. "That's enough for now. Can you tell me what happened?"

Jacob stared at the ceiling. He opened his mouth to speak, guarding his words.

"First off, Denia, there's … there's somethin you ought to know … if you don't already. Somethin I've been meanin to tell you, somethin—"

"Ma'am?" a soldier said.

Rachael turned.

"Ma'am … water."

"Hold that thought, Jacob. I'll be back."

Jacob sighed and winced. Rachael retrieved the pitcher of water.

"Barton, you're awake," Rachael said, smiling.

The corporal returned the smile. "How … how do you know—"

"Take this," Rachael said, "not too fast." Rachael lifted his head and placed a ladle of water to his lips. He sipped as Rachael's eyes met his, aqua-green and filled with appreciation. They smiled, connected. After a few swallows, Barton drifted back into unconsciousness.

Rachael leaned the ladle against its basin and wiped her hands on her apron. She turned toward Jacob and cleared her throat, remembering that a few days ago she had mentioned to Jacob her meeting Barton and giving him the lost orders she had found. Now, for reasons known only to the gods of war, they shared the same room, for the same reason.

"I'm back, Jacob." Jacob opened his eyes. Rachael glanced over her shoulder. "You … you were sayin?"

Jacob smiled. "Funny how I ended up in my own house, my own room, my own *bed*. Can't get much luckier than that." His smile left him. "These soldiers, far from their homes, from their beds … as unlucky as can be.

"Anyhow, Bigun and me, we were headin for Boonsboro until all this stuff with Claggett settled down, until after the battle. 'Tween us eatin them biscuits you made us an' us comin up on the Hog Trough Road, well, life sorta took a bend in the road, I reckon."

"A bend? You mean this battle?" asked Rachael.

"Yep. Left the house late last night, headed for Hog Trough, then up to Boonsboro. Decided to look in on all the commotion up by the church, all the soldierin goin on."

"You wanted that rifle real bad, didn't you?" Rachael asked, shaking her head.

"Maybe I did," Jacob said, his voice fading in reflection. "We decided to take a little nap in one of Reel's fields until mornin. Didn't figure on the battle crankin up so soon. Artillery woke us before the sun had a chance to, an' we scrambled.

"Wasn't long before we come across the Lee's soldiers, a whole tangle of 'em around the church. Bodies *everywhere*, Rebel an' Yank. Rebs were hollerin and carryin on like they had just whipped the whole Yankee army. I seen bluecoats runnin for their lives up the Hagerstown Pike and the Smoketown Road and through Miller's fields. Looked sure 'nough like a whippin.

"Rebs were laughin, smackin us in the back like we were kinfolk and shoutin after them Yanks, 'Run, you blue devils!' Bigun an' me just watched. It was a sight like no other.

"Some reb sent me in the direction of a stack of captured rifles by the church."

"Dunker Church? Should've got your baptism, instead," Rachael said, observing the irony.

"Yeah, well, I got me my *baptism*, all right, a *blood* baptism. I saw me a rifle layin 'cross the top of a dead Yankee, so I picked it up. Heck, I always *wanted* me one, an' this-un was *free*."

"Why a dead *Yankee*?"

"I don't know. Figured it was safer, in the midst of rebs, pickin one up off a Yankee. 'Cause it was *there*. 'Cause it'd been battle-*tested*. I don't know, Rachael. It was a *Yankee* Springfield! All I knew was, it wasn't doin *him* much good anymore."

"Then what?"

"Bigun grabbed him a rifle, too. That's where my made our mistake, pickin up rifles. A sergeant walked up to us an' strung cartridge boxes around our necks an' told us to come on. Still got my five dollar gold, I think. Wait, where's my shirt? It was in my shirt pocket."

Rachael reached into Jacob's pants pocket and pulled out the coin. "Somebody must've put this coin in your pocket so your wound could be dressed," Rachael said. "You're lucky to still have it."

A bullet-sized dent cupped the middle of the coin. Rachael showed the coin to Jacob.

Jacob examined it. "That explains the hard blow I felt right after ... This coin probably saved my life."

"Right *after?* Right after what, Jacob?"

"Me an' Bigun started down the Hagerstown Pike, holdin these rifles, me feelin like a Rebel soldier." He shook his head. "We got to Hog Trough and saw more Rebs than I ever seen in

Jacob's Baptism

one place. They'd torn down the fences and stacked the rails in front of 'em. This was no family reunion, Rachael. They'd made a battle line out of our road, Rachael, *our road*.

"A sergeant persuaded us into line, and before we could explain we weren't no soldiers, we found ourselves lookin out across Roulette's fields. Men—boys mostly—squeezed into that road like pumpkins in a harvest wagon, waitin on the Yankees to come, rifles restin on fence rails like snakes in the sun. And come they did, blue hornets at a *stingin festival*. Bull said the elephant was comin. *Damn*, was he *right!*"

Jacob fingered the bent gold.

"Bull? Elephant? Jacob—"

"Before long, the whole world blew up. Somebody gave the order to fire, and the whole world just *blew up*, ten thousand madmen in a free-for-all firefight, bullets whizzin like hell turned inside out. Me and Bigun was shootin at Yankees like I don't know what, just tryin to stay alive, shoot or get shot. They kept comin and droppin and comin and droppin. *Our road*, Rachael, and Roulette's and Piper's fields, in an *instant* changed into fertile ground for the *devil's* garden.

"Wasn't long until the boys on the line were gettin shot, too, fence rails be hanged. I never figured any man able to withstand such as I seen, Rachael. But, then, I didn't just *see* it, I was *in* it; I was *doin* it. Soldiers throwin down muskets too hot an' clogged to fire, pickin up others, takin up flags from fallen bearers, shakin their fists, darin death, takin bullets 'til their last breath.

"I seen a flag-holder hit with six or seven balls, one right after another, and he *still* managed to fling 'em the finger before they knocked him down.

"I seen a Yankee standin on a boulder out in Roulette's field, plain as a duck on a pond, firin down on rebs and shoutin at his own men to join him on that rock. Far as I know, no Reb touched him. Honor of battle, I reckon.

"I saw a man, two men, stabbed by ramrods shot from somebody's rifles. That's how frantic them boys were, in their haste to load an' fire.

"There was a fellow from North Carolina that saved my life, *twice!* I forget his name ... Tucker somethin ... but I'm not forgettin what he did. He took a saber *through the body* after shootin down a man about to shoot me. Then he killed the saber man with a Bowie knife. *Dangest* thing I *ever* seen, and it happened like a flash of lightnin!"

"Nobody had no time to think or do nothin except react. All the screamin and shoutin and explosions and curses, men laughin like it was a great big joke, an Irish weddin." Jacob paused, taking a breath. "An' God, those *poor* boys, most of 'em probably no older than me, *beggin* for their mamas or wives or girlfriends, for water, before they took their last breath of sweet air. And the *blood*, Rachael, the *blood*—"

"Shhhh! Jacob, *Jacob*. Rest. You must *rest* now," Rachael urged, her hand touching his lips.

Rachael sat next to Jacob as he dozed. Just yesterday, they had taken a walk along Hog Trough, argued about the merits of this war, about committing to one cause over the other, committing to each other, about fighting. Like the flash of lighting Jacob mentioned, death took Roswell, and Jacob had ventured into its midst.

Jacob stirred.

"More water, please?"

"Just a bit. Take slow sips. There."

"Thanks, Denia. All my jabber-jawin has worn me out."

"Jacob, there's somethin you've got to know."

"An' that would be ...?"

"You're not going to believe who I saw at Killing's Cave last evening."

Rachael dabbed Jacob's mouth.

"Killing's Cave? Who?"

"Jacob, if Bigun killed Claggett at the bridge yesterday, then we've just had the first resurrection since Jesus Christ."

"What in the name of Judas are you talkin about?"

"I'm talkin about I saw *Claggett Parker,* at the *cave!*"

"You saw—*what?* That can't *be*, Rachael. Bigun *killed* that man, put a *Bowie* through his chest! I *seen* 'im do it!"

"Calm down, Jacob. You're bleedin again." Rachael applied fresh strips of cloth to his wound. "I hear what you're sayin, but hear me, too. He *was there* at the cave; I *saw* him, and now he's got Jesse and the children. Took 'em away, to God knows where. Some old man handed me this note. Here. Read it."

Jacob sipped more water and read the paper.

"My *God*. Rachael, Bigun is outside doing a favor for me. Send him up here as soon as you see him."

Rachael heard groans, turned, and saw the groggy Union corporal stirring, semi-conscious.

"Forward, *double-quick!*" he shouted. "For God's sake, men, *come on! Faugh-a-Ballagh!*"

Rachael pushed Barton gently back to the pallet and pillow as he tried to rise.

"Shhh! You're hurt badly, Barton," she said. "You *must* lie still." She turned facing the door. "I need some opium here!"

Blood soaked the stump's dressing. Rachael peeled away the gooey linens and hastily wrapped fresh cloth around the stump.

"God, it hurts!" Barton mumbled, trying to raise his head. "Please, lift my leg so that my knee is bent. Where am I hit?"

Rachael bent the corporal's right leg.

"No, the … the *other* leg."

Rachael paused. "I cannot, Barton," she confessed.

"Why—why *not*, for the love of Pete? Where am I *hit?*"

"Your left leg, Barton. And your right hand."

Barton lowered his left hand down to his leg. Afraid of what he might encounter but resolved to know the truth, he inched his fingers toward the knee. He felt wetness. He caressed the area and jerked up his hand.

"Oh, my God, *Jesus!*" he shouted, staring at the crimson upon his fingers. He looked into Rachael's tear-filled green eyes.

Stillness descended upon Barton Brooks as he gazed into Rachael's eyes. He lowered his hand and raked the blood from his fingers onto his pallet. He brushed aside Rachael's hair tickling his neck and smiled. The shock of his loss of limb left him.

"Where—where'd they find a flower like you," he said with the calm of a June breeze. "God has been *good* to me this day."

Barton raised his fingers, took the tears from her cheek, and smeared them on his face.

"Don't," he whispered. "Angels weep for the dead."

Rachael smiled.

Chapter 29

Unnoticed amid the backdrop of

trees and underbrush, Bigun trotted with the folded Confederate colors toward the cedar, as instructed by Jacob. He stepped over bramble and rocks, his sturdy hand firm over the concealed battle flag. The heat of the mid-afternoon sun pressed against his back. Bigun stopped to wipe drops of sweat from his eye. He listened. The fight had taken a discernable shift southeastward of Sharpsburg. Limping wounded and deserters passed, heads down, ignoring Bigun.

Reaching the tree, Bigun paused to view his surroundings. He pulled the banner from his shirt and tucked it inside an opening tall enough in height to stand an artillery tube.

"Whatchu *doin* there, boy?" shouted a Confederate soldier.

Startled, Bigun stood, his back toward the soldier. "Why, I—I's just makin water, suh."

"Pissin from yer *knees*, boy?"

"I got me the pox, suh," Bigun replied, turning around. "Hard to piss anymo' lest I gits *low*," Bigun lied, hoping the Rebel's ignorance matched his disheveled appearance.

"I seen somethin *red* down yonder, boy," the soldier said, pointing, craning his neck. "Whatchu up to, anyway?"

"Nothin, sir," Bigun replied as calm as truth. "Jus' makin water's all."

"Where you b'long, anyhow?" the soldier pried. "You somebody's?"

"Yessuh, down yonduh," Bigun said, pointing to the Hoffman house.

"Why ainchu down there?"

"I has been, suh, helping wit' de wounded an' such. Jus' took me a piss break. I be goin back directly." Bigun remained steadfast in appearance, his anxiety rising.

"You look strong as an ox," the soldier observed, keeping his distance sufficient and his rifle ready. "You ain't *runnin*, are you, boy?"

"*Runnin?* Why, *no*, suh," Bigun replied, shaking his head and shifting his weight from foot to foot. "What I mean is, why would I wanna go an' do a thang like dat, what wit' de whole Rebel army right on top of me … suh?"

"A man your size too timid to piss among other men?" the soldier said as he stepped from the dust of the Landing Road into the stubble.

"White men, suh."

"Jus' the same, I reckon I'll come take me a look at whatchu got back there, boy."

Bigun closed his fist around a knife in his belt and stiffened.

"*Johnson!* Whatchu doin down there, Johnson?" shouted another soldier from the yard at the Hoffman house. "Git your butt up here!" Johnson turned in response to the command, as quickly as if he had ventured beyond his post, and without a word scampered toward it.

Bigun released a sigh and watched as the soldier melted into the confusion and commotion of the living and the half-dead. He placed a cover of branches and vines against the opening in the tree, facing opposite the road, and began his walk back to Hoffman's. He glanced back a time or two, making sure the site was out of sight.

Returning to Jacob's house-turned-hospital, Bigun slowed his gait and stared with awe at a sight bathed in the surreal of hell. Soldiers with enough life left in them writhed on the ground like maggots in a dead possum, their pleas for relief rising in the air, howls of the damned.

Surgeons' aides and stretcher-bearers, in their haste to offload wagons of supplies and men, took careful strides among the carpet of wounded. The pungency of death filled the air, overpowering the early-autumn odor of browning leaves; the sweet scent of ripened corn; and the earthy smell of cut hay. Men, soldiers no more, issued their final utterances.

"W-*Water!*" a wounded man cried.

Hearing the plea, Bigun saw the man and stopped at the well. He gazed at the soldier's wounds, the purple of blood caked on his shirt, his butternut trousers stained with grass, his expression void of the arrogance of superiority.

Son of a slave owner, Bigun reasoned. *Rebel soldier fightin to keep me in bondage.* Bigun recalled the ignominy of the auction block, the horror of families torn apart forever. *He deserves dis.*

The man stared at Bigun, his eyes begging for relief, his concerns no longer about issues of race or skin color or national loyalties.

A human being.

Bigun picked up the ladle from the ground and dipped it into a bucket. He stooped at the head this man shot through the abdomen and shoulder. The man feebly reached for the blur of motion. Bigun tilted the ladle at the man's lips, spilling a few drops on the man's chin and neck.

"*Boy!*" shouted a soldier. "That water's for the *livin!*"

"But, suh, dis man, he's—"

"Leave him be. That man's as good as *dead*. This water is for those with a *chance*. Get inside and strip some bandages."

"Yassuh, but—"

"*Now!*"

The wounded soldier's dying eyes watched as Bigun dropped the water-filled ladle back into the bucket.

"Wa—water. *Please!*"

Bigun paused. No enmity in this man, no color line, no ideological barriers in this man's eyes. Bigun reached again for the ladle and placed it at the man's opened, cotton-dry mouth. He poured in a few drops before an aide kicked the ladle from his hands. Water splashed on the dying man's face, a brief, blissful shower of cool wetness.

"I said *now*."

Bigun glared, stood, at once eager to hear the sound of the aide's neck snapping in his hands. Saying nothing, Bigun walked toward the house. He glanced back, and taking his measured steps, Bigun pondered the misery of the wounded, the foolhardy arbitration of deciders, and the nonsense of a world out of its mind. Neither national affiliation nor color of skin mattered to Bigun in this moment of abject human vulnerability. He saw only the savagery of war, the suffering of mind and flesh, the stupidity of humanity.

Surely *these* were not the ways of God. Bigun wondered what *were* God's ways. Patience, perhaps. Perseverance. Steadfastness. He thought about the centuries-old plight of generations of slaves, about himself, and about his family. So much to think about. Too much.

Bigun waded past the brutal haste of field surgery and surged up the stairs in search of Jacob.

"Bigun!"

"Miss Rachael, thank God Almighty you is awright! He'p you wit dem bandages, ma'am?"

"Made all I'm able right now, Bigun. I'm going to help the surgeons. Jacob's here, upstairs in his room. He's hurt bad, I'm afraid."

"Yes'm, I know. I brung 'im here."

"You—*you* brought Jacob here? But how?"

"I was wit' 'im, ma'am, when he got shot. We was together, down at Hog Trough. Did he tell you 'bout it?"

"He did; said y'all were fightin on the Rebel line."

"Not 'cause we wanted to, ma'am." Bigun paused. "Spect *nobody* wanted to. We found ourse'ves in a situation. Shoot or be shot, I reckon. It was a damned sight, ma'am, pardon my words."

"Yes," Rachael agreed, staring out the window. "I can see how it must have been … a damned sight." Rachael lowered her head. "You okay?"

"I doin awright, ma'am, considerin. You know the whereabouts of Jesse and the chillun?"

"They're doin fine, Bigun," Rachael lied. I'll tell you about it later."

"Tell me 'bout *what* later, Miss Rachael?"

Rachael ignored the question, her gaze to the fields.

"Can I talk wit' Jacob?" Bigun asked.

Rachael considered his request.

"Yes. Go ahead. There's something very important he needs to tell you, show you. Don't know if he's awake. Don't take too long, now. There's a Yankee soldier up with him, lost his leg and hand. Name's Barton. Let me know if he calls for me? A delirious man; don't reckon he'll make it."

"Yes'm. Thank you, ma'am."

Bigun entered Jacob's room, the smell of chloroform and blood smacking him. He saw Jacob, eyes closed.

"J-Jacob?" he whispered. "Jacob, is you awake?"

Jacob stirred. "Bigun? *Bigun!* Did you—"

"I's here, boss. Done whatchu tol' me wit' de flag. How you feelin?"

"I've had better days," Jacob said, coughing. "Cedar tree?"

"Yassuh."

"Any … problems?"

"Nawsuh, none to speak of. Had a soldier ask me what I's up to, but he didn't see nothin. How de Yankee soldier doin?"

"'Preciate it, Bigun. Yankee soldier? What Yankee?"

"On de flo', I s'pose. Rachael said he—"

"Let me see him."

"Jacob, you ain't in *no* condition—"

"Let me *see* him!" Jacob insisted, struggling to prop his body on his elbows. Bigun assisted.

Jacob stared at the soldier in blue. Images of the fight in Hog Trough Road raced through his mind as if someone had spilled a boxful of daguerreotypes into his lap. Before today, he had never seen a man missing an arm, a leg, nothing. He had read accounts of such, had heard the words of those who had witnessed such. Words only. Now his mind raced with images. Before today, Jacob Hoffman had not seen much at all.

"Handsome cuss, ain't he?" Jacob thought aloud. "Reckon who he is, where he's from?" Jacob asked.

"Rachael tol' me his name," Bigun said. "Barton, I think."

"Barton?"

At that moment, Barton stirred. He opened his eyes.

"Rachael?" he called.

"She ain't here," Jacob answered.

"Who—who said that?"

"Over here, on the bed. What's your name, Yankee?"

"My ... my leg hurts like hell," he said. "Havin a hard time of it movin to look your way. This a Union hospital? They gave us the devil's own out there, they did, but I reckon we returned the favor. What unit you with?"

"Confederate hospital. Unit? Shoot, I'm a unit all *my own*," Jacob answered, laughing.

"Confederate?" Barton replied, surprised. "I'm a prisoner?"

"Ain't no prisoner of mine," Jacob answered. "Consider yourself lucky to be alive. What's your regiment?"

"Name's Barton ... Barton Franklin Brooks, Corporal, 27th Indiana, First Division, Twelfth Corps, Mansfield's Command. This ain't—this ain't a *Union* field hospital?"

"'Fraid not, Yankee. Fact is, this is a *Confederate* field hospital. Happens to be my house, my *home*, by the way," Jacob answered, pride lacing his words. "Hard to believe, I know, but I was born and raised, right here."

"Then I *am* a prisoner," Barton said.

"Well, now, Barton, I ain't no expert on the protocol of war," Jacob replied, "but seems to me anybody who's had his leg and hand shot off ain't a prisoner of *nobody's*, 'cept himself. I reckon they'll let you walk outa here, once you get used to crutches. Why does your name sound familiar?"

Barton lifted his handless right arm.

"Jacob! Get back down on that bed this instant!" Rachael shouted as she entered the room.

"Me an' Corporal Barton here were havin a talk, Denia. War an' stuff an'—" Jacob stopped mid-sentence and looked at Rachael. "This Barton fellow … he's the … soldier you met comin from Frederick, the Yankee soldier you gave Lee's lost Special Oder 191 to."

"*That's* where I've seen you," Barton remembered, looking at Rachael. "The girl picnicking with her daddy. *You* gave me that rebel order, cigars, too. It'd take losin a leg to forget a girl like you. You were just about the *prettiest* thing I ever set my eyes upon. I don't spect it came to any good, that order. You rebs about whipped us, anyhow.

Rachael said nothing. She glanced at Barton, then back to Jacob as she inspected Jacob's dressing. The bleeding had stopped.

"Here, Jacob," she said, handing him a cup of water. "Drink this." She turned her attention to Barton, patting his forehead free of sweat with a linen cloth.

"I like that cross hanging from your neck, Rachael," Brooks observed.

Rachael felt a blush. "Thank you … Barton." She smiled. "It's an heirloom, the cross. My great-great Grandma's."

"Suits you well, embedded in that porcelain flower matte."

"More?" Rachael whispered.

"Thanks, yes." Barton took the refilled cup and drank.

"The flowers are real; they're dried, I mean."

"Smells like—like gardenia," Barton said.

"A concoction of my mother's, the matte. Gardenia and lilac. She's always mixing things together, 'fixin nature,' she calls it, like they were meant to be together all along, like nature forgot something, made a mistake." Barton touched the cross as he studied Rachael's face. "I don't rightly know how she does it."

"Could be nature's correctin itself now?" Barton asked, unable to take his gaze from Rachael's eyes.

"Rachael," Jacob asked, "may I have more water, please?"

Rachael sighed at the interruption.

"Yes."

Barton reached and touched Rachael's hand. "I think maybe they *were* meant to be together," he said about the flowers. Rachael returned his gaze with a slight smile.

"Thirsty, Rachael," Jacob said, frustrated with the perceived delay.

"Coming, Jacob."

Rachael returned with a ladle of water, spilling a few drops on Jacob's head.

"Watch it! Rachael, that's a *Yankee* you're bein all friendly with down there," Jacob whispered. "Don't forget it was *them* who killed Roswell."

"Jacob Hoffman, since when did you care about sides? You wouldn't be here if not for your selfish desire for—what was it you called it, 'a sparkling Springfield rifle', something like that. He's a human being, wounded, like you, only worse. And I'm not bein *all friendly*. He was just admirin my necklace cross. They told me to just be nice, to comfort them. I'm *bein nice*, is all!"

Jacob bristled. "Yeah, I'll just *bet* he's admirin your necklace. Looks like you're returnin the favor, the admirin part, that is."

"Let me check your bandages, Jacob. Looks to me like you're going to heal up right nicely. Wound's clean, a bit of pus. To be expected, a good sign. Have you talked to Bigun?"

"'Bout what?

"The note, remember?"

"Dang, I forgot! Bigun, get over here!"

"Right here, Missuh Jacob," he answered.

"Bigun, I got somethin to say that you ain't gonna believe." Jacob paused.

"Yassuh?"

"Seems Claggett … well, he ain't dead."

"Ain't *dead*? I put a *Bowie* through his chest. You *seen* it! He fell like a tater sack of hossshoes, bled like a pig at killin time," Bigun said through an uneasy smile. "I reckon he 'bout as dead as dey *git*, boss."

"Not accordin to Rachael, he ain't. Said she seen 'im down at the cave last night."

Bigun looked at Rachael. "Den who was it I done killed?"

"It gets worse, Bigun. Claggett has taken Jesse and the kids—"

"Whatchu say?"

"—and he wants to exchange them … for you."

Bigun stood in stunned silence.

"I don't know who you killed, Bigun. Obviously someone who looked *like* Claggett an' let us believe that's who it was. It don't matter. What matters is gettin Jesse and the kids back, without Claggett gettin hold of *you*."

"How we gawn do dat?"

"Claggett's note told us to meet him down by Rohrbach's Bridge at noon on the twenty-fourth."

"I'll meet 'im all right," Bigun said, caressing the blade edge of his Bowie knife, "an' den I'll shove dis knife up his belly, carve 'im like a trout."

"No weapons, Bigun. Claggett said he'd kill *everybody* if he even *suspects* we got weapons. I don't think it's wise to challenge him on this one."

"Sounds like you got a plan."

"Not yet, but we got a week to figure one out."

"Rachael," Barton called.

"Right here," Rachael replied.

Jacob watched, sensing his hold on Rachael loosening.

"Hurts like—"

"I know. Shhh."

Rachael took Barton's hand into hers and dabbed his forehead with a cloth dipped in the basin water. He closed his eyes and took a long sniff. The scent of gardenia from Rachael's necklace lingered, eased his pain. Rachael took in the sight of his unblemished teeth, his raven-black hair and sapphire eyes. She

Jacob's Baptism

felt her smitten spirit squeezed, Jacob's hold loosened. Despite his physical losses, this was a man in fullness, a man after Rachael's heart. Her attraction swelled, pushing aside John Jacob Hoffman.

Chapter 30

Two mornings after the great battle of
September 17, the sky dawned crisp, blue as a stand of
cornflowers. The ravaged troops occupied the same general
positions held at the opening guns. A truce called for collecting
wounded and dead had come and gone. The armies, pummeled
brawlers staggered but standing, dared the other to resume the
killing. Stretcher-bearers continued their fleet-footed scampers
across the dead-dotted fields collecting wounded and skirting
snipers. The end of the Army of Northern Virginia, the
Confederacy itself, was McClellan's for the taking.

But he would have to *take* it, and the Army of the Potomac,
pummeled in kind, suffering in its piecemeal mauling, yielded to
its commander's reluctance to engage Lee's unknown quantity.
The Army of Northern Virginia took advantage, limping across
the Potomac, leaving behind thousands of dead and wounded.

The roads on the outskirts of Sharpsburg became clogged
with the curious. Refugees began the trickle back to devastated
homes and land. The familiar was no longer so. Souvenir
hunters tramped the moonscape of no-man's-land, rifling pockets
of the remaining unburied, scavenging anything of value. Voices
of unimagined agony, each a Lazarus, begged anything on two

Jacob's Baptism

legs for a drop of water or a bullet in the head, anything to suppress, even end, the misery.

Since the morning of the seventeenth, thousands of wounded, the courses of their futures in an instant altered, filled every space in every building, every hut, shack, barn and tent for miles around. The air reeked with a nightmarish blend of putrid flesh, human and animal excrement, and the burn of thousands of pounds of powder.

A carbon haze hovered over the ground, drifting, swirling like spirits surprised by the demise of their bodies. Trees lay splintered and toppled. Trampled cornstalks splattered with red rested beside harvests of the dead. Open fields once lush with the green of grass and the rainbow of wildflowers now languished in the debris and death of war. Sobbing loved ones stepped careful paths among the deceased, amid indifferent burial details, as they grappled with the enormity of where to begin.

Armed with fresh bandages, Rachael entered Jacob's bedroom to tend the wounds of her charge. Jacob had an advantage. Though shot through the body, he rested in his own bed, in his own home, on his own land. He slept. Barton lay in a pain deepening, the quickness of his breathing and the crudeness of his amputations beginning to tell.

Rachael glanced over at Jacob. Then, she turned her attentions to Barton. Her heart jumped.

"Rachael, so good—*God, my God!*—". Barton winced, sucking in air, intermittent bolts of pain slicing through his leg, delirium through his mind. "So good to see you," Barton continued as the pain subsided, eyes closed. "Let me hold your necklace, take in its aroma."

"It's a gardenia blossom, Barton," she replied, extending her hand. "Just for you."

Barton managed a smile. "I thought Jacob said—"

"Shhh. Never mind what Jacob said."

Rachael bent over Brooks. Ends of her hair grazed Barton's face and arms. She took a quick glance at his wrist and then his leg. She was struck by the odor of rotting flesh, her head taking an abrupt, instinctive snap away. She carefully rewrapped the dressing on his leg.

"It ain't good, is it?" he asked.

Rachael paused.

"Now don't you worry about anything. It's got the pus. Doc says look for the pus. That means it's healing."

After administering morphine and redressing the stump, Rachael dampened a cloth and wiped Barton's forehead. As she patted his cheek with the cloth, Barton opened his eyes and curled his fingers around her wrist.

Rachael looked at Barton, the blue of his eyes penetrating her soul like the words of Dickinson. At once, she wanted to kiss him, a sentiment he shared. He took his right arm and nudged Rachael's neck forward. She offered no resistance. As they kissed, surrounded by Jacob's house, Jacob's room, Jacob, she surrendered any lingering affections for Jacob Hoffman.

Jacob stirred, shaking Rachael from her bliss.

"Rest, Barton," she said, placing the cloth on his forehead. "I'll be right over here."

Rachael walked to Jacob's side.

"Good morning, Jacob," she said with a musical lilt.

"Where am—," he said, dusting off the cobwebs of semi-consciousness. "Oh. Rachael ... it's you."

"Drink this water, Jacob. I'll go scramble you some eggs and—"

"No, Rachael, nothin now. Ain't up to eatin just yet."

"But you need your strength, Jacob. I'll just—"

"Rachael, please! I ain't hungry now. The water'll do."

Rachael checked Jacob's wound and changed his dressing.

"Looks good, Jacob," she said.

"*Good?* How can a hole through my body possibly look good?" he asked, irritated not so much that Rachael might be dismissive of his plight, but that she might be dismissive of *him*.

"What I meant, Jacob, was that it's looking better, healing up. I don't see any signs of infection or—"

"Rachael, you wouldn't know infection if it was a coiled rattler."

"I know what to look for; doc told me, he *showed* me. Trust me, I've seen more than I care to. Now you rest while I go make some breakfast."

"I told you, I don't *want* nothin," Jacob insisted.

"Fine. Others do. I'll be back shortly. Anything you need before I go?"

"Bedpan."

Rachael retrieved the bedpan and waited for Jacob.

"I see you got your easel set up over yonder," Jacob said, looking at the window.

"Yes, I have," Rachael answered. "Girl's got to paint."

"Whatchu paintin today? Another sunset? I reckon there ain't much of a landscape left to paint anymore."

"Nothing in particular, really. Just dabbing on some colors to see what pops up," she said, smiling.

"I know that smile," Jacob observed. "That's your smile of mischief."

"Why, John Jacob Hoffman," she said, as she used to say, "I am *not* a woman of mischief—"

"*Not* a woman of mischief? That's like sayin Lincoln's not a man of politics. You *invented* mischief." Jacob said, laughing. "Show me your canvas."

"I won't stand here and listen to your teasing. I'm going to make breakfast."

"Let me see your painting."

"It's not finished. I'll show you when it's finished, not before."

Rachael took the bedpan and cleaned it.

Jacob sighed. "You look especially beautiful today, Rachael," he offered.

"Why, thank you, Jacob."

"How *does* it look outside?" Jacob asked.

"Well, we still have wounded scattered all over the yard waiting on somebody to treat them. There're just too many of them. Supplies are all but gone. About all we can do now is give water and tend to the ones who might survive." Rachael sighed, walking to the window. "Those poor men. It's the Godawfulest thing I ever saw, Jacob."

Jacob stared at the ceiling. "Our road's a mess, Rachael."

"*Our* road?"

"Hog Trough. *That* was the Godawfulest thing I ever saw."

"Rest now," Rachael urged.

Rachael passed Barton on her way out of the room. He followed her every step, a thankful smile upon his face. She gave him a peripheral glance but did not turn her head. Each knew the other's thoughts.

Jacob's Baptism

Chapter 31

The morning of September 20

found McClellan's Army of the Potomac in complete occupation of the killing fields of Sharpsburg. Lee's battered Army of Northern Virginia had finished its retreat across the Potomac River into Shepherdstown and beyond. Though not the dominant battlefield victory Lincoln desired, Lee's abandonment of Sharpsburg and withdrawal south was victory enough. Because of this weeping of blood, this gnashing of flesh, the consequences would alter the course of the war, the opinions of the world, the futures of two nations.

Opportunities to destroy Lee's army, to end the war then and there, lay silenced among the dead and desolate of the field. History would speak of them often. The debacle of Hooker's First Corps in the Cornfield; John Sedgwick's disaster in the woods around the Dunker Church; failure of Sumner's Second Corps to press the breach at Hog Trough Road; Burnside's delayed, uninspired assault on a bridge bottleneck and its subsequent repulse by the timely arrival of A.P. Hill's Light Division on the Confederate right flank. Each of these failures carved into the country's history another two and a half years of bloodshed.

Jacob's Baptism

The great and terrible day of September 17, a horrific slinging of lead, iron, and blood on scales heretofore unmatched, produced in the days following a vacuous, resonant silence, a receding tide before a tsunami of tears from families of the slain and the pathetic cries of thousands upon thousands of wounded.

Among the more fortunate of the wounded lay Barton Brooks and Jacob Hoffman. These were among the first evacuated to field hospitals, before overcrowding became an issue of unmanageable importance.

The healing of Jacob's wound progressed more rapidly than expected, due likely to the bullet's clean passage through his body. Barton's wound took a turn for the worse. The area blackened around his amputated left leg, the pain intolerable.

"It's Corporal Brook's leg, sir," an aide reported. "Necrosis."

Doctors and volunteers, many of whom never before had seen a bullet wound, found themselves saturated with the blood from thousands of wounds inflicted by the indifferent fury of bullets and shrapnel. Now came the aftermath, born of their haste in treating the volume of shattered limbs. Gangrene.

Rachael kneeled draped over Barton, touching a damp sponge to his lips, kissing his forehead, whispering words of comfort.

"Take it off," he begged, "please, take the leg off."

"Surgeon's on his way," Rachael said, pulling the gardenia cross from around her neck and placing it in his palm. "Shhh."

Rachael lifted his hand to his nose. The sweetness of the gardenia cut through his agony and removed from his mind, if only for a moment, his doubt of survival.

"Step aside, please," the surgeon demanded.

Rachael complied.

Meanwhile, Jacob managed to prop his healing body on his elbows. He needed a bedpan, but no one had heard his requests for one. Rachael gave her complete attention to the surgeon and to Barton, a fact that did not escape Jacob's notice.

Jacob wobbled. He grabbed the bedpost and pulled himself up. As he stood, he noticed Rachael's easel near the far window. Stepping over to view her painting, he was at first aghast by what he found.

Thinking it a painting of another sunset, perhaps a painting of him and Barton recuperating, maybe a restless rendering of the sycamore outside his window, instead he found she had painted two people strolling along Hog Trough Road, a girl holding the arm of a Yankee soldier, of Barton Brooks.

He looked at Rachael. She had not noticed his discovery. The cross from her neck curled clutched in Barton's hand. The unmistakable fragrance of gardenia filled the air.

Soldiers assembled an operating table consisting of two sawhorses and a bloodstained door, borrowed from downstairs.

"We're going to give you the chloroform, now, soldier," the doctor said. "Breath slowly."

"Do good, doc," Barton said.

Rachael leaned down and whispered something into Barton's ear. Both smiled.

"Rachael, *water.*" Jacob cried.

"Coming, Jacob."

Rachael brought a cupful of water to Jacob.

"You seem to be doing *much* better, Jacob. I'm very happy for you. Now you can—"

"You love him, don't you?"

"What?"

"You're in love with Barton, ain't you?"

"Jacob, what are you talking—"

"I saw the painting, Rachael," Jacob said, pointing. "After all this, you're *still* a dreamer. The man *can't walk*, Rachael."

Rachael glanced over at the easel. "Oh, Jacob."

"It's okay, Rachael. Really, it is."

"Jacob, I never meant—"

"Answer me this. *Why?*"

Rachael stood silent, giving Jacob's question the consideration it deserved. Rachael's eyes welled.

"After all this, I have nothing left *but* dreams, Jacob."

"You have me."

"Do you have your Springfield rifle?"

"Left it on the field. Gonna get me another, though," Jacob said, excitement filling his words. "You wait an' see."

Rachael picked up her paintbrush, touched the canvas and sighed. "Jacob, when I was a little girl," she said, "I had a friend, a friend who taught me immortality. But venturing too near, himself … he never returned."

Jacob absorbed her words. "Sounds a lot like Miss Emily?" he observed.

Rachael smiled.

"I love you, Rachael. No lie." Jacob took a breath and stared at the ceiling. He issued a soft chuckle, as if for the first time he had realized the obvious answer to a great riddle. "I've been wanting to tell you, and now I said it." He sighed. "That wasn't so hard, but … I'm too late, ain't I."

A tear cut a trail down Rachael's cheek, slowly, like a raindrop on a windowpane. She had waited long for Jacob to utter those words, which now spoken rang hollow.

Chapter 32

"**I got me an idea,**" Jacob said, breaking what seemed an interminable silence. "An' I think it just might work."

It was Wednesday morning, a week after the great battle, two hours before the appointed time to meet Claggett at the Rohrbach Bridge for the exchange.

Jacob, Isaac, and Bigun spent the night at the battle-stained kitchen table, discussing the recovery of Jesse and the children, if practicable without sacrificing Bigun. Claggett had had over a week to plan, a week's head start in breaking his promise. No one knew if Bigun's family was alive, dead, or sold southward. Options appeared few for a satisfactory outcome. Bigun dismissed ideas as soon as they breathed life, weighing the risk of each.

"I hope it's a good-un, boss."

"Like all the others, I spect, Bigun," Jacob said. "Won't know 'til we try it, but we have to try *something*." Jacob glanced at the mantle clock. "Can't sit here forever, and we *can't* go to the bridge without a plan."

"You're goin at it all wrong, Jacob. What we *ought* to do is set in them trees above the bridge; *shoot* the bastard," Isaac said. "It's the obvious thing *to* do."

"An' that's why we *can't* do that, Daddy," Jacob answered. "*Too* obvious. Claggett'll be in his saddle, on the ridge, his scope trained on them trees. I know *I* would. He'd kill them *and* us."

"How 'bout I shoot Claggett b'fo' he gits close?"

"As good a shot as you are, Bigun, that plan might work, if Claggett was dumb as dung. He'll have your children strapped on either side of him, Jesse in front, like shields. Can't risk it."

"So, what's your plan, son?"

"Daddy, I figure we can get *one* of 'em free right off, just by tellin him Bigun is willin to come but he needs proof of Claggett's good faith, that he won't budge until one of 'em *is* freed."

"So you're countin on Claggett's sense of honor."

"It's a risk, I know, but hear me out. When me an' Bigun were down in the Hog Trough in the middle of the fight, there wasn't a lot of time to think about much, except rammin lead down the barrel an' pullin the trigger. I mean, I can't be sure I ever actually *shot* a man. Maybe one. Shot *at* 'em plenty. I know I kept 'em *thinkin* about it." Jacob caressed his bandaged wound.

"Anyway, thinkin back on all that, I remember how the mere sight of a regiment's colors got the blood up more'n just 'bout anything. Men would pull back from whoever or wherever it was they were aimin at an' kill the man holdin the flag. *'Kill the flag man!'* they'd shout."

"Jacob, I don't want to hear you talkin about that battle or this war anymore," Isaac demanded. "You're strayin off the path. Bigun's *family*, remember? And after we help Bigun, it's high time for your baptizin. I reckon this Sunday'll do fine."

Jacob stared at Isaac. "Ain't *nothin* you or the Dunkers can say to me about war or baptizin," he said. "Ain't nothin you can say to me about *anything*. I'm my own man, now, whether you like that or not. I've *been* baptized. I've seen an' done things you won't *never* see or do as long as you draw a breath. I figure I've earned my independence. Bigun, too."

"Keep talkin," Bigun said.

Isaac shut his mouth, anger seething inside. Freedom was one thing. Independence was another.

"I got me more than a bullet at the Hog Trough. I got me a flag, a Rebel flag."

Isaac's eyes flew open; his jaw dropped.

"Jesus of Nazareth, Jacob! How in the name of Pete did you come by another *cursed* rebel flag, of all things? Have you any idea what that flag'll do to us, after what this valley's been through?"

"Well, there *have* been a few of 'em around lately," Jacob said, reminding Isaac of the obvious. "There's bound to be a few still layin around." Seeing Isaac's blindness to the subtle joke, Jacob shifted his tender shoulder. "You had to be there. Don't expect you to understand what I saw, what I experienced. The whole affair defies words.

"But I *will* say this. Many a brave man fell defendin that very flag. Same with the Union boys an' the Stars and Stripes. I seen at least three Yankees angle their rifle barrels away from clean shots at *me* and aim instead at *unarmed* flag-bearers. *'Kill the flag man!'* That Rebel flag saved my carcass, Daddy, more'n once. That's what that flag is goin to do for us now, for Bigun's family. I got that same flag hid, an' we're going to *use* it to get Bigun's family back." Jacob smiled. "Ironic, ain't it?"

"How we gawn do dat, boss?" Bigun asked.

"As soon as we get one of the children back—which means you're gonna have to be mighty convincin, Bigun—I'm going to unfurl that reb flag, bigger'n a Richmond parade. It's the next to last thing Claggett will expect to see."

"What's the *last* thing he'll expect to see?" Isaac said, filled with stubborn doubt.

"A bullet comin straight at his face," Jacob answered.

"A *bullet!* And just *who* do you figure on pullin the trigger?" Isaac asked.

"You, of course," Jacob replied, smiling.

"Your shoulder ain't the *only* thing wounded," Isaac said."

"That big, bloodied, battle-torn flag will shine in Claggett's eyes like the afternoon sun, a distraction he *won't* be expectin. As soon as he sees it, his guard will drop. That's when you shoot 'im."

"Oh, I see. And what if I *miss?*"

"At *five feet?* Not even a Dunker Baptist misses at *five feet*."

"It's a good plan, suh," Bigun agreed.

"How is it a good plan, may I ask?" Isaac argued.

"Because, you, Isaac Hoffman, Dunker pacifist, are the *last* person on earth Claggett would expect to be armed, much less *shoot* a man. He's going to check me an' Bigun for weapons, *that* you can count on. But it won't occur to him to check *you*, a devout, *baptized* Dunker Baptist."

"Wit' what pistol?" Bigun asked.

"The pocket Colt my grandpa gave me. It's small enough to fit under your belt, above your butt. You got to be quick about it. No slips, no mistakes, no *second thoughts*." Again Jacob checked his pocket watch. "It's eleven o'clock. Bigun, you get the flag. Let's move."

"I don't like this, Jacob, not one bit," Isaac complained.

"Is there anything you *do* like, Isaac, other than doin nothin? It's all we got, Daddy," Jacob said, his hand on Isaac's shoulder. "It's all we got."

Upstairs, Rachael nursed Barton's twice-amputated leg. No recurrence of gangrene, not yet. Two voices laughed. Jacob heard. He glanced at the kitchen ceiling. How strange he felt, the love of his life rejecting him for a one-legged Yankee. How awkward he felt, Rachael and Barton upstairs in *his* bedroom.

Barton survived the Sharpsburg battle, same as Jacob. Were it not that Barton had fallen in Miller's cornfield in the hours preceding the struggle at Hog Trough Road, Jacob might have convinced himself Barton had fired the bullet that passed through his body. Now Barton passed through Jacob, taking Rachael with him. *What would Roswell say?* Jacob thought, a smile crossing his face.

Jacob walked up the stairs to his bedroom, making sure his steps produced sufficient noise to announce his approach.

"Excuse me, please," Jacob said, peeking into the room, *his* room. "We're off to get Bigun's family back. I need to get my Colt."

Jacob retrieved the mahogany box that once held his means to an adventure, its bullet-dented form now a reminder of life spared. Jacob lifted the cloth that had protected the onion, another survivor amid the mayhem at Hog Trough Road. He pulled the onion—his pocket watch—from his pocket and turned it face-down in his palm. Jacob examined the engraving, done at his behest by Bigun. He read silently.

"Beautiful," he whispered. "Just as I wanted."

Lifting the pocket Colt, he stopped. He sniffed and stared hard at the dried gardenia, marking moments of a purer past, of a time untouched by the talons of war. He smiled, despite knowing she was no longer his, not sure anymore if the fragrance he smelled was real or imagined. Though his shoulder was healing, permanency shrouded the wound to his heart.

"I love you … Denia," he whispered.

"What'd you say, Jacob?" Rachael asked, rubbing Barton's hand.

"What? Oh … nothing." Jacob checked the Colt's cylinder. "We'll be back after while. Wish us luck. We're going to need it."

"Jacob," Barton called.

Jacob stopped but did not turn.

"You're a fine man, Jacob. As honorable a man as I've ever known. Godspeed."

Jacob gave a slight nod.

"Rachael, may I have a word with you, alone?" Jacob asked.

Seeking approval, Rachael turned to Barton. He nodded once.

Rachael patted Barton's hand. "I'll be right back," she whispered.

Rachael and Jacob walked downstairs.

"What is it, Jacob?"

"Us, Rachael. What happened? What we had … how did we lose it?"

"I don't know, Jacob," Rachael answered, sighing. "Maybe we never had it to lose. It took a war to bring this country to its senses. Us, too, I reckon."

Jacob paused, reflective. "Dragonflies," he said.

"Dragonflies?"

"Devil's darnin needles. Suck your brains right out, make a mind forget everything," Jacob said, smiling. His smile dropped as he patted his chest. "Like elephants … hearts never forget."

Rachael returned the smile and lowered her head. She reached up on the tips of her toes and gave Jacob a kiss to the jaw, for old-time's sake.

"Took a ride with my Grandmother yesterday," Rachael said. "She needed the sun. We got to Hog Trough Road. I told her what had happened here, what had happened to you. She wanted to walk a bit, see it for herself. She looked around and noticed the rust-red tint of the ground, still there. Maybe it was just the sun on the dirt. You know the way light plays tricks. But the ground had a reddish hue. The red stretched in the road as far as she was able to walk. She stopped, bent over and picked up a belt buckle, CSA, a hole shot through it.

"Eyes on the buckle, she turned to me and said, 'This ain't Hog Trough no more. It's a bloody lane.' I guess we're a bit like Hog Trough. The blood of change stained *us*, colored who we truly are. We're not what we were," she said.

"Always the literary one. You were my Denia," Jacob said. "Give to Barton what you gave to me. That's my Special Order to you."

Rachael lowered her head. "Be careful with Claggett, Jacob."

Jacob touched Rachael's hair and turned to join the others outside.

"Let's get this done," he said, handing the Colt to Isaac.

Bigun gave Jacob the folded flag, bold in its red and blue design, emboldened by its coat of blood. He tucked it inside his shirt high up against his back.

"Six shots, Daddy. You might get only one."

Isaac took the pistol and shoved it between his belt and pants, just above his rear.

"Leave the talkin to me," Jacob said, looking at Bigun.

The three set out. The men said nothing during their ride to Rohrbach's Bridge. As they approached the bridge, the air stilled, silent but for the shriek of a solitary blue jay.

"That's far enough!" a voice shouted from the direction of the creek.

Isaac's wagon slowed to a stop on the Lower Bridge Road, roughly fifty yards from the bridgehead.

"I see you gentlemen came alone," Claggett said, stepping out from under the bridge to a wagon lane paralleling the creek. "Well, well, Isaac Hoffman, good to see *you* once again. Bigun, you're lookin mighty healthy … mighty healthy indeed. But, enough with the pleasantries and to the business at hand. I do believe a debt is come due."

Jacob and Isaac looked at Bigun, puzzlement in their eyes.

"Hasn't he told you? Well, then," Claggett said, "let me fill you in. Three years ago, at Harpers Ferry, Bigun participated as one of John Brown's raiders. I know of this, because I was *there*, deliverin a load of nails from the Furnace. To shorten a long story, mainly because I haven't the patience to tell it all, I kept Bigun from the hangman's noose in return for the privilege of his services, beginning, oh … now."

"Where's Jesse an' my young-uns?" Bigun shouted.

"*Calm*, my friend. They're safe. Come on out, you three. You see, normally I never would have let them leave my side, knowing how anxious you must be for their safe return, but I had to test you for weapons. Had you any weapons, surely you would have tried to kill me with those three out of the line of fire. You didn't. I took the chance, but a calculated one. So, Bigun, if you will—"

"Let Little Jim go first," Bigun demanded. "He goes, I come, or we got no deal."

"Negotiating, are we? Quite the bold one, you are. Tell you what. You can *have* Little Jim, Bigun, with my compliments. I won't be needing him. A real shame, too. Just too scrawny for Charleston summers, and he wouldn't bring enough to account for the cost of his delivery plus my profit. Planters won't give a half dollar for a scrawny black."

Little Jim looked at Jesse and at Bigun, unsure if he was free to move a muscle.

"*Go on*, boy!" Claggett shouted with impatience. "Go to your master."

Jacob let out a breath. Little Jim ran to Bigun.

"Okay, Bigun," Claggett said, "let loose of the boy and let's go. Charleston's a long way from here."

Just then, Jacob whipped out the Rebel flag, big as a tablecloth, its tattered colors flapping in the autumn air. Claggett dropped his grip on Jesse at the sight of the flag, gasping in surprise.

In the same moment, Isaac reached behind, yanked out the pocket Colt, thrust it toward Claggett's forehead. He pulled the trigger. The shot missed the intended target. Instead, the ball tore into Claggett's throat. Claggett clutched his neck, blood spurting between fingers madly probing to find and plug the hole. Bigun took the Bowie knife he had stashed in his boot and shoved it deep inside Claggett's chest. Bigun's and Claggett's eyes met.

"Debt paid," Bigun drawled as he turned the blade, shoving it harder.

Bigun released his grip on the knife and grabbed Jesse.

"Thank you, Jesus!" Jesse shouted.

Chapter 33

The spring of 1863 echoed the angry sounds of combat from the fields of Virginia. Rejuvenated by victories at Fredericksburg at the close of '62 and Chancellorsville the following May, Southern high command revisited the objectives, and the promise, of the Maryland Campaign.

By June, the Army of Northern Virginia returned to notions of invincibility. Lee's juggernaut again marched north, desperate to take the fight away from a war-torn Virginia, to thrust the final nail into the war's coffin of unpopularity, to unhinge the North's war efforts, to convince European powers, despite Lincoln's Proclamation of Emancipation, that a victory on northern soil proved the Confederacy deserved international recognition. Hopes were high that a resounding Confederate victory on Union ground would compel a war-weary North to sue for peace. Not since Second Manassas had morale been as supreme.

Jacob stood in the door of Dunker Church and watched as Southern soldiers marched northward along the Hagerstown Pike, scene of unparalleled combat just eight months earlier. The sight was eerily familiar. Men, many of them veterans of Antietam, some shoeless and lean on the bone, sang tunes of glory and home, laughed at tired jokes, spit dust stirred into their faces by the steps of men in their front. Onward they marched.

He thought of his childish pursuit of a Springfield rifle and the dead soldier from whom he had acquired it.

He thought about the savagery in the fields before him and the storm within Hog Trough Road, about Sergeant Thomas Rushin, about Bull Stokes and Tucker McGavin, about his coin, about Bigun, and about the Rebel battle flag.

He thought about the splatter of blood, the shatter of bones, the bullets flying, the bursting of Pandora's Box on the land of his home, indeed, his very house. He wiped his forehead of these thoughts trickling down. Still they came.

He thought about Roswell, wrapped in the promise of a flag, drawn to his own adventure.

His physical wound suffered in the Bloody Lane had healed, its only evidence a jagged, circular scar and an occasional itch. A Yankee for whom he had held no malice shot him down that maniacal September morning.

He thought about the irony of the survival of his flesh and the death of his spirit, his heart. He thought about darning needles and dragonflies, about Rachael, about Corporal Brooks.

Rachael was gone, married to Barton. Only God knew where they had settled. For Jacob, this was the wound worse than bullets.

Bigun, Jesse, and their two children had packed their sparse belongings in an Isaac Hoffman-made wagon and journeyed north to Boston. Jacob kept in his pocket a letter written by Bigun, his first since learning the craft, telling of his adventures as a free man out of the reach of soul drivers. Bigun spoke of joining a colored regiment at Camp Meigs, Readville, Massachusetts.

Jacob squinted, peering at the gray cloud obscuring the afternoon sun, its rays blasting out all around the cloud's edges, defying containment. *Just like Rachael*, he thought.

Jacob walked the roads and fields of the Sharpsburg battlefield day after day. He was born here. More importantly, he was reborn here. His emotional gravity took him each time to

Hog Trough Road and to his memories of Rachael. This was *their* road, Hog Trough. Now history had stolen it, a memorial to the men who struggled here, who fought in the name of all that inspired them, their blood its coronation.

As he stood and gazed along its length, Jacob now realized God's purpose for him. No other explanation satisfied his questions of deliverance from such a din of violence, of Rachael's deliverance from him.

Jacob kicked pebbles. He stepped around soldiers' rusted tins and bent to pick up smashed bullets and other debris ignored by souvenir hunters. The road was calm again, as it had been before, its fences rebuilt. Jacob wept for the poor souls destroyed that day, futures shot away, the brave men of both armies struck down in a flash of time, a moment of truth, a baptism of fire.

Near the road's apex, the point where he had fought with the Sixth Alabama, Jacob stopped and stared toward Roulette's farm, across the fields of early corn.

Here, Jacob thought. *I'll bury it here.*

The next day, Jacob rose before the sun. He and Isaac had an order of two wagons to deliver by three o'clock, but there was time. He heated day-old coffee and gulped the steaming liquid as fast as his throat allowed. He looked up the stairs for a moment and sighed.

In his room, Jacob opened the chest, swept away its cobwebs, and removed the mahogany box. He opened the box and checked its contents one last time.

The box contained the essence of what Jacob was, of what he had become.

A few cats' eyes, childhood marbles and games of attrition.

A broken antler-handle knife, marking a transition from childhood.

A gold coin, the currency for adventure, dented, its purpose fulfilled.

"Buy an adventure," Jacob said with a laugh, a rush of emotion pushing a tear to his eye.

A string-bound fascicle of Emily Dickinson's poems, given to Rachael with a shrug of indifference by her cousin. Rachael had given the volume to Jacob. He held it in his palm.

"Rachael," he said, "this is who *you* were, the spirit I too often ignored."

One of Rachael's paint brushes, blotched with the coagulation of red paint.

"This brush you used to paint your sunset scenes," Jacob observed as he tucked it snug against the box's wall. "And so it did."

Flowers of dried gardenia, three four-leaf clovers, one black-eyed Susan.

"These I'll place inside Miss Emily's book. Poetry should be pretty, you always said. A bit lucky, too, I'd say."

The cloth-wrapped onion. Jacob removed the pocket watch and read aloud its inscription.

"'For my friend, Tucker," Jacob read. "'Though I knew you only minutes, your memory is timeless. You saved my life. Thank you'." Jacob gazed at the watch. "Rest in peace, my friend."

Finally, a folded parchment, written by Jacob.

"For history."

Jacob lowered the lid and closed the latch. He brushed both palms across its top, as if he were saying goodbye at a funeral. He reached under his mattress, removing the bloodstained, bullet-torn Rebel battle flag. With gentle respect, he spread the flag open on his bed and placed the box upside down in its middle. He folded the flag around the box, its center star shining center-top of the box.

Jacob gave a deep sigh and turned to go downstairs.

"Where you headed, son?" Isaac asked as he dressed.

"Out," Jacob replied.

"Out where?"

"I'll be back in a while. Biscuits and coffee on the table."

"We got those wagons to deliver," Isaac said. "Don't want to be late."

"We won't. Deliveries are always on time," Jacob replied with a smile, "even when we think they're not."

"You ready for Sunday?" Isaac asked.

"Couldn't be readier."

An hour later, Jacob set the box on the northern embankment of Hog Trough Road, near the apex. He took his shovel and began. Piling chunks of dirt aside, stopping on occasion to wipe the spring sweat from his face, Jacob cut a hole in the earth two cubic feet deep. Finished, he plunged the shovel into the embankment and watched Roulette work the same fields through which thousands of Union soldiers had charged and died. He lifted the box one last time, placing it in the hole, in the middle of the road, and returned the dirt.

"Done," he said with a wipe of his hands. "Time to heal."

Jacob Hoffman hoisted the shovel onto his shoulder. He stood erect and gave a salute as he stared down the length of the road.

"To you, fine soldiers of gray and blue. May you bury *your* past, *your* trinkets of a former life, as I have buried mine."

Jacob turned and began his slow trek home.

No going back now, he thought, as he glanced over his shoulder at the site one last time. *Bloody lane.*

Sunday came quickly. Jacob stood at the front door of Dunker Baptist Church, holding it open, greeting his congregants.

"Lookin forward to hearin your message today, preacher," an old man said, entering.

"Lookin forward to deliverin it, sir," replied Jacob.

Chapter 34

Mark parked his car in the lot facing the
Bloody Lane. He had spent the morning touring the northern
portions of the Sharpsburg battlefield. The day started chilly for
April, spits of rain from time to time and void of the stampede of
tourists. He grabbed his digital camera and walked toward the
intersection of Roulette's Lane and the Bloody Lane.

Mark took scores of photos from an array of angles. He
formed mental images of what occurred here nearly one hundred
fifty years earlier, imagining charging troops dropped by volleys
of musketry, courage amid chaos. The breeze against his face, he
paced head-down the sharp uphill grade at the bend in the eroded
lane. As he walked, his shoe caught an object on the ground,
tripping him. Mark investigated, finding the guilty object, the
rounded point of a corner, like a root with no tree, protruding
from the ground in the middle of the road.

Curious, Mark examined the object. He reached down to
touch it, loosen it. The damp ground held it firm. It was wooden,
but this was no root. Mark saw no other persons in the lane. He
began to scrape the ground away from the object. Each removal
of soil revealed a bit more.

After careful excavating, Mark freed the box from the hole. He took it to his car and rested it in his lap. Using his car key, he pried loose the latch. Lifting the lid, he discovered its remarkable contents. He sifted through each item, most of them well-preserved, stunned with his find. He held the gold coin, running his fingers over the dent. He tried opening the pocket watch but could not. Marbles rolled from side to side as he tilted the box. Then he discovered wrapped in a two embroidered handkerchiefs a folded parchment projecting from a string-bound booklet.

He laid the paper on his lap and gently lifted each fold. Inside he found the magnificent swirls and curves of nineteenth century penmanship. The date, though faded, read "June 17, 1863." He fingered the antler-handle knife and read.

'Greetings to you from this place of sadness. Folks call it bloody lane. For me, it shall remain Hog Trough Road. That's a piece of my past I can never bury.

It is three months until the first anniversary of the great battle at Sharpsburg.

Though you and I shall never meet, I trust this box and its once-treasured contents will give you clues as to person I was.

I am certain history has recorded the events of September 17, so I will not encumber your time reciting facts you already know.

Instead, I will say this. Rebel and Yankee fought with passion in these solemn fields of the Antietam Valley, fought for what they believed important, as they did here in this road. Each fought for his own reasons, valid in his own mind. Those killed and wounded left their reasons in the blood they spilled here. I fought among them and witnessed their courage and their struggle. I should think all Americans are still as brave.

Bravery as I shall never know again was common among the men who trod these fields and died in the clover and black-eyed Susans. Commitment and dedication were as sweet as gardenia.

Battle is anything but poetic, though some would disagree. Miss Emily wrote, "When that which is and that which was, apart, intrinsic, stand; and this brief tragedy of flesh is shifted like a sand." Sometimes it takes a poet to reveal battle's truth.

The gold coin bears the impact of a Yankee bullet. Were it not for this coin in my pocket in this road, given to me by my Grandfather two years earlier, you would not be reading this note, nor thumbing through the contents of this box. He told me to buy an adventure. I got my money's worth. Read the engraving on the watch's back. Tucker was a man among men, the quintessential American soldier.

This box was wrapped in a battle flag of the Sixth Alabama. Render its remains to solemn keepsake, and never forget the valor of the men of both armies, what each won and what each surrendered on 17 September, 1862.

> *John Jacob Hoffman*
> *Sharpsburg civilian*

Jacob's Baptism

Mark searched the soil but found no remnant of the flag, it long having surrendered to the elements and to time. He folded the parchment and placed it inside the string-bound booklet, which he returned to the box. He picked handfuls of clover and, with dirt, filled the hole, patching the resurrection of a one-hundred-and-fifty-year-old wound. He waved his hand, shooing away a pesky dragonfly, and laid a black-eyed Susan on top of the clover. He sat next to the spot, box in his lap, and thought. For thought was all Mark could muster.

Cherry blossoms, colors in full, spilled unbrowned from their branches, coating the ground around him. He looked up. A great horned owl screeched overhead, its eyes upon the prey of the fields.

About the Author:

Mark Randolph Watters is a dedicated father, husband, author, and civil war history enthusiast. He resides in rural PA with his family, but still holds dear his roots deep in his old Northwest Georgia stomping grounds. He's been known to haunt the riverbanks and forests there, searching for historical treasures.

To date, Mark has had three other titles published by King's Way Press, including: *The Ghosts of Benevolence* (a novel of suspense and intrigue), and two young adult titles; *Taylor Smart and The Chamber of Skulls* and *Blythington's Game*. He's also an accomplished Children's book author with several children's titles in print.

Mark is currently busy writing the third installment in *The Raventon Mysteries.*

www.ingramcontent.com/pod-product-compliance
Lightning Source LLC
Chambersburg PA
CBHW020600260626
47157CB00003B/799